ACCOUNTING FOR LOVE

ACE OF BAES
BOOK 1

BELLAMY WEST

Copyright © 2025 by Bellamy West

www.bellamywestwrites.com

All rights reserved.

No part of this book may be reproduced in any form or by any electronic or mechanical means, including information storage and retrieval systems, without written permission from the author, except for the use of brief quotations in a book review.

NO AI TRAINING: Without in any way limiting the author's exclusive rights under copyright, any use of this publication to "train" generative artificial intelligence (AI) technologies to generate text is expressly prohibited. The author reserves all rights to license uses of this work for generative AI training and development of machine learning language models.

Whether you're a spreadsheet freak or a freak in the sheets, this book is for you.

CONTENT AWARENESS

Taylor and Gabriel's story centers queer joy. While light-hearted and fun, Accounting for Love does contain the following:

- Biphobia
- Childhood cancer (side character who is now a healthy adult)
- Medical scare and fainting related to burnout
- Alcohol consumption
- Explicit sexual content between consenting adults

1

TAYLOR

Universal rule number one: when I had somewhere important to be, I was definitely going to be waylaid by a host of complications.

We were a few days into January, and the background hum of the office was already a little more frantic. Last month, everyone promised to 'loop back after the new year.' Now, all those checks were being cashed. The printer's whirring was more insistent, the coffee machine buzzed more frequently, and the soundtrack of constantly ringing phones replaced the repetitive holiday music.

The phone on my desk rang for the hundredth time, and I leaned back in my chair, adjusting my tie. The suit was my corporate armor of choice.

"JPL Accounting, Taylor speaking," I said, doing my best to keep the exhaustion from my voice.

"Hey there!" A bright voice came from the other side of the line. "Just calling to confirm our meeting on Thursday. I know I wrote down the time somewhere, but I can't find that slip of paper now."

I breathed out a sigh of relief. It was just Fiona—easily one of my favorite clients. "Absolutely. I have you scheduled for nine that morning."

Fiona chattered on the other line as knuckles rapped against my office door. It flew open before I could respond, the gust from Kai's dramatic entrance blowing over all the piles of invoices I'd already sorted. He managed to look like he didn't have a care in the world, despite being in our busy season, with the top two buttons of his short-sleeved button-up undone.

"See you then!" I said quickly to Fiona before hanging up the phone.

Kai shoved the rest of the papers off my spare chair and brushed his long, dark hair out of his face before taking a seat. His haircut made him look like a young Keanu Reeves.

"*Kai*." I groaned, throwing a pen at him.

"Forgot your lunch again, didn't you?"

I looked down at my watch in surprise; it was lunchtime. I swear I'd never eat if I didn't live with a roommate. Reaching into his lunch bag, Kai produced a banana and a protein bar with a flourish.

I grumbled under my breath but still grabbed the offering when he slid it onto my desk.

"That's what I thought." Kai bent over to pick up the now-disordered invoices and placed them in a haphazard stack on the corner of my desk. "Do I need to drag you to the break room, or do you promise to eat?"

"Yes, yes, I promise." I waved him off as I arranged the snack beside my yellow legal pad and collection of black ballpoint pens. "I have to meet Margo in a few hours, so I'm trying to rush through these emails."

"It's so strange your little sister is getting married," Kai mused. "I feel like she was just a kid when we met."

"That's because she was." My eyes darted to my empty coffee

mug emblazoned with the words 'World's Best Brother'—the only personal item I kept at work. It was a college graduation gift from Margo, who was only fourteen at the time. "I don't think I'm ready for her to grow up."

We were each other's whole world until she met Benji. I wasn't the one Margo relied on anymore, at least not in the same way she had when we were growing up. Margo, the eternal optimist, insisted she'd always have time for me, and we'd always be close, but I had my doubts. I knew lovers came first at the expense of everyone else.

Our parents taught me that.

"I think that ship has sailed, babe," Kai said. "Aren't you helping her pick out a wedding dress today?"

I narrowed my eyes at him accusingly—he was supposed to be on my side.

He raised his hands in surrender.

"Close the door on your way out," I hissed, and Kai cackled mischievously as he left it slightly ajar.

I blinked at my screen, trying to remember what I'd been working on before Kai invaded my office, then back at my coffee mug. A third cup couldn't hurt, could it? I straightened my notebook and laptop before grabbing the mug and heading to the break room.

I popped a mocha latte pod into the coffee machine and leaned against the counter with my back to the room, where tables were full of coworkers on their lunch breaks. The chatter echoed off the ceiling.

Just as the sweet, caffeinated elixir filled my mug, a notification from my email pinged on my cell.

Urgent: Late Payment Notification.

I fumbled my mug, and the scalding mocha spilled over my hand and across the countertop.

"Need a hand?" My boss's voice pierced through the chaos.

I flushed with embarrassment.

Rachel was a curly-haired, five-foot-two powerhouse, but she was also one of the best bosses I'd had. She was never afraid to get her hands dirty, attacking the spill with an abundance of paper towels.

I shot her a grateful look while wetting a small dishrag to wipe down the counter. "You're a lifesaver."

"These things happen," she said with a kind smile. "Enjoy your time off this afternoon."

It had been almost a decade since I passed the CPA exam and started working at this firm. In those nine years, I'd never taken a day off except when Margo needed me: the long weekend when her high school softball team went to the state championships, a whole week for her college graduation and our celebratory road trip to Napa, and a few hours this afternoon to help her choose a wedding dress.

This wedding was the culmination of all my goals—well, almost, but the last one would hopefully be accomplished soon. It hung over me, just out of reach. At least now that I was helping her plan her wedding, we'd be able to spend more time together like we used to.

Once the wedding was over, everything would change.

WHEN I SAID I was taking the afternoon off work to help my sister, it would have been more accurate to say I was taking the afternoon off to sit in gridlocked traffic. Office Space taught me that as soon as you changed lanes, the one you'd been in would start flying past you, so I stood my ground resolutely. I'd spent at least forty-five minutes staring at the same billboard for a motorcycle accident attorney.

I hated being late, especially for Margo.

With a deep sigh, I pulled up my sister's number on my car's Bluetooth and dialed.

Margo's voice teased over the speakers. "Please do not tell me you're still at work!"

"Of course not," I grumbled. "I left just after three, but I feel like I've been sitting in the same spot for an hour."

"Maybe there's an accident? I can check online." There was a brief pause as Margo scrolled in search of updates. "Oh shit, Channel Seven says a semi overturned and blocked the road. I bet that's what's causing the backup."

I chewed my lip and thrummed my fingers on the steering wheel. "Crap. I have to get off this freeway."

"Hey, no need to panic." Margo laughed. "This is the first dress shop I have an appointment at. You know my picky ass isn't going to find the one on the first try."

"Says the woman marrying her college sweetheart."

Margo and Benji had met in a graphic design class in her senior year and were obnoxiously in love. I hated that my anxiety was waiting for everything to crumble, like I knew all relationships did. Maybe their soulmate bond was a karmic apology for putting her through the absolute nightmare of childhood leukemia.

"I'm going to head into the appointment now," Margo said. "It lasts an hour, so hopefully, you can make it before I drink too much bubbly and they kick me out."

"I promised I'd be there. I'll figure it out."

The car was too quiet after I ended the call with Margo, and I put my head down on the steering wheel to think through my options. If I could get over three lanes before the next exit, I could get around the accident and make it to the dress shop before her appointment ended. She said it didn't matter, but I had been there for all her significant milestones.

I couldn't miss this one.

A honk from beside me startled me out of my contemplation. At last, traffic had begun to inch forward. As I caught up to the car ahead of me, I glanced around to find the source of the honk.

In the car beside me, grinning and looking right at me, was the most beautiful man I'd ever seen. Curly dark hair, brown skin, a nose ring, and a tank top that showed off the toned arm he rested on the center console of his yellow VW bug. The low-hanging winter sun shone from behind him like a halo, and my eyes widened as he gave me a playful salute and returned to singing along to the radio.

Despite the brief forward momentum, things reached a standstill again. I couldn't help but sneak furtive glances at the yellow bug, hoping to glimpse the mesmerizing stranger. Every time I caught his eye, he smiled wider. And was that a wink?

No way this guy was flirting with me on the highway.

I glanced away quickly, caught with my hand in the cookie jar.

"Dammit," I muttered.

Too distracted looking at handsome men, I missed my opening to change lanes.

And again. And again. Why couldn't I pull myself away?

When I noticed the progress flag hanging from the man's rearview mirror, it gave me a glimmer of hope—which I immediately shut down. What was I supposed to do, roll down my window and shout some cheesy pickup line across the freeway? Absolutely not.

I tired long ago of playing pointless dating games. If fancy algorithms couldn't track down my soulmate, the patron saint of the California Department of Transportation and an overturned semi certainly couldn't pull it off.

Besides, there was too much on my plate between overtime

and wedding planning. Once I had spare money in the budget and Margo no longer needed me, I could think about dating. She was my priority, not some sexy stranger.

I needed to get out of this damn traffic and get to that dress shop.

The next time I got the courage to look over, the man was rummaging in his glove box. He pulled out what appeared to be a small sheet of paper, scribbled something quickly, and folded it into a paper airplane.

When he looked up, he smirked—as if he caught me staring. Hopefully, he couldn't see me blushing from so far away.

The stranger gestured the universal sign for 'roll down your window' and laughed at my perplexed expression. It was like my brain-to-hand connection had been severed under his attention. Once my mind rebooted, I hit the button to lower my window.

My heart skipped a beat as the little paper airplane left the yellow bug and floated into my lap. I unfolded it gently, and my cheeks flushed as I read a number and a name. Gabriel.

Shit, now the ball was in my court.

I stared down at the number. Surely Gabriel didn't expect me to call him now.

I looked back over to see him holding his hand up by his ear and mouthing, 'Call me.'

Ok, then.

I swallowed hard, rolled up my window, typed the number into my phone, and dialed.

The phone rang a few times, and doubt crept in. Maybe I'd misunderstood him? What was I doing calling him in the first place? The phone kept ringing, and he appeared to be staring at his car radio in confusion.

He snapped out of his trance, and I saw him tap his dashboard. "Hello?"

"Uh, hi." I sent a little wave when he looked back over at my car. "This is Taylor. Your next-door neighbor in this absolute clusterfuck."

"I didn't mean for you to call this instant, but I can't say I have any complaints."

With a self-conscious shrug, I moved one hand from the steering wheel to the back of my neck.

"So, Taylor, where are you heading this afternoon that's got you so stressed?" The way he said my name sent a chill down my spine in the best way.

"Everything is going wrong today, and now I'm late to meet my sister. She's trying on wedding dresses, and if I don't get out of this traffic soon, I'll miss it."

Why was it so easy to unload my stress on him? His soft smile and relaxed voice eased the ache in my shoulders—usually, talking to strangers piled on the stress rather than alleviating it.

I couldn't help the hint of desperation in my voice. "I can't miss it."

"LA traffic is a real bitch sometimes."

"Yeah, and Margo says there's a big accident ahead, so I don't think we're going anywhere anytime soon. I need to get off this freeway as soon as possible, but I'll admit, I've been distracted."

"I've been known to be very distracting." He grinned when I looked his way, and I let out a loud, surprised laugh.

I huffed. "That's not what I meant."

"Whatever you say, cutie. I'll let you merge in front of me once this car moves, but in exchange, I wanna see you this weekend."

The words "It's a date" left my mouth without my permission, and I turned my face so he couldn't see me wince.

Too bad I was going to ghost Gabriel. He seemed so sweet, but that's what had to happen.

All the wedding talk had put me in a mood. I wasn't actually lonely. Love was not for me, and I knew that. I had Kai, who would be single for the foreseeable future, right along with me, and I had Margo, at least for a few more weeks. I knew how falling in love worked out in the end.

And I was never going to put myself through that.

2

GABRIEL

"Don't let me keep you, then," I told Taylor. "We can text later."

From what I could see through his car window, Taylor looked totally put-together and handsome in a grey suit with a navy tie. His light brown hair had a hint of red undertones when the sun hit it, although his pale complexion indicated he probably didn't spend much time outside.

I wished I could see the color of his eyes.

Taylor continued. "How close do you think we are to the accident? It looks like traffic opens up just past this underpass."

I guess we weren't hanging up after all. I let him merge in front of me like I'd promised, even though that meant I could no longer see his face.

"I think you're right," I said.

The lanes in front of me slowly merged into one on the far left, only to reveal an absolute carnage of rubber ducks in every color of the rainbow spilling out of an overturned semi. I couldn't help cracking up at the ridiculousness of the scene.

And then I heard a magical sound—Taylor's laugh. It was deep and breathless but sounded a little unpracticed.

"Oh my god, this is not real," I heard him say when he'd finally caught his breath.

I wiped tears from the corners of my eyes. The truck's cab seemed ok, and if there had been an ambulance, it was long gone. I sent a wish up for the driver's health anyway before snapping a quick photo of the chaos with my phone.

"If you're dreaming, then so am I," I said, needing to hear him laugh again.

Taylor's laughter echoed over the phone. "Stop, that is so cheesy."

Score. I blew him a kiss through his rear-view mirror. Damn, was I glad he called. I could tell he'd almost surprised himself, and I found that endearing.

After we hung up, I quickly lost sight of Taylor's car as he rushed to his sister's appointment, and I turned the volume back up on my music. Growing up in Southern California, I'd been singing along with the radio to pass the time in traffic since I was small, although these days it was more Mad Tsai than Maná.

A text pinged on my phone while I was at a red light, and I glanced down to check it.

> MAMÁ
>
> Have you forgotten that you have parents?
> Papá needs your help in the garage.

If I needed something to burst my bubble, that was it.

I'd been putting off my next visit home to Santa Ana for a month, but I wouldn't be able to avoid my mom's texts and calls for much longer. Ever since Abuela moved back to Mexico to enjoy her retirement, the house had felt too empty, and my mom had been focusing all her hovering energy on me in my grandmother's absence.

Best to bite the bullet. I dialed my mother's number.

"Hola, mijo," my mother's voice filled my car. "It's good to hear you're still alive."

I sighed. "The botanical gardens are busy this time of year, but I'll be able to visit soon."

"Your work isn't that important. You can take time to visit your parents. We aren't going to be around forever."

"I know, Mamá."

My parents loved me, but they always managed to remind me of my shortcomings. I was their only son, bearing the weight of all their expectations. I loved my work as a horticulturalist planning public gardens, but they didn't understand why I needed expensive student loans to do the same job as my father did at his landscaping company. After changing my declared major a few times, I even had to stay an extra year to finish my degree.

I wasn't exactly making them proud. I wasn't doing anything they could brag about at church or around the neighborhood. I couldn't even hang on to a romantic partner.

"Did you hear that Oscar is going to be made a partner in his law firm?" Mamá asked.

Oscar—my responsible older cousin and a high-powered lawyer. A benchmark I was always held against. Now that I was staring down my thirtieth birthday, measuring up was starting to feel more and more out of reach.

"Tía Rosa is so proud," she said.

"I'm happy for him." I fought to keep the bitterness out of my voice. I *was* happy for him, as much as I was tired of living in his shadow. "He's a lot older than I am."

Why was it so hard for me to commit to a life plan? It seemed like everyone else had an internal compass guiding them to the same finish line, and mine was defunct, pointing me in the wrong direction.

Money was their security, and I understood that deeply, but I wanted more.

I wanted a life that was free and expansive. Why did every day have to be a series of sacrifices and obligations? Why couldn't it be fun?

She continued. "When I was your age, I had two jobs and an eight-year-old to take care of."

There was nothing really to say to that, and she knew it, which was why she said it. Mamá was smart, managing all the scheduling for Papá's landscaping business while working as a receptionist for a dentist's office.

I fell quiet and let her talk for the remainder of my drive, halfway listening to all the chisme about her church ladies, the neighbors down the street, and parents of friends I'd had in elementary school that I no longer kept in touch with. I'd heard half of these stories before, but despite what my mom implied, I cared about her. She just made it hard sometimes.

"...I'm going to invite the Lopez family. They have a single daughter who's your age."

I cut in. "Anyway, Mamá. I just wanted to let you know I'll be down soon to help Papá with his projects. I have to run into the store now."

She sighed. "Sale, hijo."

Thankfully, it was easier for Mamá to say goodbye once I'd promised a visit. I was too distracted by the display case of sprinkled donuts in front of me to process that I'd only been half-listening while she was orchestrating a set-up between the Lopezes' daughter and me.

IF MY LIFE WERE A MOVIE, I'd want it to start with the following montage: me in my yellow VW bug, driving down the Pacific

Coast Highway, with a box of donuts in the front seat. As far as I was concerned, there was nothing better.

"Just call off from work, Oscar. It'll be worth it."

I'd been at my job for a year but never managed to rack up much PTO because I did things like call my cousin on a random Tuesday afternoon and convince him to play hooky with me. As far as I was concerned, time off was intended to be taken, and I found reasons to use it.

"It's a beautiful day, and it's January!" I said. "We have to take advantage."

"We live in Los Angeles. The weather is always gorgeous." Oscar had on his professional voice, the one he used at work, and his keyboard clacked in the background. "I have adult responsibilities to handle."

I winced but tried to let the unintentional dig slide off my shoulders. It's not that I didn't like my work at the botanical gardens. It was as close to an ideal full-time job as I could get. But even still, it was just a job. Days like today, I'd never get back. It was hard to explain that to someone as career-driven and successful as Oscar.

Oscar and I grew up together in the same neighborhood. I didn't have siblings, but I had him. I was bigger than him in build, but he had me in height. He was five years older than me, which he loved to rib me about in childhood because he got to do everything fun before I did.

How the tables had turned now that he's in his mid-thirties.

"Whatever," I said. "I'm not forcing you to do anything. It's just an invite, but it will be fun." I dragged out the last word, adding some teasing to my voice.

"I'll see what I can do, but no promises." Oscar sighed. "You're a bad influence on me."

"Yeah." Even I could admit that was true. Much to the

chagrin of my mother, who wished it worked in the reverse. That wasn't Oscar's fault, though.

"You know where we'll be." I kept my voice cheerful before hanging up the phone. There was no point in dwelling on my shortcomings; there was too much fun to be had.

Aside from a few tourists and a lone surfer trying to catch a break, the beach was practically abandoned. Tiny whitecaps broke on the wooden supports beneath the pier. The sun was shining, sparkling on the water, and the cool ocean breeze would keep me from sweating too much while we played. Our ragtag group had become close after joining an intramural queer volleyball league together. Now, we were always finding an excuse to make it to the beach.

We named our team Ace of Baes. It could be hard to negotiate all six of our schedules, but we did our best. Everyone except Oscar was already gathered at Huntington Beach when I arrived.

"I come bearing gifts," I shouted, raising the purple specialty donut box over my head and kicking off my flip-flops. There weren't many things I liked better than dirt under my fingernails or sand between my toes. I was a lucky bastard to be able to regularly have both.

"Dude, thank you." Brian was the first to reach his hand into the donut box, as usual. He was our resident gym bro, with tan muscles covered in tattoos and a short dark beard.

"Yeah, man," I said. "I saw this place online, and I couldn't resist checking it out."

"You're going to make us all need extra gym time with your impulse purchases." Lucas ran his hand through his blond, wavy hair. He was the only one who'd played volleyball in college until an injury sidelined him. As our most experienced player, he took on the role of captain and led our practices. Even though he could be a bit of a stickler, he was a great teammate, and I appreciated that one of us was organized.

Several of us needed full-time wranglers.

"Hey, no toxic diet culture here." Kat shoved Lucas aside. "Sugar isn't evil; you don't have to punish yourself to enjoy it."

We'd all heard plenty of stories about Kat's country club almond mom, but Kat embraced her curves. She grabbed the donut with the most sprinkles, split it down the middle, and handed one half to Alex.

Alex—the Wednesday Adams of our crew—eyed the rainbow sprinkles as if they'd infect her.

Kat tugged playfully on her braid. "They won't bite."

The six of us were a bit of an odd group, but I wouldn't trade it for anything. I loved my teammates like my siblings. I was a fish out of water in my family, but the Baes accepted me no matter what.

We'd put up the net and started running drills when Oscar finally showed. He'd abandoned his fancy suit for shorts and a razorback tank that showed off his long limbs. He still wore his designer shades, though, and his hair—wavy to my curls—was styled back.

"Yes! Now we can play three-on-three." I fist-bumped Brian.

"Good of you to make time for us in your demanding schedule, esquire." Lucas gave a mock salute.

"I'm only going to be able to stay for an hour or so," Oscar said, grinning. "I made up an excuse to take a long lunch, but I do have to actually work today, unlike you assholes."

"Yeah, yeah. Let's not waste time then." Brian shooed Oscar onto our makeshift court.

Kat, Brian, and I ended up on one side, with Lucas, Alex, and Oscar on the other. We played six-on-six against other teams in the league, but we tried to change the matchups as much as possible when we practiced so that we'd all be able to read each other.

Physical activity was calming, even when my lungs were burning, and my muscles were spent. My mind never felt as still as when I was in motion. There was no way I could have worked a desk job like Oscar, even if I'd been academically inclined. I needed to feel the fresh air and be on my feet, or my mind would swallow me whole. I threw myself into the volleyball game like an enthusiastic puppy, and even though I was mediocre, I liked to think I'd get an A for effort.

The hour Oscar granted us went by way too fast. Despite collective peer pressure, he ended up going back to work. Lucas was the next to peel off after receiving a text from his husband, and Kat called it a day so she could shower and get ready for her evening shift at the bar. Once we'd packed up the net, Alex and I helped Brian carry everything back to his Jeep.

"I'm starving." I slammed the trunk shut. "Dinner?"

"Can't," Brian said. "I work early tomorrow, but there is a place near here that does really good quinoa bowls. You should check it out."

"Has anyone ever told you that for a meathead, you sure do eat like a rabbit?"

"That's how you keep the muscle definition, baby." Brian teased back, lifting his shirt to flex his abs. Between volleyball and the gym, I could keep in pretty good shape, but I was not willing to sacrifice my sweet tooth on the altar of a six-pack.

I laughed and reached in to tickle him, and he shrieked before escaping to the safety of his vehicle.

Once Alex and I sat down with our bowls, hers with salmon and mine with shredded beef, I had to admit defeat. "Don't tell Brian, but he was right. These are delicious."

"Your secret is safe with me." Alex rolled her eyes.

I joked that Alex was my platonic goth girlfriend—we could

not be more different when it came to our aesthetics. She was always in black, even in the heat of the LA summers. Always put on Chelsea Wolfe whenever I handed her the aux. Always told the darkest jokes. Meanwhile, my friends told me I had chaotic golden retriever energy.

"I meant to ask how things went with that gorgeous woman you were talking to at the bar last weekend," she said. "The one with the neck tattoos?"

"She was stunning." I shrugged. "But I wasn't feeling it. I got her number, though."

"No?" she said, raising a single manicured eyebrow.

I laughed, and my mind drifted to Taylor. "I guess I didn't feel the spark?"

Alex gave me a skeptical look. "Are you asking me or telling me?"

"I dunno. I'm not sure what was missing." And thirty was looming like a final exam I hadn't studied for. "But my mom's been threatening to set me up on dates if I don't settle down soon, and I'm starting to think she's serious."

"There's no rush to have everything figured out." Her eyes narrowed. "You have a job you like and awesome friends—that's not nothing in this economy."

I hummed as I considered her words. "You're right. What I'm doing now is a lot of fun. I'm sure things will work out the way they're supposed to."

"You know I'll support you, whatever you decide." She smiled slyly. "And if you want to hook your best friend up with that smoke show from the bar, I'll gladly take her off your hands."

"What a martyr." I laughed, steering the conversation to the upcoming volleyball tournament and away from these strange feelings of dissatisfaction.

So many people had told me I wasn't cut out for a serious

relationship that, even though I was tired of the hookup culture, I wasn't sure I could pull it off. I was the good-time guy—the fun one—my ex, Maria's, voice echoing in my head every time I let myself entertain delusions about happily ever afters.

No matter how much I wanted one.

No-strings was rejection-proof, and whether it happened with my new Highway Hottie or someone else didn't matter.

If I said it enough, maybe I would believe it.

3

TAYLOR

I'd made it to Fairy Godmother, the queer-owned boutique where Margo was trying on wedding dresses, with fifteen minutes left in the appointment. Thankfully, that was plenty of time for her to pour me a glass of champagne, shove me down on the sofa, and try on her top contenders for me.

We had our own little nook in the boutique, sectioned off with velvet curtains. Several mirrors surrounded the dais where Margo would model her dresses. A bouquet of fresh roses was on the small table with the champagne ice bucket, close enough to the small, tufted couch where I sat that I could smell them. Margo's consultant, a cute enby with gauged ears and a mint green jumpsuit, hovered just outside her dressing room, waiting to zip up the first dress Margo wanted to show me.

As I waited for Margo to change, my mind wandered to Gabriel. Did he make it to... damn, I hadn't even asked him where he was going. I hoped he wasn't still stuck on the 5, anyway.

"You're not even looking!" Margo had come out of the fitting room in a satin mermaid-style dress with a sweetheart neckline.

I shook myself back to the moment and looked her up and

down with a raised eyebrow. Her shoulder-length hair was dyed purple, a change from when we'd had lunch last week.

"It looks nice on you, but it's not the one. It doesn't have enough personality."

"Ugh, you're so right." Margo nodded decisively as she turned back toward the fitting room, swishing the dress behind her. "Ok, next!"

All this hoopla over a wedding made my skin itch. At sixteen, I'd decided I'd never get married, and as soon as Margo declared Benji 'the one,' I'd been dreading this process with a hefty serving of guilt. February would be here before we knew it, and it would all be over. I wasn't sure if I was relieved or sad.

I tried not to think too much about what life would have been like had Margo not gotten sick, if I hadn't needed to become a mini-parent at fifteen. I got all my driving hours for my learner's permit by shuttling her to appointments and picking up medications at the pharmacy.

I dropped my extracurriculars to be there for Margo's treatment, and I chose accounting in college so the salary from a stable, well-paying career could tackle those medical bills. I'd do it all over again, knowing she's here in the next room, putting on a wedding dress.

No use dwelling on what-ifs.

My phone buzzed, and my heart sped up when I saw the name flash across my screen.

Gabriel.

When I opened the photo, I couldn't help but laugh at the rainbow rubber ducky explosion we'd witnessed on the 5. Margo walked out in the next dress and grabbed my phone from my hands, evading my attempts to take it back.

Younger siblings have no boundaries.

"What's so funny?" She zoomed in on the photo. "What the hell is this?"

"This is what was blocking the 5 and messing up the traffic today." I snatched my phone back and assessed her dress: a princess style with rhinestones on the bodice. Margo was not at all a princess-dress kind of girl. I narrowed my eyes at her. "Who are you, and what have you done with my sister?"

"You don't like it?" Margo twirled on the small platform in front of the mirror. She tried to look innocent, but the mischief in her eyes gave her away.

"You already have a dress picked out, don't you? And you're trying on these random dresses so that I'll cry with relief when you put it on at last?"

Or, more likely, so I wouldn't feel too bad for being late and missing the moment.

The consultant snorted, covering their mouth to hide a smile.

Margo laughed. "You know me so well."

"Well, let me see it then! Stop torturing me with subpar dresses."

"Fine, fine, but the reveal will be worth it." She kissed my cheek and returned to the fitting room.

I took the opportunity to text Gabriel back.

TAYLOR

> I still don't believe that was real, even after seeing it with my own eyes.

He responded right away.

GABRIEL

> Did you know that a shipping container full of rubber ducks once fell into the Pacific Ocean, and people were finding them floating around Greenland a decade later?

> I have literally never contemplated the logistics of rubber ducky transportation until this very afternoon.

> Did you make it to your sister's appointment in time?

I snapped a quick photo of my hand holding the champagne as an answer. I had removed my suit jacket when I arrived at the appointment and rolled up my shirt sleeves. Apparently, I wasn't above teasing a little forearm porn, which came as quite a shock to me, even as I was hitting send. I was, to my knowledge, neither a flirt nor a tease, but something about this man made me forget myself.

TAYLOR

> I hope you made it to your destination safely as well.

"Get ready," Margo called out. "Here comes the grand reveal!"

Nothing prepared me for the sight as she stepped out from behind the curtain. The dress was form-fitting on top and long-sleeved, with strategic mesh panels that gave it a modern, geometric look. The skirt was full, with layers of tulle. It was avant-garde, feminine, and suited her perfectly.

"Damn, sis." I rushed to my feet and pulled her into a hug. Tears filled my eyes as I pulled back to look at her. "This is definitely the winner."

"Oh, stop." She swatted at me. "You're going to make me cry, too—but yeah, you're right. This is the one. It's the perfect vibe for the gallery venue, and I can buy it off the rack, so it'll be ready next month."

"Remember when you told me there was no chance you'd be finding your dress today?" I teased.

Benji had proposed over Christmas, and they'd rushed into wedding planning full speed ahead. I thought they were out of their minds for planning a wedding in six weeks, but Margo was understandably never one to waste time. Despite all my skepticism around relationships, I was glad Margo was having the wedding she wanted, even if it meant I'd have to see our parents in person for the first time since her college graduation.

There wasn't a single day that I didn't thank my lucky stars for still being able to see Margo living her best life.

I hugged her one more time, snapped a few photos of her in the dress, and we toasted with the last of the champagne.

"Who sent you that photo of the duck truck?" she asked from behind the curtain as she changed back into her street clothes.

I was hoping she wouldn't come back around to that, but at least she was still out of sight, so my flushed cheeks couldn't give me away.

"Turns out I made a friend on the 5 today."

"You don't say." Margo peeked her head out. "Is he cute?"

"Uhhhh..."

"I knew it. So, when are you taking him on a date?"

"This is the first time we've spoken. You need to relax."

I tended to be a bit cynical after having to mediate my parents' relationship as a teen and wading through a lot of failed dating app interactions in my twenties.

I would admit, however, that if there's one place to believe in love, it might be a wedding dress boutique. As if a sign from the universe, a bottle of champagne popped in a fitting room, followed by a round of cheers.

My phone buzzed with another text from Gabriel. My breath caught as I took in the selfie of Gabriel at the beach, curls framing his face, a wide grin, and sparkling hazel eyes.

GABRIEL
Safe and sound.

TAYLOR
Ugh, jealous. Can't wait to get home and get out of this suit.

Tease ;)

"Can't wait to have him at the wedding," Margo said in a singsong voice when she reappeared from the dressing room with a large garment bag in tow.

I sighed as we made our way outside. "You're ten steps ahead of reality, as always. It will probably lose momentum since I don't have much free time right now."

"Whatever you say, Debbie Downer. It wouldn't hurt to think positively now and then. You never know when the right person will surprise you."

Margo was a hopeless romantic, which was probably my fault. I took pride in having shielded her from the worst of the drama in our childhood.

As far as I was concerned, the only promise love made was that one day, you'd be without it again, worse off than when you began. I wasn't about to rain on her parade during what was supposed to be a happy time, though. There weren't two people more in love than Margo and Benji.

"Thanks for inviting me today," I said. "The dress is perfect."

She rolled her eyes as she pulled me into a hug. "Of course, you idiot."

As much as it would be nice to have someone on my arm for their wedding, I didn't need a date to have a good time. There was no reason to make anything work with Gabriel. The conversation would run its course, and that would be that. We spent our family's allotment of luck on Margo, so I was shit out of it.

My phone buzzed again, and my heart raced for a different reason—my father.

> **JOHN**
>
> Why did I just get a late payment notification on Margo's loan?
>
> You better take care of that ASAP. It's going to look bad on my credit.

Something stabbed at my chest, a sudden sharpness that made my phone slip from my loosened grip. I pressed my hand to my left pec, dragging in a labored inhale. My heartbeat stuttered.

Margo rushed toward me. If she was speaking, I couldn't hear her. Her garment bag lay abandoned on the asphalt.

I slumped toward the pavement.

And everything went black.

I DON'T KNOW how much time passed before I opened my eyes to beige acoustic ceiling tiles, an incessant beeping, and various sensors connected to my chest and hands.

"Oh, thank goodness." Margo appeared by my side. "How are you feeling?"

I groaned. "Like I face-planted on concrete."

"You had me so scared. I'm not used to being the one on this side of the hospital bed." It was probably supposed to be a joke, but I could hear the fear beneath it.

I was the big brother. I was supposed to be looking out for her.

"Did you actually eat that snack I dropped off, asshole?" I finally noticed Kai sitting in a chair in the corner of the room, his feet kicked up on his laptop bag, still in his work clothes.

I shrugged. "I can't remember."

"So, no." Kai grunted and shook his head. "You're lucky I love you. You scared us both."

"The doctors are going to want to run a bunch of tests. They said your bloodwork looks like you might have had a heart attack. I told them about my leukemia, too, just in case."

Margo squeezed my hand so tightly that I briefly wondered if it would mess up whatever measurement the sensor on my finger was tracking.

Fear coursed through me. I could remember everything Margo went through at just eight years old.

It couldn't be that. Not now. Not ever. I didn't have time to be sick.

I shoved the panic aside, putting on a brave face for her. "A heart attack? I'm thirty-two. It definitely wasn't that. I'm just tired and had low blood sugar, that's all."

"You've been losing weight. Don't think I haven't noticed." Margo pushed my hair back from my forehead and scanned my face. "Kai says you're barely sleeping or eating."

I glared at Kai. He was the one person who knew why I'd been working so hard, and he'd ratted me out to my sister. She was worried for nothing. I had everything under control.

"That's because it's tax season and we have a lot to do," I said. "Everything is fine, Margo."

"I appreciate you trying to make me feel better, but it's not working." Margo shook her head. "I'm not going to be able to relax until you get all the tests they recommend, and maybe a few extras."

I sighed and silently prayed that this hospital was in-network. I didn't need a second medical debt hanging over my head.

As soon as I got my phone back, I was making that loan

payment. I didn't want to hear from my father any more than I had to.

Over the next few hours, people flowed in and out: a nurse to draw my blood, an EKG tech, and a cardiologist. Benji came to drop off food and a change of clothes for Margo. I had more blood drawn, and Kai watched like a hawk while I forced myself to eat the biggest, blandest bowl of split pea soup I'd ever encountered. Finally, someone appeared to do a bone marrow biopsy on my hip. Margo wouldn't let it go until I'd had that last one, even though the nurse said my white blood cell count was only elevated a small amount.

With each new visitor, the bill kept tallying higher and higher in my mind.

4

GABRIEL

Over the following days, my Highway Hottie went radio silent.

It had been two days, but I couldn't stop thinking about him. He almost seemed like a figment of my imagination: a suit-wearing specter I could use to hang all my daydreams on. It got to the point that I was worried that if we did ever bump into each other again, he wouldn't live up to my fantasies.

In a city as big as LA, we'd never see each other again, but if I ran into him at the bars one day, I wasn't going to let him leave without going down on him at least once.

Just to get him out of my system.

It was Thursday morning when I made a quick stop for supplies at The Gnomery, my favorite neighborhood garden center, on my way to work. My plant babies deserved the best. I had become good friends with the owner, Fiona, since I came in so often. She started giving me the small business discount when she found out about my bitters brewing hobby, and in exchange, I brought her samples from each batch for free.

"Great to see you," Fiona called out.

"I have a new flavor for you," I said, making my way to the

counter. "I think it's going to be my summer special, lavender hibiscus."

"Oh, what a treat!" Fiona's box braids were tied back behind a light blue handkerchief, and she wore a pair of olive green coveralls. "Any serving suggestions?"

"Gin, I think." I turned to where I knew I'd find my favorite soil blends, then stopped. "Or tequila. Everything tastes great with tequila."

Fiona's laughter followed me down the aisle.

I'd picked out everything I needed, plus a pretty terracotta pot, and was standing at the checkout counter when I heard the bell chime over the front door.

"Be right with you, Taylor," Fiona called out to someone behind me.

I froze.

No way this was *my* Taylor. But sure enough, when I turned to look, there was no mistaking him—tall, tailored suit, reddish brown hair—standing by the pretty display of fairy houses Fiona always decorated.

The pot I was holding slipped from my fingers, crashing onto the concrete floor and breaking into pieces.

"Oh shit," I whispered.

Taylor turned at the sound, and he was just as hot as I remembered. I wished he were getting a better second impression. My hair was a disaster, and I was dressed for work at the botanical gardens—a white polo with our logo, khaki cargo pants, and thick-toed boots. I could finally see the color of Taylor's blue eyes, the freckles across his cheeks, and the way his suit fit every line of his lean body to perfection.

My cheeks heated when I remembered the promise I made to myself just this morning. A blow job in the back aisles of The Gnomery had not been on my bingo card, but if he'd let me...

Fiona's movement seemed to break the spell I was under as

she rounded the counter, holding a broom. "Are you ok, Gabriel?"

"Oh my god, I'm so sorry!" I quickly knelt to start collecting the broken pottery. "It slipped right through my fingers."

I glanced up at Taylor through my lashes. His cheeks flushed, and I couldn't help imagining whether it continued under his buttoned-up collar. My tongue darted out to lick my lips, and I watched his eyes follow the movement. Of course, he could simply be embarrassed for ghosting me, but in case the blush was from the sight of me on my knees, I'd play into it a little.

Turns out I hadn't been exaggerating the chemistry, at least on my end.

Taylor cleared his throat and loosened his tie, his pink cheeks darkening to red. Oh, it was so on.

"It's no problem," Fiona said, her voice pulling me away. "Let's get you another pot and a fresh bag of this potting soil, shall we?"

"You don't need to—" I start.

"Nonsense." Fiona waves a dismissive hand.

Taylor finally spoke, a playful seriousness to his words. "Are you sure you should be giving away inventory in front of your accountant?"

He made his way toward us, his movements brisk and precise.

"Oh, hush, you," Fiona replied, threatening him with her broom. "I get to run this business however I want. All you do around here is make sure I won't lose the farm if I get audited."

I chuckled as I took the broom out of Fiona's hands. Time to go in for the kill. "Careful, I'm taking this guy out tomorrow, and I want him in one piece."

Fiona's eyebrows shot up.

Taylor quickly added, "We met recently."

"Small world." She pressed her lips together in a smile and hustled away down one of the aisles, with a mischievous twinkle in her eye. "Taylor, let me go find those papers I had for you—and Gabriel, I'll grab your pot and soil. Be right back."

Subtle as a sledgehammer, that woman. I loved her for it, because now I had my opening.

"It's nice to meet you, officially." I brushed my hand off on my pants before reaching out to offer it.

He gave a little squeeze before letting go, and I melted. It was going to be so fun to take this put-together man apart.

"Likewise," Taylor said.

"So, tomorrow night?"

"What?"

"For our date." I smiled up at him, stepping a little closer.

"I work late..."

"If I didn't know better, I'd think you're trying to get out of our agreement," I teased.

Taylor worried his lip between his teeth and avoided my eyes.

I wanted to take that plump lip in my mouth instead, treat it with a little more care.

I brushed my fingers against his hand. It was a touch so light it could be explained away as unintentional, but I felt it in every fiber of my body. I took one step closer. "It's fine if you don't want to go out. I think you're stunning, but I'm not going to force you into anything if it's one-sided."

"It's, uh, definitely not one-sided," Taylor replied, giving a little self-conscious grin. "You think I'm stunning, do you?"

"Hell, yeah. Even better up close than from my car window." My eyes dropped to his lips, and I heard his breath catch. "So, about that date..."

Fiona slammed her office door as she made her way back to the checkout counter. Taylor startled and stepped back, and I felt a cool breeze in place of the warmth from his body. I was a confident guy, but I wasn't going to pressure anyone to go out with me. I mentally started writing him off, but...

He touched my elbow and leaned in to whisper, "Tomorrow."

Fiona passed me my purchases before handing Taylor a manila envelope. "Here are those receipts you asked for. I'm sorry I couldn't figure out the online portal. You know I'm hopeless with technology."

"It's fine. It wasn't out of my way to swing by for them," Taylor said, taking the envelope. He flipped through the contents with a small smile. "I know you wanted an excuse to see my face."

"I wasn't expecting to see you at all, actually," Fiona said, her lips pursed. "A coworker of yours called yesterday to say you'd been in the hospital."

I hovered by the front door, pretending to be fascinated by the seed carousel and not at all in their conversation. A hospital visit? Why did that make my chest ache? I didn't even know this guy.

That explained why he'd stopped texting.

"I'm fine, thank you," Taylor said. "I'll call if I have any other questions while I'm working on your return. It'll probably be the first or second week of February."

Ok, so he clearly didn't want to talk about it, and I certainly didn't know him well enough to ask.

"Sure thing." Fiona pushed Taylor toward the door. "Now get out of here."

I squinted into the sunlight as I stepped outside, adjusting the large pot in my grip as Taylor followed. If I flexed my biceps a little extra for the benefit of my audience, that was within my rights. "Were you serious about tomorrow?"

"Yeah, I should be able to meet you around eight p.m." Taylor typed away on his phone.

Maybe he would ghost me a second time, especially since he was glued to his phone. I felt a buzz in my pocket.

"I just sent you a calendar invite," he said as he slid his phone into his pocket.

I wanted to ask about the hospital. I wanted to ask why he was working so late. I wanted to kiss him. Instead, I simply said, "Works for me. You going to buy me dinner?"

"I MET A BOY," I whispered conspiratorially to Magdalena, as I misted her large Monstera leaves. She remained as stoic as ever, hard to impress as she was.

The little jungle I'd created in my tiny apartment was like an oasis. I had twinkle lights hung over the top of the greenhouses like indoor stars, and the walls were painted a warm coral color, making me smile every time I opened the front door.

"He's kind of shy and funny and has the prettiest blue eyes."

I pulled up my phone to show Magdalena the selfie he'd sent me, but she was unmoved. Maybe she wasn't into guys; that's the only reason I could think of as to why she wouldn't immediately be in love.

Not that I was in love, either. Obviously.

"Do you think I can really do this whole dating thing?" I toyed mindlessly with the gold hoop in my nose. Magdalena didn't answer, and I sighed. "No, you're right. I'm overthinking. It's just a casual dinner at a bar. Maybe some dancing if I'm lucky. No pressure."

I continued misting the plant babies. Several hung from the ceiling in macramé hangers. Then, I had the greenhouse cabinets, the smaller pots lining my TV console, and several bigger floor pots lined up under the windows. They all had names and personalities, and I liked to imagine the telenovela-style dramas that unfolded between them while I was at work. I should have known I'd end up working with plants, but it was a long, winding road.

When I finally made it into the bathroom to brush my teeth before bed, my eyes landed on the bathtub full of oranges I'd completely forgotten about. My winter bitters flavor was orange agave, and it was my most popular. However, those damn oranges were standing between me and my ability to take a shower—something I definitely needed to do before my date with Taylor tomorrow.

I wasn't trying to disrupt the cocktail industry or anything. It just felt good to make something delicious and share it with friends. Downtime made me itchy, and I'd had many hobbies come and go, but this one had stuck so far.

Even though part of me wanted something in my life to be permanent, I never let myself get too attached. Whether it was hobbies, careers, or people, things always ended. I was waiting for the spark, for something to consume me. Why bother settling without that burn-the-world-for-you feeling?

"You couldn't have reminded me about this earlier?" I called out to Magdalena in accusation as I stared down the oranges.

Silence. Typical.

I was tempted to call Taylor so he could keep me company while I worked. It was a strange impulse, considering we'd barely interacted. There was definitely a spark, though, and I was prepared to chase it. What did Taylor get up to on a Thursday night? I connected my headphones and hit dial. No overthinking.

While the phone rang, I began gathering oranges into my largest stock pot, carrying from the shower to the kitchen sink to wash and juice them.

"Gabriel?" a groggy voice said.

I glanced down at my phone and realized that it was after midnight. Ok, so I should probably have tempered my impulsiveness long enough to check the time.

"Oh, my goodness, I'm so sorry," I said quickly. "I didn't realize it was so late."

"Is everything ok?"

"Yeah, everything is fine. I'm elbows deep in a bathtub full of oranges and thought it'd be nice to have your company, but I don't want to interrupt your sleep. We can talk tomorrow."

"A bathtub full of what?" His voice was husky with sleep. "I'll be honest, this is the strangest booty call I've ever received."

My mind finally processed that I was mostly naked and he was in bed, and suddenly, that was all I could think about. Was he naked, too? He'd looked so goddamn good in that suit when he showed up at The Gnomery, all long, elegant lines. I couldn't help imagining what he might look like dressed down. He seemed the type to have silk pajamas or some shit.

"Gabriel?"

I'd been internally panicking for too long, so I panicked externally instead. "I really wasn't trying to booty call you, I swear. Please go back to sleep and let me die of embarrassment in peace."

Taylor chuckled softly through the phone. "It's fine."

I could hear Taylor shuffling around in his sheets, and I bit the inside of my cheek to stop myself from asking him what he was wearing. "It's not, but I appreciate you saying that. I can't wait to see you tomorrow."

"Goodnight, Gabriel," he said in that sexy, sleepy voice.

Did he get bedhead, or was his hair always perfectly in place? I got half-hard just imagining it.

"Sweet dreams," I said.

By the time I piled the bucket of peels and the gallons of orange juice into the fridge, it was close to three in the morning.

I stepped under the shower spray to rinse off the sticky orange juice residue. I was still mortified that Taylor thought I was trying to booty call him. While I *was* trying to sleep with him eventually, a midnight 'u up?' was not my style. I might have made a fool of myself, but I wouldn't let myself regret it.

I shivered and ran a soapy hand over my body, finally palming my hardening cock.

My breath quickened. I leaned my free arm against the shower wall for support as I let my mind wander into sexy territory, filling with my usual shower spank bank material of wet, soapy bodies.

A pair of particularly compelling blue eyes invaded my imagination.

Hey, Taylor was the one who put the idea of a late-night booty call in my mind. I was just running with it.

I whimpered, tracing my thumb over the head of my cock, sliding the foreskin around.

Fantasy Taylor pressed against my back, his arm reaching around to take control of my handjob, whispering in my ear with that deep, scratchy voice. Those soft, delicate fingers wrapped around me. The pounding stream from the shower head above became kisses on the back of my neck.

A moan fell from my mouth.

If only he were here to hear it.

Speeding up my strokes and tightening my grip, it wasn't long before I was painting the tile with my release.

5

TAYLOR

I was stationed in the break room in front of the coffee machine, daydreaming about that midnight phone call from Gabriel and guarding my in-process mocha latte, when Kai bumped his hip into mine.

"Don't get enough of me at home, so you have to come harass me at work, too?" I said.

"You know it." He groaned. "My eyes are going cross-eyed staring at spreadsheets, and it's only the first official week of January."

"It happens every year."

"And every year, I am unprepared. Why are you surprised by this?"

I wasn't surprised, not really; we'd been attached at the hip since our CPA study sessions in college when he became my emotional support extrovert.

"Got any plans for this weekend?" Kai asked as I grabbed my mocha, and he popped his coffee pod into the machine.

"Actually... I have a date tonight."

Not that I particularly wanted this information to be widely known, but I wasn't going to be keeping anything from my roommate slash nosey AF bestie for long. Might as well surrender willingly.

"You. Have a date," Kai repeated. "You never go on dates! You hardly leave the house unless it's for work."

"You exaggerate." I left the house for more than work, in fact, almost every week I had lunch with—

"...or Margo. I can hardly get you to hit the bars with me anymore. Where did you meet this magical man?"

Ok, fine. Maybe he wasn't exaggerating that much. "We met in a traffic jam on Monday afternoon when I left work early."

"Ooh, damn. You can pull even in that basic Honda Civic, huh? Of course, you can."

I rolled my eyes and deflected. "It's probably going to be a casual thing, but I don't think it'll be terrible as far as first dates go. We've been texting, and he seems decent."

"Decent, huh?" He chuckled. "Well, it's a good thing you're setting the bar so high."

"Don't get me started on Mark or Mike or whatever gym bro you're currently getting under these days."

"Hey!" His usually unflappable demeanor wavered slightly before a mischievous smile spread across his face.

"I never claimed to be looking for true love. I'm just in it for the excellent dicking down, obviously. And Matt knew what he was doing in that department." Kai waggled his eyebrows at me suggestively. "But he's old news now."

I laughed at his straightforwardness. I was neither a prude nor a virgin, but I didn't go broadcasting things as unabashedly as Kai did. He insisted that being blunt meant fewer misunderstandings when you finally made it to the bedroom.

I wasn't hurting in the hookup department. I got my needs met. So what if it felt a little transactional? Transactions were clean. So what if I was lonely?

It was better to be lonely than hurt.

"Rachel wanted to see you," Kai said, grabbing his mug from the machine. "She didn't say why, just that she wanted you to stop into her office before you left for the day."

I grimaced. Rachel was a great boss, but I couldn't think of a positive reason she would want to meet with me out of the blue. I walked to her office with my feet feeling like lead.

Rachel's corner office was well-appointed, with colorful modern art painted by one of our accounting clients. She was backlit by the floor-to-ceiling windows, so I couldn't immediately see her face. Why was I so nervous? My heartbeat fluttered.

Were these the palpitations the doctor was referring to that I should watch out for?

"Are you alright, Taylor?" Rachel sounded concerned. "Sit, sit."

"I am." I plopped into the chair and rubbed my chest before remembering where I was. I immediately dropped my hands and squared my shoulders. "How can I help you?"

"Actually, I'm hoping I can help you. Did you know our company offers medical leave?"

My brow furrowed as Rachel continued.

"As your boss, I'm going to strongly suggest that you avail yourself of it. Alternatively, you have almost six weeks of PTO banked up."

"I don't understand."

"You're a great employee, and we're so grateful for the work you do for our clients," Rachel said, "but I'm concerned about your health. You regularly clock in at six a.m. and don't clock out until eight p.m. And with your hospitalization earlier this week..."

"I'm fine. Everything is fine!" The frustration seeped into my voice, although I tried to keep it professional. "Have you received complaints about my work?"

"No. Your clients love you and consistently give you wonderful reviews."

"Then why am I being punished?" I was so close to the finish line of paying off those debts, so close to being free. Now my body and my boss were betraying me.

"This is not a punishment. Think of it like a sabbatical."

"What will happen to my clients? We're right in the middle of the busiest time of year. I can't abandon them."

Lately, every little task felt like moving a boulder. All my love for the job had evaporated, but I wasn't about to abandon Fiona and the others.

"Your projects will be handed off to others on the team. I'd like for you to take at least a month off. Focus on your health and your family, and you can pick things up when you get back."

"It sounds like I don't have a choice."

"You do... but compliance is strongly encouraged."

I stood abruptly. "Understood."

"Fill Kai in on where all your current clients are in the workflow before you head out today and enjoy your time off." Rachel rounded her desk to shake my hand.

"Will do," I grunted. I knew I was being rude, but I struggled to make sense of what was happening.

Aside from Margo, my work was everything to me. Now, both were being taken away at the same time. I walked back to my desk in a haze. I contemplated texting Gabriel and canceling our date, but being alone with my thoughts felt equally terrifying.

BUTTERFLIES SWAM in my belly as I sat in the car outside the bar, my chest tight with nerves. It was my last chance to get out of this—I could turn the car around and never text Gabriel again. But knowing he was inside waiting for me, I couldn't bring myself to do it.

I allowed myself three deep breaths before rolling back my shoulders, pulling myself out of the vehicle, and making my way inside.

I pushed the door open, letting my eyes adjust to the lowered lights of the bar, and scanned the room. The dance floor was abandoned this early in the evening, but every seat at the bar was full.

When I finally spotted Gabriel sliding out of a booth in the back corner, I couldn't help but smile despite my anxiety.

Holy sex on a stick, the man was hot. Gabriel wore a loose-fit grey tee, and the V-neck showed off his sharp collarbones. His cuffed jeans hugged his legs, and he wore white sneakers. When our eyes met, his dimpled smile was totally captivating.

Shit, how did you greet someone on a first date? If he'd stayed in the booth, that would have been easier, but he was getting up. A handshake seemed too formal. Jumping right to peeling him out of those jeans was probably presumptuous, even though I could admit, at least to myself, that it was what I wanted.

Gabriel made me think ridiculous things.

Thankfully, he made the decision for me as he threw his arms around my neck and wrapped me in a hug. My mind quieted immediately as I put my hands around his waist and held him close. He was maybe two inches shorter than me, and he felt good in my arms.

After a beat, he leaned back and said, "It's really good to see you."

We were pressed against each other, looking into each other's eyes like we were lovers who'd spent months apart, not relative strangers who'd chatted a few times and were now on a first date.

I laughed lightly to alleviate the tension. "You, too."

He let his arms fall from my shoulders and stepped back, the moment broken.

"I hope this booth is ok," Gabriel said, sliding onto the bench seat. "I figured it'd be easier to talk back here, although the dance floor doesn't start to get rowdy until around eleven, so we have a few hours yet."

I sat across from him. "Oh, have you been here before?"

Gabriel gave a rueful smile. "Yeah, a handful of times. Some of my buddies work here. In retrospect, I should have asked to meet somewhere else because I'm pretty sure at least one of them will try hard to embarrass me tonight."

As if summoned, a waitress with dirty blonde hair, dark brown eyes, and hot pink lipstick appeared at the table. She gasped. "We would never."

"So, it begins." Gabriel rolled his eyes. "Taylor, meet Kat."

"Hey, hun," Kat said, looking me up and down.

I shifted under her gaze.

"Can I get you anything to drink? We have an excellent seasonal cocktail made with mezcal and orange agave bitters."

"Nice to meet you," I said. "That sounds awesome, actually. I'll take one."

Kat shot Gabriel a quick smile as if she was in on a secret. He ordered an old-fashioned, and we both decided on the burgers with fries. Once Kat left the table with our orders, Gabriel visibly relaxed.

"How do you two know each other?" I asked.

"I bartended for a few years after college, so we met when we worked at the same bar. Now we play in a volleyball league together."

"What do you do for work now?"

"I'm in horticulture at the Beachside Botanic Gardens. I help care for the plants and plan exhibits, among other things." Gabriel smiled. "I also, uh, make small batch bitters at home for fun."

My eyes widened. "Like the kind, for example, that they might use at a gay bar for seasonal cocktail specials?"

He looked sheepish, sinking slightly in his seat. "Um, yeah, actually. Exactly like that."

"Wow, ok, plant daddy. You are far too cool for me." My eyes widened when I realized what came out of my mouth. Embarrassed, I covered my face with my hands.

Gabriel laughed. "Plant daddy. Oh my god."

"So, when you said you were in a bathtub full of oranges last night..."

"They're in season right now!" Gabriel peeled my fingers away from my face and held them lightly. "I really did have like three hundred oranges in my bathtub."

I couldn't believe this guy. Not only was he hot, but he also had fun hobbies, an interesting job, and a side hustle. I was so out of my league.

He smiled at me, and I got lost momentarily, noticing how thick his eyelashes were. When Kat reappeared with our drinks, I pulled my hands back reluctantly.

"Anyway," Gabriel said. "It's not like a real business or anything. Just a hobby."

"Hey," I said, more forcefully than I intended. "Just because you're doing it for fun doesn't mean it's not a real business. I think it's awesome."

Gabriel peered at me. "Thanks, Taylor. What about you? How do you spend your time?"

"Well, I work in accounting, as you know. Although I just got forced into medical leave, which is a long story."

Gabriel's brow furrowed.

"Other than that, I'm helping my sister with her wedding. That's practically a full-time job, since the woman decided to plan the whole thing in six weeks. I haven't had time for hobbies or anything in a while."

I sounded boring even to my own ears. *You're supposed to be putting your best foot forward here, Taylor.* "Thrilling, I know."

"I find you very thrilling." Gabriel's voice was low and warm.

My cheeks flushed. "Whatever. I know I'm not that interesting. I'm like the Honda Civic of people."

"C'mon, Civics are reliable and low maintenance." He winked. "There's a reason so many people like them, but if it's more fun you want to have, I can definitely help you."

I couldn't help smiling back at him and nodding. Gabriel had this way of off-roading across my carefully constructed plans and intentions. It wasn't like me to sign a contract without reading the terms and conditions. What did I agree to, exactly?

"Let's start with getting you out of the house. I have a volleyball tournament tomorrow. It's a queer league, and we play at Huntington Beach. You should come."

"Oh, uh... sure?" Normally, I worked at least a half day on the weekends during tax season, but now I'd have to find a new way to fill my time. This seemed as fine a plan as any.

"Great," Gabriel said. "That's settled, then. Sounds like you and your sister are close."

"We are." I was simultaneously grateful for the subject change and not about to walk into that whole mess. "She's eight years younger than me, but we've been close since we were kids. Our parents weren't exactly around a lot. Although I think if I want you to like me, I should keep the family trauma dump for at least date three or four."

That made Gabriel laugh. "Can't wait."

6

GABRIEL

"Speaking of my sister, would you mind taking a photo of me?" Taylor asked as Kat dropped off our burgers. "She apparently needs daily proof of life now."

Kat jumped in to offer, as she reached for Taylor's phone. "I can take one of both of you."

He hesitantly gave it to her, and my hand rested on his forearm across the table as we leaned in for the photo.

I was in so much fucking trouble with this guy. I should have been terrified that he was already hinting at more dates when we hadn't even made it one drink into the first one. And yet...

I was the perfect person to help Taylor let loose a little bit, and I was already brainstorming ideas in the back of my mind for places I could drag him.

"Text it to me, too?" I asked Taylor when he got his phone back from Kat.

It was our first photo together, and I was not being sentimental or cute about it in any way.

When Kat remained at the table, hovering, I cleared my throat. "I think we're good here, Kat."

"Ok," she chirped. "Just holler if you need anything else!"

Alex eyed us from behind the bar.

I didn't know what I was thinking, inviting Taylor to volleyball. These hoes were going to be all up in our business. For now, I had him to myself, and I directed all my attention his way.

"I'm trying so hard not to be nosy," I said at last, picking up my burger. "But I overheard Fiona talking about the hospital, and now you mentioned medical leave. You don't have to tell me anything if you don't want to, but I'm also here to listen if you need it."

"I don't know why everyone is making a big deal out of this. I passed out Tuesday night, and Margo took me to the ER for a bunch of tests. Now, even my boss is treating me like I'm made of glass. But I feel normal!" Taylor took a deep breath.

I hummed. It seemed like he had more to get off his chest.

He sighed. "I don't want to be off work on some kind of corporately sanctioned bed rest, especially during our busiest time of year. My clients deserve better."

"You don't have to worry about any of that from me." I smirked. "I'm planning on handling you as roughly as you'll let me."

The tension drained from his posture as he laughed. That was my gift, keeping it light, and I could tell Taylor needed it.

The conversation wove from there through the usual first date suspects: favorite movies, where we'd grown up and gone to college, and the best concert we'd ever attended.

"Ok." I gained confidence now that I was on drink number two. "What do you think is the most dateable type of cookie?"

Taylor tilted his head to the side. "Hmm. I want to say chocolate chip because that feels like the obvious answer. But honestly, my favorite cookie has always been a gingersnap."

I could appreciate a man who took my ridiculousness in stride.

"Ooh, a little spicy, I like it." I wiggled my eyebrows at him over my drink, and that pretty blush returned to his face. "In my opinion, it's those peanut butter cookies with the Hershey's candy on top. They're dependable and classic, but also an excellent kisser."

Taylor chuckled at that, and I couldn't resist taking the questions in a little more PG-13 direction. "Tell me about your first kiss."

Taylor glanced to the side before answering, clearly hesitating. I was about to retract my question when he finally answered.

"Will Chan, backstage after a dress rehearsal for the school play when I was fifteen. We were both on the stage crew. It was awkward, as I guess most first kisses are, but it definitely confirmed that I was gay." Taylor shook his head and a little bit of the light left his eyes.

"I had to drop out of theater not long after that, so it never went anywhere," he said. "You?"

I wanted to ask why he quit theater, but I should answer his question first.

"My first kiss with a girl was my neighbor, Sara, when we were both thirteen. We were playing a game of truth or dare, but we ended up making out in her backyard again after everyone else went home. The first guy I kissed was my college roommate, Henry. It happened kind of spur of the moment during a threesome with him and this girl he was seeing."

I looked across at Taylor, his cheeks stained pink. He cleared his throat. "Is that something you're into?"

I started to feel a little defensive, worried that maybe he'd have an issue with my being bi, until he clarified.

"Threesomes, I mean."

"It's not something I seek out, but it's happened a few times over the years when the circumstances felt right." I winked.

"Honestly, I prefer to focus my attention on one person at a time."

His shoulders relaxed, though the flush in his cheeks didn't fade. "Good, ok, yeah."

I waited to see if he'd elaborate, but he stayed quiet, those pensive blue eyes scanning my face.

Finishing off the rest of my drink, I assessed the bar. Since I'd be competing in a volleyball tournament, I didn't want to keep drinking, but I wasn't ready for the night to end.

Maybe the first step in encouraging Taylor to have more fun was spending a little time on the dance floor. It was now around ten, and while it was not as crowded as it would get, there were enough people on the dance floor that I could risk the invite. "Want to close out here and dance for a little bit?"

"As long as you don't take it personally when I turn into a pumpkin soon. At the risk of sounding like an old man, it is past my bedtime. But a dance before we go sounds fun."

Taylor insisted on paying, and I promised that next time it would be my turn. We both scooted out of the booth, and I took his hand, dragging him into the crowd of moving bodies.

Even though we began in our own space, it wasn't long before we were pressed against each other, his front to my back. Taylor seemed shy with words, but it was clear he had confidence in his body. He held my hips in a solid grip as we moved together, and I leaned my head back onto his shoulder, nuzzling my face into his neck. Taylor smelled amazing, like spiced vanilla. He was a couple of inches taller than me, the perfect height to tuck myself against.

His hands moved across my chest, and I could tell the moment he felt the bars through my nipples.

"I was wondering if you had any other piercings." Taylor toyed with the jewelry through my shirt, and I held back a moan as I pushed back against him.

When the music transitioned to something with more bass, he spun me around so we were face to face, our thighs interlocking. We moved so well together, like waves against the shore, totally in sync. Now that I could see his face, I wanted to kiss him badly.

We were inches apart, and I thought he was going to move in and meet my lips. My breath hitched as he hovered near my mouth. His attention moved down to my lips.

But at the last minute, he diverted to my ear instead.

"You make it difficult to be responsible," he whispered.

I could feel him getting hard against my leg as we ground against each other, and there was no way he couldn't tell how turned on I was with as tight as these jeans were.

"Responsible is overrated." I ran my finger across his skin, tracing the chains he had around his neck.

Taylor shivered.

After another few songs, he grabbed my hand and dragged me toward the front of the bar. As we emerged into the relative quiet of the night, he pulled me against him again.

"Thank you for the dance." Taylor looked into my eyes as he spoke, and I believed each word. "It was just what I needed."

I was caught in his tractor beam, waiting for him to make a move. Our faces were inches apart, and I closed my eyes as he leaned forward, my lips parting.

He pressed a light kiss to my cheek, near where my jaw met my ear, and pulled away. "I'm going to call it a night. Text me when you get home?"

"Yeah, of course," I said, flustered. "I'm gonna run back inside for a minute to say bye to my friends, but I'll text you the tournament details before I go to bed."

"Goodnight," Taylor said as I leaned my back up against the brick wall of the bar. "I'll see you tomorrow."

He was really leaving without kissing me? I'm sure my

surprise showed on my face. I hadn't read things that wrong tonight, had I? I'd talked a big game to myself about blowing him in the bathroom, and now I was letting him walk away. Maybe I knew once we hooked up, my excuses to see him again would run out, and I wasn't quite ready for that.

"Night." I blew him a kiss with a playful smile, and he caught it in his hand before turning away and disappearing down the street toward his car.

WHEN I WALKED BACK INSIDE and squeezed into a seat at the bar, Alex and Kat were already hovering, waiting for the post-date analysis.

I put my elbows on the bar and groaned into my hands. "Damn it, he's so hot."

"Hun, we have eyes," Kat said. "Tell us something we don't know. How was the kiss?"

"He, uh...we didn't kiss." I glanced away. The rejection was still fresh.

As much as I wanted to shake Taylor for ghosting me and teasing me, I could see the desire in his eyes tonight. I had a hunch it wasn't personal—or maybe I needed to believe that.

"You didn't kiss?" Kat shrieked. "You were practically humping his leg out on the dance floor! I assumed he'd dragged you outside to make out."

Alex had stepped away to help another customer, but she gave us both side eye at Kat's outburst.

"Shhhhh, Jesus. I don't need the whole bar in my business," I hissed.

"That's your fault for bringing him here when you knew we'd be working," Kat said.

I shrugged. "Taylor suggested it, and he'd sounded excited. I couldn't say no."

Alex and Kat exchanged a look.

"Hey, hey, what was that about?" I pointed at them accusingly.

"Just not like you to move so slowly," Alex said. "So, are you seeing him again?"

"I invited him to the tournament tomorrow. Hopefully he'll show, but we're definitely going to see each other again. I've appointed myself his shenanigans instigator."

They glanced at each other again, and I narrowed my eyes.

"His... what?" Kat asked.

"Shenanigans instigator. It's like the opposite of the fun police. He said he needed to have more fun, and you know how fun I am." This seemed perfectly logical to me, but both Kat and Alex were staring at me like I'd grown a second head.

Well, it was clearly time to leave my annoying friends behind. "Anyway, I just came to say bye before I head out. See you tomorrow, babes."

I couldn't get our almost-kiss out of my head for the rest of the night. It was impossible to deny the spark I felt with Taylor. And I was sure it was mutual. So, what was holding him back?

There were so many things I liked about him, but the moment that made this feel like something extraordinary was when he was so quick to support my hobby. Aside from my Ace of Baes crew, no one believed in me like that. Especially not so quickly.

Taylor hardly knew me, yet he'd known exactly what to say.

Fuck waiting for him to make the first move. The next time I saw him, I was going to kiss him.

7

TAYLOR

When I got Gabriel's goodnight text last night, I regretted not kissing him. More accurately, I regretted not kissing him as soon as I'd let him walk back into the bar. The text only served to remind me what an idiot I was.

It had taken me a long time to fall asleep. I spent so much time second-guessing myself and every word I'd said—and what I hadn't said. In the end, I slept just as much as I would have if I'd brought him home with me, except in this scenario, I woke up alone.

Now, I was awake way too early, glaring at the coffee machine on our kitchen counter like it had personally wronged me.

Kai rummaged in the fridge behind me, pulling out a jar of overnight oats. He was headed to work, and I forgot I wouldn't be joining him until I was already dressed.

"Want one of these?" he asked.

"Only if there's a raspberry one. Blueberries are the worst."

"You're in luck." Kai pulled out a second jar and placed it on the counter beside me. "You look terrible. Was the date a bust?"

"The date was perfect," I grumbled.

I wished it had been less perfect because it made it hard to keep him at a safe distance.

"Ok. So, what's the issue? Did he sneak out before you woke up or something?"

"I didn't bring him here. We didn't even kiss."

Kai narrowed his eyes. "Why not?"

I loaded up my mug with coffee. "First of all, not everyone is as quick to bed as you are. Second of all, he's playing in a volleyball tournament today, and I knew he needed sleep. If I kissed him, I wouldn't have been able to stop."

"That's sweet in a very you-fucked-up kind of way. Did you make plans to see each other again?"

Kai handed me his mug, so I filled it as well.

"He invited me to the tournament this afternoon, but I'm not sure I'm going to go. I feel all out of sorts." I sighed. "It feels too soon to meet his friends, right?"

"Yeah, makes sense. A workaholic has a few hours with nothing on his calendar, and it prompts a whole-ass crisis."

I glared at Kai as he sipped his coffee.

Kai continued, unbothered. "Here's what we're gonna do. I'm gonna go to work, and you're going to sit your cute butt on the sofa and binge-watch some mindless reality TV. I'll swing by here at lunchtime to pick you up, and we'll go to his game."

"We?"

"Yeah." Kai slid his laptop into his cross-body bag before throwing it over his shoulder. "If you're meeting his friends, it's only fair I get to tag along and vet him, too. Plus, what gay man is going to turn down an IRL Top Gun volleyball montage moment? That movie turned a whole generation of boys into members of the alphabet mafia."

I rolled my eyes, but he wasn't wrong. I definitely wanted to see Gabriel jumping around in some little volleyball shorts.

Would he want to be with someone like me? Who was I without this job? Would I be able to continue paying all these medical bills if I started getting lazy now, when I was so close to the finish line?

"I can hear you overthinking." Kai ushered me to the couch, forced me out of my suit coat, and turned on the TV. "Nothing will blow up if you have a little fun."

I responded with a noncommittal grunt. It was annoying as shit when Kai could read my mind, but I wasn't about to admit it out loud.

"I'd better see you in that same spot when I get home," he said. "You're only allowed to get up for snacks or to change into beach clothes. See you at noon!"

And with that, he was gone.

PROMPTLY AT NOON, I hopped into the passenger seat of Kai's BMW, and we were off to the beach.

I texted Gabriel to let him know I'd see him soon and that I was bringing a friend. I didn't expect an answer since I figured he'd be playing or busy with his teammates, but it wasn't long before I got a party emoji and a location pin.

After we parked, I made Kai stop at a convenience store to grab a few lemonades and sports drinks.

"You haven't even kissed yet, and you're already taking care of the man." Kai tugged my earlobe affectionately. It was something he'd done since college.

I punched him in the arm and threw the bottles in our beach bag.

I was thankful Gabriel had sent the pin and saved us the hassle of checking every court for his team; the crowds on the way to the courts were intense. We arrived mid-game and found a spot on the bleachers to watch.

"Which one is he?" Kai asked.

"Toward the front with the incredible hair and the hot pink shorts."

They were all wearing matching team shirts. Gabriel's was cropped, which was the best thing I'd ever seen.

Kai fanned his face. "If you don't kiss that man today, I will."

"You absolutely will not."

"Hurry up and mark your territory then."

We fell under the game's spell after that. Kai whistled loudly each time a player stripped off their shirt and muttered about Tom Cruise and aviators. I didn't know enough about volleyball to know what made a team or player good, but it was fun to cheer regardless. Plus, watching Gabriel's strong thighs as he jumped around was a definite bonus.

I could get used to this.

Wait, I'm not getting used to anything. Promise.

"I am *so* glad I made you bring me here," Kai said when Gabriel's team scored the winning point. He stood and shoved me down toward the sand.

"I'm going to regret this, aren't I?"

"Absolutely."

I finally caught Gabriel's eye and waved as he celebrated with his teammates on the sidelines. His smile got almost impossibly wider, and he ran over to me.

He jumped up the remaining bleacher steps that separated us two at a time, and time seemed to slow as he approached. All I could think about was that almost-kiss last night and how good it would feel when it finally happened. While I knew I wouldn't be making the same mistake today that I made last night, I was absolutely not expecting Gabriel to run up and kiss me first thing.

Before I could process it, his hands were on my face, and his lips were against mine.

I was glad Kai had the beach bag because my arms went around Gabriel immediately, one hand at his lower back and the other sliding up into his hair.

He smelled like salty ocean waves and orange trees.

It was the best first kiss I'd ever had. My racing thoughts faded to white noise, and a small moan escaped me when he took my lower lip between his teeth.

I'd completely forgotten where we were and that we had an audience of our friends. That kiss could have lasted ten seconds or ten years, as far as I was concerned. Before I could coax my tongue into his mouth, someone cleared their throat behind me.

We broke apart from each other, startled, and Gabriel looked as dazed as I felt.

"Sorry for jumping you like that," he said, shaking his head with a small smile. "I've been thinking about kissing you since last night."

I laughed. "Oh, trust me. That was not a problem. The opposite, in fact."

"You must be Gabriel," Kai said from behind me. "Or at least I hope you are. I'm Kai, Taylor's best friend."

Gabriel broke eye contact with me and stuck his hand out toward Kai. "Yeah, that's me. Nice to meet you."

"Are any of your teammates single? After watching that volleyball performance and the free after-show, I am horny as fuck."

I groaned. "Oh my god, Kai."

Gabriel cracked up. "Yeah, just dive into the fray, and I'm sure you'll do fine."

Kai wiggled his eyebrows at me and handed me the beach bag, and then he was off to do his flirty extrovert thing.

Once we were alone, I stepped closer to Gabriel. "Are you thirsty? I brought electrolytes."

"Ooo, do you have the blue one? It's my favorite."

"Obviously." I pulled out a blue sports drink from the bag. "It's the best one."

He cracked the lid and started swallowing it down. I attempted, to no avail, not to stare as his throat bobbed. When he finished, I leaned in for another kiss and tasted the blue drink on his lips.

He beamed up at me when we parted.

"Thanks for the drink." He nudged me toward his teammates with his shoulder. "Let me introduce you to my friends."

"Yeah, we probably shouldn't leave Kai unattended for too long."

He touched his hand to my lower back, sending a shiver up my spine.

"You met Kat last night at Whiskey Sour, and you might have seen Alex behind the bar. Brian is the guy with all the tattoos, Lucas is the blond, and that's my cousin, Oscar."

"Nice to meet everyone. I'm Taylor. That was a great game."

Kai's attention was focused on Brian, who was exactly his type: a shirtless behemoth covered in ink.

"Yeah, you played so well," Kai said as he squeezed Brian's arm. "Was that your last game of the day? Anyone want to grab a drink?"

"I'm down." Brian swung his arm around Kai. "We usually head to this bar a few blocks off the beach to avoid the tourist madness."

"I'm glad you made it today," Gabriel said as we walked to the bar together.

"Me too." I entwined our fingers. "I'm sorry for not kissing you last night."

"No need to apologize. That was the best first date I've ever been on."

I blushed. "Me too."

NOW THAT THE kiss seal had been broken and Gabriel and I had a few drinks in our systems, it was impossible to keep our hands to ourselves. His leg pressed against mine under the table, his fingers trailed along my thigh, and damn, it felt good. It had been so long since I'd had that closeness with anyone other than Margo or Kai, and even though they both were touchy-feely people, this was different.

I let the conversation flow around me and soaked up Gabriel's exuberance with my arm on the back of his chair, running my fingers along his shoulder as he talked with his friends. Kai fit right in, as he always did, keeping the group laughing and making eyes at Brian as he sipped his margarita.

This whole thing was messing with my head.

I told myself I didn't want to date, didn't have time, didn't want to commit. Yet here I was, meeting Gabriel's friends and holding onto him like he was my boyfriend after just one date, even though he hadn't indicated anything more than us having a bit of fun.

What was I doing? An anxious buzz filled my stomach, and I scooted out of the booth.

Gabriel startled at my quick movement.

"Gonna run to the restroom," I said by way of explanation as I wiped my sweaty palms on my shorts.

Kai looked at me appraisingly and opened his mouth to say something when I shook my head subtly. Gabriel glanced between us, but I turned and fled down the hall to the bathrooms.

Safely hidden away, I washed my hands and stared at myself in the mirror.

I'd always controlled my anxiety with an iron fist, sticking to the plan, carrying out the objectives toward a clear, quantifiable goal. My hands clenched with frustration when I thought about how close I'd gotten. Now, the guardrails I'd constructed had been ripped to shreds, and my map had been turned upside down.

Then there was Gabriel, who was YOLO personified. Thinking about him made my heart race, and isn't that exactly what the doctor had told me to avoid?

Stepping up to the hand dryer, I knew I'd already been in the bathroom for too long.

Three. Deep. Breaths.

Then I had to get back out there.

8

GABRIEL

I raised an eyebrow in Kai's direction after Taylor left the table. Something was up, and I could tell; Taylor had tensed up before he pulled away to make his escape.

Kai leaned in my direction, speaking low enough that only I could hear. "I'd give him a few minutes, then go check on him."

I nodded, grateful he seemed to trust me even though we'd just met. They were obviously close.

"How long have you two been friends?" I asked, a little louder to include the rest of the group in our conversation.

"We met our senior year of college, when we were both studying for the CPA exam. Bonded over our shared trauma," Kai said with a laugh. "Now he can't get rid of me. We live together and work at the same accounting firm."

"Sounds like Kat and me," Alex said. "She's attached herself to me like a barnacle, and I can't shake her no matter how hard I try."

Kat gasped. "Lies. You love me."

Alex ruffled Kat's hair but didn't deny it.

"Are you seeing anyone?" I asked Kai.

A cloud passed over Kai's face before it was plastered with a bright smile. "Oh no. I am firmly in my ho phase. Just trying to get laid as often as possible, ya know?"

"To getting laid." Brian toasted as the others joined in.

I used that moment to slip out of the booth and make my way toward the restroom. I leaned against the wall outside the bathroom door. I didn't have to wait long before Taylor emerged. His posture was rigid, as if he were bracing for battle instead of drinks with friends.

"Hey," I said. "Is everything ok?"

Taylor sighed, rubbing his jaw. "Just getting in my head. Groups of new people can be hard for me."

I could tell that wasn't the whole truth, but it seemed somewhat honest. I could work with that.

"I know something that might help get you out of your head." I grabbed his shoulders and turned us so his back was against the wall.

"Oh yeah?" Taylor asked, a little breathless.

I loved how responsive he was to my body in his space. Humming appreciatively, I leaned in to kiss him. It started slow, with soft kisses and hands moving gently up and down my sides under my crop top. The feeling of his soft fingers on my bare skin was next level.

Finally, he relaxed against the wall, and I did an internal fist pump at my success. It surprised me how much I cared about how he was feeling, but ever since I laid eyes on him in that traffic jam, all I'd wanted was to melt his stress away and put a smile on his face. I could feel that smile against my mouth now, and it was the sweetest reward.

Taylor spread his legs and grabbed my ass to pull me closer. Then, the real fun began. I canted my hips against him, and he moaned into my mouth. He clearly had a thing for my curls, his fingers finding their way there at every opportunity. Fortunately for both of us, I loved having my hair played with. I grunted when he tugged at the hair at the nape of my neck and thrust up against me.

"Come home with me," I said as he used his grip to pull my head to the side, exposing my neck to his kisses.

"Yes," Taylor breathed into my neck. "Please."

I grabbed his hand and dragged him out of the bar's back exit. Taylor texted Kai to let him know we were leaving and not to forget the beach bag.

"With the number of times he's bailed on me for a hookup, I don't feel bad at all," he said.

"You think you're getting lucky, do you?" I rearranged myself so we could walk to our ride-share pickup without offending the public.

Taylor tracked my hand with his eyes. "I don't think I'd be the only one disappointed if I didn't."

He was dressed more casually than I'd seen him, in a white T-shirt, thigh-hugging jeans, and the same necklaces I'd noticed last night around his neck. I willed myself to stop tracking my gaze over his body, or I'd never be able to leave this alley.

Taking his hand in mine, I led him down the street until our car came into view. Seeing him squeeze his long legs into the back seat was a riot, and soon, we were on our way.

"What were you listening to when we met?" Taylor asked. "You looked like you were having way too much fun to be stuck in traffic."

"Oh, I don't remember. Probably Gaga, because she's mother. I like singing along to her music."

"She's an icon."

As we chatted quietly in the backseat of the car, he trailed his fingers up and down my thigh, inching closer and then farther away from where I wanted his attention.

TENSION BUILT between us as we climbed the stairs to my apartment. We made it through the door, and Taylor kicked off his sandals without my even having to ask.

"Wow, it's like a rainforest in here," he said as he looked around.

I shrugged. "Yeah, I don't have a lot of space for my plants, so I have to maximize it. I built most of these greenhouses myself."

"You're incredible." Taylor leaned over and kissed the shell of my ear.

Although I didn't visibly blush, I could feel my cheeks heating under his praise. "Well, this is basically the full house tour. I can't wait to get a bigger place someday, maybe even a yard for a garden, but that won't be in the budget for a while."

"And where's the bedroom?" Taylor nipped my earlobe and toyed with the small gold earring with his tongue.

"You'd like to see that, would you?" I turned toward him, caught his bottom lip in between my teeth, and sucked it into my mouth.

He moaned, and it was like a dam breaking.

I pushed him backward with urgency. "This way."

He pulled my T-shirt over my head once we tripped down the short hallway and into my bedroom. Bending over, he took one nipple into his mouth and used his teeth to tease the piercing. I moaned and grabbed at the back of his shirt, pulling it up.

"Yours too," I urged.

He reached behind his neck to pull it the rest of the way off, and my hands immediately went to the smattering of light hair across his chest. Taylor was leaner than I was, and I ran my hands from his pecs over his shoulders and down his biceps. He had a trail of hair leading down from his belly button, soft against his pale skin. Squeezing the backs of his arms, I pulled him closer.

"God, you're gorgeous," Taylor whispered into my mouth

before he began kissing me in earnest. His fingers teased just inside the waistband of my shorts at the top of my ass, and his thumbs pressed into my hip bones.

I let out a satisfied sound as I worked open the fly of his jeans, pulling them down with his boxer briefs. He had a tiny rainbow tattoo near his hip, just inside his V-line, and I was pretty sure it was his only ink. It was sexy as hell.

I backed up toward the bed and watched his face as I tugged down on my shorts. I preened under his gaze; I worked hard for this body, and I knew I looked good. It felt great to be appreciated, and I definitely was. Taylor's pupils dilated, each breath coming out as a harsh pant. He wrapped his hand around his erection.

He stroked himself slowly as I dragged out the show to tease him. "Let me see you, Gabriel."

Putting him out of his misery, I tugged my shorts all the way down, my hard cock slapping against my abs as it was freed. Naked at last, I fell back onto the bed, and Taylor was on me in an instant. We scooted up toward the pillows, and he settled in between my spread legs. I loved feeling his weight on me, and we groaned as our cocks finally pressed together with nothing in between.

He dove back into my mouth with urgency as he rutted against me. I reached my hand out, fumbling toward the top drawer of my nightstand until I felt the bottle. I wasted no time slicking my fingers with lube and wrapping my hand around both of us together. His cock felt so good against me—a little longer than mine, but not as thick.

I couldn't wait for him to fuck me. Not tonight, but soon.

I didn't normally make plans for a second round before I'd even come the first time, but I wanted it all with Taylor. I wanted to be inside him, and I wanted him inside me. I should have been scared, but all those fantasies of future fuckings just made more precum spill out of me. I threw my head back, tightening my grip around us, and he grunted into my neck.

Taylor pushed my legs apart with his knees as he changed the angle of his body, sliding his dick along mine as he rolled his hips. Pushing himself up on his hands, he looked into my eyes as we frotted against each other, gasping and panting. His eyes were so blue, his reddened lips slightly parted, and I wanted to kiss every freckle that was painted across his cheekbones.

"Fuck, fuck, *fuck*, Gabriel," Taylor cried as he sped up his thrusts. His face as he came was a goddamn masterpiece. The feeling of his cum hitting my hand and stomach did me in, and I followed him over the edge.

Taylor collapsed on top of me, all the tension finally draining from his muscles. I stared up at the ceiling as I wrapped my arms around him and let my soul return to my body. His weight was comforting and warm in the post-orgasm haze. He slid off to my side, still tucked under my arms, and rested his head on my shoulder.

Dragging his fingers across my abs, Taylor sighed. "You look fucking hot covered in cum."

"I look fucking hot all the time." I teased, pretending to be offended. It was that or admit how much my world had just shifted under my feet.

"That's true," Taylor said as he grinned up at me. It was a struggle to maintain eye contact; there was so much between us at that moment. "But I particularly like this look."

I leaned over to kiss him languidly, the urgency of our orgasms behind us. "I am starting to feel sticky, though. Shower?"

"Yeah." Taylor followed me into the bathroom and under the spray.

A few days ago, I had imagined this man in my shower with me, and now we were here.

Taylor grabbed my citrus soap and the washcloth, running it over my shoulders and pulling me close so he could reach my back. His tongue peeked out from his lips as he focused extra attention on cleaning the cum off my stomach and chest.

I'd only known him a short time, but I could tell that Taylor was someone who cared deeply.

It was quite an experience to have that energy focused in my direction.

Determined to return the favor, I ran my soapy hands over every inch of his body. His face and chest flushed from the heat of the water, or maybe from how intimate the moment was.

As Taylor towel-dried his hair, I watched his eyes dart from me to his pile of discarded clothes and back. I wasn't sure if what we'd shared had outweighed the moment in the bar when he'd seemed so skittish and anxious, but I didn't want him to think I didn't want him here.

"Stay," I whispered. "For a little bit. If you don't want to sleep over, that's fine, but I'm not done with you."

The moment stretched out, awkward and silent, as I waited for an answer. Taylor's eyes darted back to his clothes as he chewed the inside of his cheek.

"I can stay." A small smile came over his face as I pulled him into bed with me. I tucked myself under his arm, and with the sound of his heartbeat steady in my ear, I fell fast asleep.

9

TAYLOR

I woke up with Gabriel in my arms, his back to my front, and my morning wood nestled against his incredible ass. I didn't want to rush things physically; something told me it would be hard to protect my heart once I'd been inside him. Most of my hookups these days were exclusively handjobs or blow jobs. That was quick and to the point, but damn it, frotting against Gabriel and looking into his hazel eyes had been intense enough.

Nothing about this felt like a hookup.

I hadn't slept over at someone's house since my last long-term relationship, either, but it had been so easy to tumble naked into bed with Gabriel after our shower and cuddle until we'd both drifted off to sleep. Waking up next to a warm, hard body was so nice.

Gabriel still slept against me, but I knew I'd have to leave soon to help Margo with wedding things. I ran my fingers across Gabriel's chest, tugging on his nipple piercing, and he grunted.

"Gabriel." I trailed my hand down the plane of his stomach. "Time to wake up."

"Ngh," Gabriel protested, though he pushed against me. "Too early."

"Promise I'll make it worth your while." I let my cock slide between his thighs.

My fingers teased along his length, spending extra time on the sensitive spot under the head before I took him in my hand. He arched into me, and I thrust against his taint and the back of his balls. Gabriel must have grabbed the lube from the nightstand, because I soon felt its cool slick under my hand.

"Tay, baby, please," Gabriel said, sounding more awake. He gripped my forearm with one hand, and the other reached for the headboard.

Now that I was sure he was on board, my grip on his erection tightened, and I moved my hips with more intention. He moaned and writhed as I jerked him off, twisting my hand around the head of his cock with each pass. God, the sounds he made should have been illegal. He crossed his ankles and squeezed his thighs together, gripping me as I thrust between his legs.

I was too close, too fast.

"Come on, Gabriel," I said against his neck. "Come for me."

"Fuck," he cried as he thrust quicker into my hand.

Soon, his warm, sticky release coated my fingers. I kissed the top of his spine as I stroked him through the aftershocks of his orgasm.

"Oh my god. That is the best way to wake up."

"My pleasure," I whispered as I nuzzled into his hair.

His shampoo smelled like delicious, sweet oranges.

"Oh, it's about to be," Gabriel replied with a mischievous grin as he turned to face me and rolled me onto my back. He climbed on top of me and kissed me deeply, apparently unconcerned with morning breath.

My breath hitched as his kisses trailed along my jaw and down my throat to my collarbone. He licked and nipped at what felt like every inch of my skin as he worked his way lower to my aching cock.

Gabriel nuzzled his face into the crease between my thigh and my groin, moaning. "I love the way you smell."

"You're good for the ego." I huffed. "But I'm going to need you to suck my dick, like right now."

He laughed into my thigh, kissed my rainbow tattoo, turned his head, and dragged his tongue up the underside of my cock. "Is this what you need, baby?"

My ability to speak completely left the building as he put his mouth around me. All I could do was groan in relief. He twirled his tongue around the tip, then took my cock into his throat so suddenly I shouted in surprise, struggling not to thrust my hips. His hot mouth was heaven, and the suction as he swallowed around me brought me to the edge quickly.

Gabriel stilled, lips stretched wide around me, long lashes wet, until I put my hand on the back of his head and tested a few small thrusts into his mouth. He encouraged me to bend my knees and get some leverage by gently tapping on the back of my thighs. The vibrations from his moan when I hit the back of his throat finally snapped the last bit of my control.

I hovered on the edge of my orgasm, thrusting deeper and faster into his mouth until his slick fingers trailed through the saliva that had pooled onto my balls and down to my ass. When they circled my rim and applied light pressure there, it was like an instant O-button. Before I could warn him, I shot my cum down his throat.

He gagged a little but recovered quickly and swallowed down everything I gave him.

I have mostly topped these days; I found it hard to trust a

hookup enough to bottom. But by the way my body reacted to Gabriel there, I wondered if maybe… *well, let's not get ahead of ourselves.*

"Sorry, that snuck up on me."

"I will take it as a compliment." Gabriel's eyes sparkled as he wiped his mouth with the back of his hand.

I pulled him up to me, and he slotted under my arm against my chest.

"What time is it?" he asked eventually.

"Almost nine. I hate to rush you out of bed on a Sunday, but I'm meeting Margo in a little bit to help her with some wedding errands, and I was hoping we could get breakfast before I have to go."

"I'd like that," Gabriel said as he popped out of bed. "There's a café down the block that makes delicious breakfast sandwiches. We can walk over."

He tossed me a burgundy colored T-shirt and a pair of briefs as he dug around in his dresser.

His ass as he bent over the long drawer distracted me, and the clothes hit my face.

"In case you don't want to wear the same thing as yesterday. I think I have a spare toothbrush under the sink, too. I'll go check."

Gabriel grabbed his pile of clothes and made his way to the bathroom. Once he was gone, I pulled on the underwear before grabbing my jeans from yesterday off the floor. The shirt fit better than I expected, despite being a little baggy, and Gabriel's citrusy ocean scent wrapped around me. How long could I delay returning this thing to him before it got weird?

Dammit, I should not be thinking these things.

By the time I was dressed, Gabriel made his way back into the bedroom—clothed, regrettably—and tossed me a toothbrush wrapped in plastic. "Help yourself to whatever's in the bathroom."

His eyes heated as he took me in. I'd steal his whole wardrobe if he kept looking at me like that.

"Thanks." I fled to the bathroom to escape my treacherous thoughts of the future.

Breakfast passed too quickly, and before I knew it, I was in a ride share headed back to my apartment to grab my car and meet up with Margo.

My mood dampened when I unlocked the apartment doors to Kai's applause from the living room couch. I knew I wouldn't escape his inquisition, but I was hoping I could put it off for a little longer while I was still basking in the afterglow.

"I am so proud of you," Kai said with a shit-eating grin.

"Oh, shut up. It's not like that."

"Really." Kai lifted an eyebrow. "Where were you last night, then?"

"Exactly where you think I was." I pushed him back onto the couch from the arm where he'd been perched. "How did things go with Brian?"

"Exactly how you think they went." Kai smirked. "The man has a massive—"

"Nope, no, thank you. I will never be able to look at him again if you don't stop talking."

"He didn't stay the night, though, since he's just a hookup." Kai looked at me with an assessing gaze. "Are you wearing Gabriel's clothes?"

I rolled my eyes. "He lent me a shirt, so I didn't have to wear yesterday's clothes to breakfast. It's nothing."

Kai narrowed his eyes and handed me a cup of coffee, but he seemed content to end the interrogation for the time being. Thank goodness. I had to change before seeing Margo. She was observant enough to notice Gabriel's shirt as something I wouldn't have bought for myself, and she would have questions. I threw on a button-up in the same color and fixed my hair before rushing out the door.

I'd left my phone in the car. I hadn't meant to, but now I was committed. I definitely didn't want to address why I was so antsy about it with my sister.

Margo and I were seated around a small table, with about twenty cake samples between us. Benji was diabetic, and as much as I was sure my sister would rather have her fiancé here than her brother, I was willing to make the sacrifice. Once we'd narrowed down our top three flavors, Benji could try the samples Margo would bring home without sending his blood sugar through the roof.

As much as I was trying to be a good brother and focus on the task at hand, all I could think about was my damn phone sitting in the cupholder of my car a few blocks away, maybe buzzing with a text from Gabriel. I hoped today wasn't the day my car window got broken into.

Margo's voice filtered into my brain. "What do you think of the pickle vanilla? Or maybe the one with taco seasoning sprinkles?"

I responded automatically. "Delicious. This place is great."

My hand kept reaching into the pocket where I always kept it, only to find it empty.

"Ok, what the hell?" She whacked me on the back of the head, snapping me out of my stupor. "Pickle cupcakes? Where is your mind right now?"

I blinked at her. "Sorry, I haven't gotten much sleep the past few nights. I feel like a zombie."

I was a bit of an old man about my bedtime. Two late nights

in a row had me all twisted up inside, not to mention this fixation on Gabriel that I didn't know what to do with.

"You are *supposed* to be resting," Margo said as she handed me another sample. This one looked like a chocolate-coconut combination.

"It's hard to magically change your sleep schedule when you're used to early mornings and late nights." And when you had a new man keeping you out until all hours.

Margo tutted. "That job works you way too hard. I don't know why you let it happen."

Margo didn't know I was helping our parents with her medical debt, and she'd likely kill me if she found out. I was so, so close to paying it off, and I promised myself yet again that as soon as it was off my shoulders, I'd scale back the overtime.

"You know I'm grateful for everything you've done for me." Margo softened her voice, almost as if she'd read my mind. "I literally wouldn't be here without you. If I were having someone walk me down the aisle next month, it would be you."

I sniffed and looked up at the ceiling. There was nothing I was more grateful for than Margo being alive. I'd given up almost everything for it, and I'd do it again.

"All I want is for you to be happy," she said. "Have a bit of fun every once in a while."

A blush stained my cheeks when I remembered Gabriel's offer on our first date. I'd already had more fun with him in one weekend than I'd probably had in a year. I stuffed another cake sample into my mouth, so I didn't blurt anything too embarrassing.

She would latch onto Gabriel and never let go.

Margo poked me in the side. "Whatever's on your mind that's making you make that face, I want more of that. Now, let's figure out this cake thing. I think we have about twelve flavors left to try."

I groaned and rubbed my stomach. "Torture, but someone has to do it."

Margo laughed, and we settled into an afternoon of shoving cake into our faces.

When we'd finally narrowed down the options to key lime, vanilla butterscotch, and red velvet, I practically had to roll myself out of the store. While the specter of my abandoned phone still lingered in the back of my mind, I thought I did a reasonably good job of staying in the moment with Margo.

"Which way did you park?" I asked when we left the store.

"That way"—she pointed down the street—"but you don't need to walk me."

"I absolutely do." I hooked my arm with hers.

Margo rolled her eyes, but she let me lead her down the street. "When are you going to accept that I'm a grown woman?"

"I know you're a grown woman."

Margo protested with a *hmpf*.

"I do, I swear, but it's still polite to walk a lady to her car."

Margo snorted. "I am *not* a lady."

As soon as we said goodbye, my abandoned phone was all I could think about.

Hopefully, Gabriel wasn't mad I'd ignored him all day—if he'd texted at all. Surely, he had. Right? Then again, I hadn't reached out to him either. Not that I'd been able to in the first place, but he wouldn't know that.

The anxiety curled inside me like a constrictor, my heart pounding and my pace quickening until I could see my car, thankfully with all its windows still intact.

When I slumped into my front seat and opened my phone, I couldn't help laughing out loud at the text waiting for me. Gabriel had sent a GIF of Britney Spears with a birthday cake and asked if we'd picked a winner. Of course, he'd texted me to check in, and he found a way to make me smile even when I'd been spiraling.

My heart was doing somersaults as I flipped between infatuated and terrified.

I'd always envisioned myself being single forever, but the perfect man had crashed into my life, and I didn't know what to do with myself.

10

GABRIEL

I had no business texting Taylor as much as I did. Or, at least as much as I did while also telling myself it was casual. And he was texting me as if he *liked* me. Taylor was perfect, and he deserved more.

I wasn't sure I was willing to risk that. Yet, whenever he texted, I found myself replying within minutes.

> **TAYLOR**
> Do you have plans after work?
>
> **GABRIEL**
> Looks like I do now ;)

That's how we ended up at a small table in a trendy bubble tea café I'd seen on social media.

I was dressed casually, in gym shorts and a tie-dye hoodie I changed into after work, but Taylor looked shockingly put together for a guy who was taking time off. The navy dress pants and button-up with rolled-up sleeves worked for him, though, so I wasn't going to complain.

"I'm going stir-crazy in the apartment by myself all day," Taylor grouched. "I can feel my brain atrophying."

"Want to do my accounting for me? If I never had to do math again, I would be happy."

"Yes!" Taylor practically jumped out of his seat, and I burst into laughter.

"I was kidding. You do not have to do my accounting."

Taylor crossed his arms over his chest and frowned, which only made me laugh harder. "What if I want to?"

I considered his offer as I sipped my taro milk tea. I really hated all the numbers involved with making the bitters, and it was only going to get worse if I decided to make it an official business like I'd been daydreaming about. "Eh, I mean, I won't stop you."

"Thank god." Taylor slumped back into his seat. "If I had one more day of doing nothing, I would have lost it."

"You are a weird dude." I smiled, and he narrowed his eyes at me. "I like weird."

Taylor's face relaxed. "Send me what you have, and I'll take a look at it."

I stood and stuck out my hand. When he took it, I pulled him up from his chair.

"Now that we've made a business deal, let's get to the fun part." I pointed to the prize machines lining the store's wall. "You pick one for me, and I'll pick one for you."

Taylor released my hand to survey our options. Some of the machines had small plushies, while others had keychains and figurines. "Ok, but you can't look. Otherwise, you won't be surprised."

It was harder than I expected not to follow Taylor's magnetic presence with my eyes, but he looked so cute, bent over to peer into the different machines, his tongue barely peeking out.

When he caught me looking, he pointed an accusing finger in my direction.

I stuck my tongue out in return. "You can't peek either."

After five minutes of chasing each other around the store, stealing glances, and pretending we weren't, we reconvened on the store's patio with our loot.

"Now you have three hundred and one oranges to deal with," Taylor said with a wry grin.

I was confused until he pulled a small keychain from behind his back, revealing a cartoon orange making a cute little winky face. My face broke out into a wide grin. "It's perfect."

Grabbing the keychain from Taylor, I immediately added it to my keyring.

"This made me think of you." I revealed a small tuxedo cat plushie from where it had been hiding in my hoodie pocket. "I thought you could keep it on your desk when you go back to work."

Taylor took it with a soft smile and threaded his fingers with mine. "Thank you for meeting up with me tonight."

He pulled me close enough that our chests bumped together, and his gaze was all tender and sweet. I licked my lips, and his eyes followed the movement.

"You know, I—"

"I found a bar in West Hollywood that does cosmic mini golf," I blurted, overwhelmed by how intense this moment felt.

Cosmic mini golf was fun. Fun was my comfort zone.

Taylor's eyes widened. "I'm afraid to know why you're telling me that."

"It's my turn to pick our next date." I smirked.

"Doesn't this count?" Taylor grumbled. "That means it's my turn to pick next."

"Nope, this is a bonus." I threaded my arm around his waist.

"Friday night is still my choice, and I say we're going to cosmic mini golf."

"Fine, fine." Taylor looped his arm over my shoulder with a sigh, but his smile betrayed that he was only giving me a hard time.

I already couldn't wait for Friday to arrive.

LATER THAT WEEK, I worked on my bitters, and Alex perched on a bar stool on the opposite side of my kitchen counter, filling out a Sudoku puzzle with enviable focus.

The only things we had in common at the start of our friendship were the volleyball team and our taste in women, but when I'd told her about the first glass IKEA cabinet I was planning on rigging as a greenhouse, she'd gotten excited and told me about her plans for a goth garden. That immediate support had cemented her bestie status. We'd made her very own cabinet greenhouse the following weekend. In return, she'd bought liquid eyeliner and taught me how to perfect the cat eye.

"I think I've decided on a name for this thing," I said. I liked that she and I could shift between catching up and sitting in companionable silence. "Plant Daddy Botanicals."

Alex snorted, which was as close to a belly laugh as I could expect from her, so I counted it as a win. "Where'd you come up with that? And you know, you can call it a business. You have the paperwork and everything."

To start supplying the bitters to my friends at the Whiskey Sour, I'd had to apply for an in-home cottage food license and take a food handling test, but I hadn't filed an LLC or a business name. Somehow, that made it more real, and nothing had felt right yet.

"Someone said it as a joke the other day, but I kind of love it."

"I think it works for you," she said. "I'm going to start sending you links for the LLC application until you finish it."

I sighed.

I didn't want to go through all the trouble of paperwork and applications if it wasn't going to stick. Things never stuck, no matter how badly I wanted them to. I was a little bit like a tumbleweed, getting tossed around from idea to idea with no control over when my brain would latch onto something else. The fact that I'd been working on this same project for a few years now didn't seem enough to prove a lifetime of evidence wrong. I had a whole closet that I called the craft graveyard to show for it. The remnants of hobbies past lingered there, haunting me.

"I dunno, girl. Do I have to?"

"Um, yeah, you do." She pointed her pen at me. "It's beyond time for you to make it official."

My phone buzzed from the other room, and my mind went to Taylor.

"That was just me," Alex said. "With the link to the LLC paperwork."

"Fine, you win. I'll do it tonight."

"I'm going to text you daily until I get receipts."

I huffed as I cleaned the mason jars I used to ferment the orange bitters. Once the peels were soaking in vodka, they'd go into the cabinet under the kitchen sink, shaken daily for two weeks until they were ready to be sweetened and bottled.

"Hey, do you have plans this weekend?" Alex asked. "I'm going to see a burlesque show at Bar Sinister, and I have an extra ticket."

"Busy, sorry. I have a date on Friday, and then I have to head out to Santa Ana to visit my parents. They've been pestering me. I don't think I can put it off any longer before they put in a missing person's report."

I was both willing the weekend to come sooner and dreading its arrival for those exact reasons. I couldn't wait to kiss Taylor again, but I could wait another lifetime to hear my mom compare my life choices to hers.

Alex eyed me skeptically. "I didn't think you dated."

I refused to make eye contact in case she saw too much. "Yeah, well, turns out this guy is very dateable."

"Same guy we met at the tournament? Taylor, right?"

I nodded.

"I'm intrigued, but I'll let you keep your secrets for now. I'd better be the first to hear the details once you make it public, though."

"We're keeping it pretty casual."

"Mmhmm."

"Look, I just—I'm not cut out for serious relationships. People are with me for a good time, not a long time, ya know?" I pulled on my nose ring before huffing in frustration at contaminating my hands and heading to the sink to wash them. "Casual is better."

I had my back to Alex, but I could imagine her unimpressed expression. "I know that girl in college messed you up, but at some point, you're going to want to let someone love you."

"She got engaged to someone else," I cried. "Six months later!"

"Sounds like she was a shitty person. Do you really think Taylor's playing you?"

"I don't know."

Alex gave me an unimpressed look before returning to her puzzle, letting my answer hang in the silence.

Usually, I got so much more done when someone was keeping me company. Tonight, with Alex's questions floating around in my head, it felt like hours until I finally finished preparing the bitters and stored them in one of my kitchen cabinets to infuse.

On her way to her car, Alex helped me carry the trash to the apartment dumpsters. "Let me know if you need me to manufacture a crisis this weekend to get you out of your parents' house."

About once a month, I needed to bite the bullet and head home for the weekend to help Papá with house projects, ensure their DVD player was still connected to their TV, and reassure Mamá that I wouldn't die alone and poor.

My time was up.

"Thanks, but I think I'm good," I said with a laugh. "I am afraid of the type of crisis you'd manufacture."

Alex frowned at me. "Ungrateful."

After walking Alex to her car, I looked up at the moon.

With all the light pollution in the LA area, we couldn't see many stars, but I'd always loved the moon. Goose bumps ran along my bare arms as the winds kicked up. Abuela used to tell us that whenever she felt homesick, she gazed at the moon and remembered how it looked over the mountains near her tiny hometown in Michoacán, how the rabbit had been put there by Quetzalcóatl to be honored. The whole family was Catholic, of course, but I always found Abuela's myths and legends more comforting than the rote prayers and readings at Mass.

I could never quite pin down where I was supposed to be homesick for.

TAYLOR

Are you absolutely sure we have to go mini golfing tomorrow?

GABRIEL

Don't worry. I'll make sure you have a good time ;)

...

> I trust you.

My stomach dropped like I'd crested the top of a roller-coaster. *I trust you.*

How could he, when I wasn't sure I could trust myself?

At this exact moment, everything felt too perfect. I had a job I loved, amazing friends, a house full of plants, and a handsome man who wanted to wish me goodnight.

But if I let my mind drift to the future, everything felt changeable and tenuous.

I was glad I'd get to see Taylor again before I left for Santa Ana. He had this grounding energy that calmed down my frenetic mind. If my time with my parents left me too overwhelmed and sad to continue to be his appointed shenanigans instigator, at least I would have succeeded in getting him out of the house one more time.

11

TAYLOR

It was finally Friday night. I was uncertain about Gabriel's choice of venue, but I'd chosen last time, so I was trying to be a good sport. He'd promised to help me have more fun, and he seemed to take the assignment seriously.

I leaned up against the wall outside the bar where he'd told me to meet him, looking down at my phone. I felt a hand on my shoulder and a quick kiss on my cheek before Gabriel said, "Hey, baby."

I tried not to let my surprise show at the pet name. He'd called me baby in between kisses last weekend, but oxytocin and serotonin made you say all kinds of things you didn't mean. I chalked it up to the afterglow, which was fine. We hadn't defined the relationship yet—although the thought of him calling anyone else baby made my stomach twist.

Was this a word he used liberally or only with me?

Did it mean something to him now?

"I missed you this week." I wrapped him in a hug and buried my face in his hair. "How was work?"

Gabriel felt good in my arms. The floral shirt he wore open over a white tank hugged his biceps just right, and the dark hair on his thighs peeking out from the holes in his ripped jeans had my pulse quickening as I remembered what it had felt like against my skin.

Keeping him at arm's length was not working—literally or figuratively. The way I ran my hands down his back, pulling him closer, felt like showing too many cards, but when I saw how Gabriel smiled at me, I couldn't bring myself to stop.

"No talking about work tonight." Gabriel squeezed my ribs as he pulled free from my embrace. "It's shenanigans time!"

He grabbed my hand and dragged me into the bar as I followed him, laughing. My stomach did that sour flip-flopping thing again when Gabriel turned his sparkling hazel gaze at the beautiful bartender. It had been so long since I'd felt jealous that the emotion startled me. His hand didn't leave mine, even when she brought over our drinks and those tiny pencils for our scorecards.

It turned out I was terrible at mini golf. And not even in the damsel-in-distress way, to convince Gabriel to stand behind me and show me how to swing, the heat from his body and his breath on my neck sending chills up my spine. This reckless part of me that Gabriel seemed to bring out wanted to push back against him, while the rational part of my brain flushed and stepped away to retrieve my ball that bounced off course and rolled underneath an alien spacecraft.

We took a break for more drinks before lining up to start the second course, and I scooted into the bar booth behind him so I could tuck him under my arm. His hand went immediately to my leg as he perused the menu.

"So, what are you up to the rest of the weekend?" I asked.

"I have to visit my parents in Santa Ana." He huffed, blowing one of his curls around in the process.

A pit sank in my stomach at the tone of his voice. "Are they not accepting of you?"

"It's not that, exactly. They mean well, but they have this specific roadmap for my life. And I don't know if you've noticed, but I can be a bit of a chaos gremlin."

"A shenanigans instigator."

"It's true." Gabriel let out a self-deprecating puff of laughter, but he didn't quite smile like I'd been hoping. "My parents aren't unsupportive directly, but they don't exactly know what to do with me. I want to make them proud."

"I don't know how anyone could look at you and not feel proud. You're an amazing human." I tilted his chin up and brought my lips to his. "I don't have the best examples to draw from, but it seems to me that a good parent would want their child to feel happy and fulfilled."

Gabriel studied me from under those long eyelashes, and the corner of his lips tipped up. Not enough to make his dimples pop, but at least he was smiling. "Thanks. I make it out to see them about once a month, and I can manage to suffer through it for their sake. The guilt keeps me away and keeps me coming back, you know?"

"Yeah." I squeezed his shoulder as the waiter approached the table with our fries. "Good thing we ordered potatoes. They make everything better."

He chuckled at that, looking grateful for my willingness to move the conversation elsewhere.

I'd made peace with my parental situation a long time ago, but it still stung that the people who brought me into this world didn't have much interest in being a part of my life—aside from my financial contributions. They'd been all too happy to put me in the middle of their battles, blame us kids for their unhappiness, and hand the adult responsibilities over to me as soon as they could.

In some ways, that was a gift. I was free to be who I was without their expectations. But it had been awful in other ways.

I had to grow up too fast and give up too many things. Playing mini golf on a date at thirty-two brought back a bit of that childhood crush energy I hadn't experienced since I was fifteen.

I couldn't understand how anyone would fail to see what an incredible person Gabriel was. The electricity of being around him. He put on this front as the confident life of the party, and this was the first time I'd seen him looking vulnerable and unsure. God, I wanted to fix it all for him. I ran a finger through the curls above his ear.

Gabriel's voice pulled me from my thoughts. "You're obsessed with my hair."

We weren't far apart in height, but I liked the way he looked up at me when he was tucked against my side. He ran his hand down my thigh.

"Have you seen your hair?" I tugged on one of his curls. "These are a national treasure. So soft, and you smell like a creamsicle on the beach."

Gabriel tilted his head back and laughed. "I'm hiring you to run my PR."

"I'd consider a career change as long as the benefits are good."

"Oh, I think you've experienced how good the benefits are. But I'd be happy to provide a refresher."

Gabriel licked into my mouth. He tasted salty from the fries and sweet from his margarita, which was a delicious combination. In fact, Gabriel was my new favorite flavor.

By the end of the second round of mini golf, my score was more than double Gabriel's, but the tension had unwound from my neck, and my abs hurt from laughing. I should have been thinking about getting enough sleep so that I'd be able to get through everything tomorrow: grocery shopping and meal prepping with Kai, and wedding planning with Margo.

All I was worried about was getting enough Gabriel—impossible, it turns out. The limit did not exist.

WE LINGERED in the parking lot, facing each other and leaning up against my car. Neither of us seemed quite ready to say good night. Our fingers threaded together, with my thumb rubbing over the back of his hand.

I felt like a teenager again.

I'd run out of words, but Gabriel kept right on chugging, and I found that I didn't mind listening to him explain the decision process behind the botanical garden's new sustainable landscaping exhibit or his thoughts on the bisexual Bachelorette or why he would never turn down tres leches even though lemon bars were his favorite.

Gabriel had taken a ride share to meet me tonight, so I contemplated bringing him home with me. I'd learned my lesson the first time, hadn't I? The groceries, the wedding planning, the work email—nothing made me feel alive like his fingers trailing up and down my arm mindlessly as he rambled.

It was disorienting, thinking not only of tonight but all the nights together in the foreseeable future. The buzz was better than the margaritas, and I wanted to drown in it. I wanted to forget that all relationships inevitably ended in tragedy. I wanted to pretend that some of the luck Margo lived by was left over for me.

"Hey," I blurted, realizing when I saw Gabriel's startled face that I'd probably interrupted him. "Look, I know I don't have much to give right now when it comes to my time and energy. My work will be crazy for months, and it gets like this every year. Then there's Margo's wedding coming up so fast..."

Gabriel stepped back and eyed me skeptically. "What are you saying?"

"Agh, no, this is coming out all wrong." I shook my head and took a deep breath. "What I meant was, the timing's not ideal, but I like you a lot, and I was thinking that maybe we could give this a try? I want to try. Being exclusive, I mean. Boyfriends? If you'd be into that."

The longer I spoke, the more Gabriel stiffened, his hands releasing mine and tucking into his pockets.

The silence stretched out between us, and... I must have overstepped. I thought we were both really into each other, but maybe Gabriel was more liberal with his use of pet names. I'd read too much into it.

I had no idea what made Gabriel close up on me, but I needed to fix it as soon as possible. I needed him smiling again. It had been two weeks, and I already couldn't imagine being without his constant texts, random GIFs, and goodnight phone calls. I didn't want another Friday night without his company.

"I'm not..."

"Never mind," I said, mirroring his pose, my hands in pockets. "Forget I said anything. I didn't even ask if you were looking for a relationship, and we've only been on a handful of dates. We can totally keep things casual."

I lied out of my ass, even though every other time I'd said those words, I'd meant it. But I hadn't met Gabriel then. It was fine. I had plenty of experience with casual. At least this way, I wouldn't end up like my parents. I certainly did *not* want to end up like my parents.

Gabriel was still frozen, his mouth open and his eyes wide. I turned to lean my back against the car because I didn't want him to read the humiliation on my face. I tilted my head to examine the bar's neon sign hanging above us.

"Taylor," Gabriel said cautiously.

"We're good. I hope everything goes ok with your parents this weekend." I pulled my keys from my pocket and hit the unlock button as I looked down at my feet. God, anywhere but Gabriel's face right now.

It was strange to find myself in this place, wanting a relationship for the first time in forever, and I'd jumped in with both feet before checking the temperature of the water. An uncalculated risk was unlike me, and the embarrassment scratching against my skin like a too-small wool sweater reminded me why.

Tomorrow, I would blame the alcohol I'd had at the bar, say I was drunk enough that I could pretend the whole conversation away, even though that would be a lie. At that moment, I felt painfully sober.

"Taylor," Gabriel said again, but not making a move to close the distance between us.

"I'll see you next Friday, maybe?" I stepped around him to get to the front door of my car.

A large group of laughing people tumbled from the bar behind us, and I braced my shoulders against the intrusion of cheerful sounds. That was us an hour ago.

"Yeah," he said, "of course, baby."

I couldn't help wincing. I was unsure how this evening had gotten so far off plan. Wasn't it just a few hours ago that the word baby in Gabriel's mouth was a revelation?

"I'll text you, and we can make plans?" He had the decency to look sorry, but it didn't do much to ease my anxiety.

"Sure," I said, plastering a smile on my face.

My mind couldn't help crunching the numbers again, analyzing the data to see where I went wrong. The chemistry, the nicknames, the way he'd spend all day texting with me and still call to say goodnight—that went beyond a casual fuck, didn't it? I'd been out of the game for so long that perhaps I'd forgotten the applicable equation.

I sank into the driver's seat, started the car, and got the hell out of that damn parking lot as quickly as legally possible.

12

GABRIEL

Well, I'd messed that up quicker than I expected.

Even when he freaked out at my reaction, it was like I had forgotten how to speak English. I couldn't put two words together and was powerless to stop him from driving away from me.

The worst part was that I wanted to say yes.

Aside from a thumbs up to my text letting him know I'd made it home safely, I hadn't heard anything from Taylor since. When I'd texted him good morning, he'd left me on read.

I couldn't get his face out of my head, the one he made when I'd called him baby. It felt right to call him that. At the beginning of the night, it had made the corners of his eyes crinkle in surprise and delight. But when he was running away at the end of the night, it was like the word cut him like a knife.

I was an asshole.

My hesitation didn't have anything to do with Taylor. He was the kind of man who deserved something real—even only having spent a few weeks with him, I knew that. Everything he did was for the benefit of someone else. He needed to be with someone who could take care of him for a change. I wasn't sure I could be that person—at least, no one seemed to think I could be that person.

I'd always told myself I'd never taken any of my past relationships seriously because I was waiting for *the spark*. That magic that would reveal my perfect person and somehow keep me safe from rejection.

I couldn't deny that I felt sparks with Taylor, more than I had with anyone else, but I couldn't be what he needed. Now that I finally felt the magic I'd been waiting for, the risk felt that much greater.

I was terrified.

The low soundtrack of Mamá's telenovelas filtered from the kitchen to where I was seated at my parents' dining table, sorting the mail to ensure no essential bills had been missed. I had a long list of projects to handle, and I'd told my dad I'd help him assemble a storage rack he'd bought for the garage. I was sure I'd need to make at least one or two customer service calls to the cable company or cell-phone provider.

On the upside, time passed quickly while I bounced from project to project. Plus, it gave me an excuse to avoid my mother's questions and think about Taylor. On the downside, dinner was approaching, and I'd have to make eye contact with my parents without any distractions.

Mamá made my favorite, enchiladas de carnitas, which she always did when I came home. I set the table while she brought the serving dishes out of the kitchen, and Papá made his way in from the garage to wash his hands, kicking off his work boots. I was about to sit down when there was a knock at the door.

"Set out a few more plates, mijo," Mamá said as she rushed to the door.

I looked at Papá in confusion, but he gave a guilty sideways glance and a shrug.

"You know what your mother is like," he said as he seated himself at the head of the table. "She loves having guests."

I heard voices in the front room, then Mamá reappeared with three strangers trailing behind her. "Gabriel, you remember me telling you about the Lopez family. This is their daughter, Daniela."

Oh no. While I'd been distracted from flirting with Taylor on the 5, I'd somehow agreed to a blind date. My mouth hung open.

Daniela reached across the table to shake my hand. "Nice to finally meet you. I've heard so many stories."

"That sounds ominous." I chuckled. "Excuse me, I have to go grab a few extra plates for the table."

I rushed into the kitchen, and even though everything in my mother's kitchen was exactly where it always was, I fumbled around in the cabinets to buy myself a few moments. Mamá had made comments about setting me up, but I didn't actually think she was serious. Turns out I underestimated her.

"I take it you didn't know you were having dinner with the matchmakers tonight," Daniela murmured from behind me.

She really was pretty, with long black hair and dark pink lips, but all I could think about was how she wasn't Taylor and how wrong it felt not to have him here with me.

"Sorry, no. I'm sure you're lovely, but..." I struggled. "I'm kind of seeing someone. It's pretty new."

Daniela smiled. "Honestly, it's fine. I'm moving out of state in a month and don't want to start anything before I go. I'm only here because my parents wouldn't stop talking about how wonderful your mother's cooking is."

If we'd met somewhere else, we might have become friends.

"It really is the best." I smiled back, thankful to have an ally at the table tonight.

"So, your mom sent me in here for the limonada. Shall we

head back out before they start to assume you're in here defiling me?"

We laughed together and walked out with the lemonade and extra place settings.

"It's so lovely to have the whole family together," Mamá said as I finally sat down. "I wish you would come home more often, mijo."

I just hummed. "How do you all know each other?"

"We met at church," Sra. Lopez answered with a kind smile. I could see the apple didn't fall far from the tree; she and Daniela had the same eyes. "Your mother and I signed up to do a reading for the same Sunday Mass, and the rest is history."

As soon as it was polite, I escaped back into the kitchen with a stack of dirty plates. I got started on the cleanup; I wasn't leaving Mamá with a messy kitchen.

This time, the soft footsteps following me were my mother's. "Mijo, are you going to call Daniela?"

"She's very sweet, but I'm not interested." I continued loading the dishwasher with my back to her.

Mamá wrung her hands. "We just want what's best for you."

"I'm happy with my life, Mamá, and I want you to be happy for me."

When she remained silent, I closed the dishwasher and left the kitchen. I knew Mamá would think it was rude of me to walk out without saying goodbye to our guests, but I couldn't be bothered.

Eventually, my parents would either come to terms with how I lived or they wouldn't. Since I was never going to live up to their expectations, I might as well stop trying. I grabbed my car keys and headed out the door. For now, I knew where I needed to be, and it was with my boyfriend.

If he'd still have me.

"Kai speaking." It took some wheeling and dealing, but I was able to get Kai's number from Brian.

"It's Gabriel."

A beat of silence passed, and I almost thought he'd hung up on me.

"Forgive me for not being thrilled to hear from you," Kai finally said.

"I get it. I want to fix this, but Taylor's not picking up my calls. Just tell me where to find him so I can apologize."

Another agonizing stretch of silence while I waited for his verdict. I stared down the grocery store display of flowers, bouncing from foot to foot.

"I like you for him," Kai said. "Don't fuck this up."

I wasn't intending to—at least any more than I had already. I grabbed the biggest bouquet I could find and a pint of mint chocolate chip ice cream. I didn't know Taylor's favorites yet, but he'd told me a story about tubing on the lake in Wisconsin with his grandparents as a kid and how he and Margo had eaten their body weight in mint chocolate chip. So, I was confident he wouldn't hate it.

I texted Kai to let him know I was at the apartment, and he replied that he'd stepped out to run some errands and give us privacy. I was going to have to get him an apology gift, too.

My palms were sweaty as I stood in front of Taylor's apartment. I lifted my hand three times and put it back down without knocking.

Could I be a boyfriend?

I'd tried and given up on so many things in my life. I'm an experiential learner, and I don't think I would have found the right career or a hobby I loved—small business, I corrected myself internally—had I not tried a bunch of things.

And yeah, maybe this wouldn't be my one great love story, but I'd never find it if I didn't even let myself try. Maybe I'd discover that I couldn't be serious after all, but I wasn't even giving myself the chance.

Before I could talk myself out of it again, I knocked.

"Did you forget your key, or what..." Taylor trailed off as he opened the door and processed me standing there.

"Hi," I said, holding out the grocery store bouquet. Next time, I would do it right and get a fancy arrangement from a florist.

Taylor looked down at the flowers in my hand before tentatively taking them from me. "What are you doing here?"

"I'm here to apologize to my boyfriend," I murmured. "If he'll let me."

Taylor looked at me for a long moment, head cocked as if trying to decide what he was going to do with me. *You and me both, baby.* Finally, he stepped aside and let me into the apartment. He mumbled something under his breath that sounded a lot like, "fucking Kai."

"I brought ice cream." I held up the reusable grocery store bag.

His eyes softened, and he lunged at me, wrapping me in a hug. My chest hit his chest, and I let out a soft *oomph*.

"I'm sorry for freaking out at you," I said, muffled into his neck. "Nobody's ever wanted to date me before, so it caught me off guard."

"No one?" Shock laced Taylor's voice. "Impossible."

"Possible. So possible. The one time I asked someone to be my girlfriend, she laughed at me."

"She didn't know how good she had it."

"Turns out she was seeing someone else at the same time. Married him, and now she's got three kids." My face was still buried against Taylor's throat. "What do I have?"

"Do you even want kids?" His chest rumbled against mine with a chuckle.

"No," I whined.

"Then it's all for the better that she found someone else, and I get to have you." The gentleness in his voice made me lift my head and meet his eyes.

Taylor made a self-deprecating huff and squeezed me tighter. "I'm sorry, too. I should have let you talk instead of running away like a baby."

"You're my baby." I risked the word again, and even though I could tell he was holding in a smile, his eyes were crinkled around the edges again.

"It's not fair," he grumbled. "I turn to goo when you call me that."

"I promise to only use my powers for good,"

I leaned up and kissed him. It was tender, tentative, and in a way, it felt like the first time I'd been kissed.

"I've never been a boyfriend before," I whispered. "I hope I'm not bad at it."

"I don't have a lot of experience at this either." Taylor pulled back, tucking a curl behind my ear. "We don't have to use the word boyfriends if you don't want to. I just really like kissing you, and I'd like to be the only one who gets to, for now."

"Exclusive make-out buddies, huh?" I should have been thrilled at his willingness to keep things casual—it was what I'd always claimed to want from past relationships—but I couldn't help the sting of disappointment at his words. "I dunno, I like boyfriends."

Taylor assessed my face, and I could see the conflict in his eyes. "You scared me."

"I'm sorry."

I didn't like the distance Taylor was putting between us; it hadn't been there before. It was my fault, though, and I was determined to fix it. I'd show him I could be the best boyfriend he'd ever had.

"Ok," Taylor whispered, and I let out the breath I'd been holding.

"So, ice cream?" I asked, and he laughed, stepping back.

I missed having his body against mine immediately, but he put his hand on my lower back and ushered me to the kitchen.

"Let's put that in the freezer for a few minutes. There's something else I want to do before Kai gets home and interrupts us." His mouth was on my neck, and I shivered as his hand slipped around my waist and down the front of my pants. My cock thickened under his attention.

"Yes, yeah, ice cream can wait." I pushed forward into his hand, and he chuckled.

"Hey, weren't you supposed to be in Santa Ana at your parents' this weekend?"

I blinked at the change in subject, trying to redirect some of my blood back to my brain. "Dude, do not talk about my parents with your hand on my dick."

"Sorry, sorry." Taylor smiled as he grabbed my hand and pulled me to his bedroom.

We were a flurry of hands and clothes and kisses as we tumbled onto the bed together.

I lay on my back and maneuvered him over me so we could sixty-nine. When his lips closed around my cock for the first time, I couldn't help but arch my back and moan. He lapped around the crown, his tongue toying gently with my foreskin, and held me in his mouth with the perfect amount of suction. My moans made precum leak from his dick, dripping toward my face—holy shit, that was hot. I licked him clean. He was salty and tangy and perfect. When I took him into my mouth, he thrust to the back of my throat.

I loved having my face fucked, but tonight I wanted something different. I released his erection from my mouth and licked my hand before gripping and stroking him. Then I kissed back toward his balls, giving each one some attention with my tongue. It was hard to focus while getting the best head of my life, but the way he made me feel spurred me on.

I wanted him to lose his mind like I was losing mine.

Using my hands to spread his cheeks apart so I could get at what I really wanted, I licked up his taint and right over his hole.

He released me with a gasp. "Holy fuck."

"Is this ok, baby?"

I knew not everyone liked being eaten out, but I'd be disappointed if he stopped me.

"You better not stop," he hissed, licking up my cock and making it twitch.

I teased around his rim with my tongue.

"God, Gabriel, that feels so good."

Satisfied with the green light, I dove back into my boyfriend's ass with enthusiasm.

13

TAYLOR

Gabriel was going to kill me.

He was tongue-fucking me to within an inch of my life, and I was sure I was giving him the worst blow job I'd given since I'd been a clueless college student. The filthy sounds Gabriel was making spurred me on as I took his cock into my mouth, bobbing up and down.

When his tongue and hands left me, I lifted my head and glanced down at him. He sucked two fingers into his mouth, and the heat in his eyes as he stared at me had me whimpering. His chest was streaked with my precum, his hazel eyes dilated, and his hair absolutely wild across the pillow.

He looked like a dream.

He adjusted the angle of my hips again. My cock was back in his mouth, and he was encouraging me to thrust against his tongue. His wet finger slid up my crack and gently pressed into my hole.

"Fuck. Gabriel, please," I gasped.

He worked a second finger inside me as he continued to take my length into his mouth, swirling his tongue across my tip each time I pulled out.

"More."

At this point, I could barely focus on my task, just holding his dick in my mouth and groaning around him. When he crooked his fingers and grazed my prostate, I was done for. He pulled off me at the last second, and I covered his face and chest with rope after rope of cum.

As I rode out my orgasm, I took him to the back of my throat, burying my nose against his balls, and swallowed around him. He shouted my name as he thrust up once, twice, and came in my mouth. I gagged as cum hit the back of my throat, and his release dripped down my chin.

Once I could tell he was too sensitive to continue, I rolled over so we were face-to-face. I reached for my shirt, handing it to him so he could clean off, and I collapsed against him. When I dove into his mouth, he tasted like me. I'd never kissed anyone who'd made me want to forget the rest of the world before, but every thought, every feeling, was wrapped in Gabriel.

I didn't know what I was doing, trying to lock him down, but I couldn't help wanting him to myself. I could keep this casual if that was what he needed. I didn't have more than casual in me, anyway.

"I like having a boyfriend." Gabriel sighed. His eyes were glazed with afterglow, and his cheeks were flushed as I tangled my fingers in his chest hair. This was what I'd asked for, but it didn't make the panic go away. If anything, it raised the stakes.

My heart pounded in my chest, and I wasn't sure if it was from the incredible orgasm, the mystery illness that was plaguing me, or plain old store-brand anxiety.

I decided to kiss him instead of worrying about it, at least for tonight.

From our cocoon in my bed, I heard the front door open and Kai's footsteps echoing through the apartment.

"Shall we share our ice cream with the little shit who told you where I live?" I asked.

"Don't hold it against him. I can be very persuasive."

I nibbled on his ear. "Well, I hope you use different methods of persuasion on him than you do on me."

He rolled us over and straddled me as he grinned widely. "You know I reserve all kinds of things just for you. That's how boyfriends work, right?"

Gabriel fluttered his eyelashes at me, and I couldn't help but tickle his ribs, even though my heart skipped a beat.

He yelped and jumped off me. "Ok, ok. Let's get up, or I'm not going to leave. I need to get back to Santa Ana tonight."

I tried to hide my disappointment. "You can't stay?"

"Sorry, baby. I want to, but I kind of walked out on my parents, and I know they'll be worried if I don't go back."

I opened my mouth to ask what had happened when he cut me off. "I promise I'll tell you about it, but not right now. Let's go eat that ice cream."

I hummed but didn't press him further, and we threw on our sweats before heading out to the kitchen. As we emerged, Kai was sprawled out on the couch, scrolling on his phone.

"Oh, good," he said, glancing up. "You're clothed."

Sometimes, it was annoying to have a friend who'd known you so long they had a catalog of your every facial expression. It became impossible to hide anything from them.

Kai had guessed something was up as soon as I'd walked out of my room this morning and wouldn't let it go until I'd told him the whole story. He'd chastised me for running off before Gabriel could get a word in, even though ultimately, I thought he was on my side. I wouldn't forget how easily he'd turned on me. I narrowed my eyes at him in accusation. After tilting his head in assessment for a moment longer, he slapped his thighs and gave me a slight nod before he stood from the couch.

"I have ice cream," Gabriel said from the kitchen, where he was bent over the freezer drawer. "Join us?"

"Nah, I'm gonna head to bed. Besides, if you know Taylor at all—which I hope you do—you brought mint chocolate chip, and I can't stand that flavor."

Gabriel was holding the tub of ice cream in his hand, and we both looked at it in surprise.

Kai nodded in approval as he passed the kitchen doorway. "Oh, yeah, well done. Cookies and cream or bust for me."

He continued down the hall and into his room, and we were alone again.

"I don't even remember telling you my favorite ice cream flavor," I said.

Gabriel shrugged. "You told that story about your sister. I made a lucky guess."

He turned toward the cabinets to look for bowls and spoons. I stepped up behind him and wrapped my arms around him, tucking my face into his hair. I knew the ice cream was not a big deal in the grand scheme of things, but I was not used to people paying that much attention to my preferences. And wow, did it make me feel things that he'd listened to and remembered a small detail like that.

"You're going to have to un-octopus yourself from me if we're going to eat this," he said.

I nipped at the back of his neck and let him go to grab the ice cream scoop. Once we'd portioned out some ice cream, Gabriel jumped up onto the counter and grabbed his bowl.

"Challenge accepted," I said, grabbing my bowl and stepping between his legs.

He tucked his ankle around the back of my thigh and smiled. All I wanted was to be close to him.

I wasn't sure how I was going to balance that with helping Margo once I was back to my regular hours, but I'd been pulling more than my weight since I was fifteen, so I'd find a way to make it work.

By the time we finished our ice cream and did the dishes, it was late.

"I know you don't want to talk about your parents right now, and I respect that," I said, "but is there anything I can do to support you?"

Gabriel looked up from where he was bent over by the front door, putting on his shoes. The soft, smitten look on his face had my heart pounding. I didn't want to let him leave. When he stood and slipped on his hoodie, he pulled me into a hug.

"Nothing right now, baby. They're having a hard time accepting my choices since they're not the ones they'd make for me, but I'm an adult, and they'll get there." He tilted his head to the side. "Or not. Anyway, seeing your face tonight has made life a lot better."

"I'm glad you came." I kissed him, trying to keep things light. I knew he was about to walk out the door.

He dragged himself reluctantly out of my embrace. "Me too."

I knew Gabriel had agreed to be exclusive, but a part of my heart still needed to hold back. It didn't feel safe to let feelings get involved—we were having fun. Together. Exclusively.

Yup, everything was fine.

KAI WASTED ABSOLUTELY no time outing me to my sister as soon as we walked into their townhome. "Taylor has a boyfriend."

Margo gasped, and I glared at him.

"I'm not one hundred percent sure I do." We'd said a lot of things last night, but had Gabriel said it was what he wanted? Or was he giving me what he thought I wanted?

"Semantics," Kai said with an eye roll as he fist-bumped Benji and made his way farther into the house.

"I promise I wasn't keeping him a secret, Margo. It's new. Kai just wanted to steal my thunder, the drama queen that he is."

Margo squeezed me tight. She gave the best hugs, although Gabriel might give her a run for her money now.

"Well," she said, "hurry up and get in here so you can tell me all about it."

Benji smiled at his fiancée indulgently. "Maybe pour the mimosas first, love."

Margo clapped with glee. "You're right. This calls for champagne. A boyfriend!"

"Let's not get ahead of ourselves." I accepted the mimosa from Margo, and we made our way out to their small back patio.

Benji had assembled a row of narrow planter boxes filled with tall snake plants, creating a private oasis on the patio, even though their townhome was sandwiched between several others. It was just big enough for four chairs around a round table and the grill. Café lights hung above us, a reminder of all the evenings we'd spent out here with cocktails and card games.

They rented the place, like Kai and I, but I was proud of the home Margo and Benji had created here. Sometimes, it still felt impossible that Margo was a full-grown adult, even though I'd watched it happen.

"Ok, I've waited long enough," Margo whined. "Spill."

"You've waited three minutes," Benji said.

We all laughed. Margo had always been impatient.

"His name is Gabriel. He's the guy I met the day we found your dress." I looked at my sister.

"I knew it!" She shrieked. "You're inviting him to the wedding, right?"

I rolled my eyes at her theatrics, but my cheeks flushed.

"We've only been on a few dates, and it's casual. But yeah, I'll probably invite him to the wedding."

I pulled up a selfie we took at the cosmic mini golf place to show them. "He works at the botanical gardens and plays volleyball. I think you'll like him."

"They are nauseatingly sweet together," Kai said, making a gagging noise. "I am going to have to get noise-cancelling headphones."

"You act like you never bring people over." I scrunched up my nose at him.

Margo laughed. "Maybe it's time for the two of you to get your own places. I know you both could afford it."

Kai and I scoffed. He was the only person who knew the real reason we'd kept living together. And he covered for me like he always did.

"You know we're codependent as hell," Kai said. "I couldn't live without your brother around to mother-hen me. If I have to listen to his sex noises, it's a sacrifice I'm willing to make."

"What a martyr." I huffed, finishing off my mimosa.

"Well, that's settled then," Margo said with a determined nod. "We'll visit the botanical gardens for lunch so I can meet him."

Benji laughed. "Now you've done it. Margo's cupid alter ego has been activated."

I groaned. He was right. It came from a good place, wanting me to be as happy as she was with Benji. Honestly, I wasn't worried about Margo and Gabriel not getting along. I was worried about them getting along too well.

"Any chance we could finish planning your wedding before you start planning mine?" I asked, reaching over to top off Margo's glass. "I promise we'll make plans for you to meet him soon."

The buzzy, bubbly feeling in my gut wasn't from the champagne, and it didn't settle even as our brunch conversation carried on to other topics—mainly Margo and Benji's impending nuptials. When my phone lit up with a text from Gabriel, that feeling intensified.

14

GABRIEL

When Taylor told me how little time he'd have for a relationship, I hadn't been that worried. I'd never been in a relationship, and I considered myself to be pretty independent. I didn't anticipate what it would feel like to start to fall in love.

Even still, with as busy as he was, when I told Taylor about setting up the LLC for Plant Daddy Botanicals, he was over that same night with his laptop. He sat in the same stool Alex always chose and said he'd hang out for as long as it took. He promised he wasn't working, but a spreadsheet was open on his screen, so I was skeptical.

It was probably my fault for accepting his offer to handle my folder of business receipts.

"I have to do this thing with my parents in a few weeks," I said, looking up from my paperwork. I was nervous to ask, but I couldn't hold it in any longer. "It's a Saturday night, and I'm almost positive they're going to try to bring someone to set me up with. Would you come play boyfriend and protect me?"

"I can make it work. I don't need anyone encroaching on my turf," Taylor teased. "What's the event?"

"A neighborhood block party, but I always end up getting roped into helping my parents with things."

Everything within me fought against talking about my complicated relationship with my family. I had so much to be grateful for, and there were so many parents out there who were even worse, but I'd promised Taylor I'd fill him in eventually. If I wanted him to be my backup, I needed him to know the whole story.

"That's part of why I left last weekend and drove to your house. We were at dinner, and my mom ambushed me with a blind date. The whole family showed up with their single daughter, like we were on Mexican Matchmaking. My mom can't handle that my life hasn't followed the exact timeline she envisioned, so she's taken matters into her own hands."

Taylor nodded sympathetically. "That sucks. I'll be there if you need me to be."

"Thanks. I know it's too early for you to meet my parents, but I could use the support."

"If it weren't for Margo's wedding, you probably wouldn't be meeting mine ever." Taylor grimaced. "Not if I could help it, anyway."

I couldn't blame him. Part of me was already anticipating that the block party would go terribly.

"That's fine; meeting the parents is kind of a serious thing," I said.

"It's not that I would want to hide you from them. They just haven't been invested in my life. As soon as I turned eighteen, it was made clear I was on my own. So, I don't make an effort to keep in touch with them. The only reason I do is because of Margo."

"Why does Margo still talk to them?"

"She was diagnosed with cancer when she was seven," Taylor said. "My parents checked out after that. I don't think they really wanted us to begin with, but when shit hit the fan, it became too much. I took her to all her appointments as soon as I got my license, and I tried to shield her from how bad things got when they divorced."

"Yikes." I winced. "You were just a kid."

"Yeah, but Margo was younger, and she was sick. I didn't want her to shoulder that responsibility. I wanted her to get better and stay better, and she did." Taylor rubbed the back of his neck the way he did when he was stressed.

I rounded the corner and started massaging his shoulders.

"Anyway, she doesn't know or remember most of how things went down, so she still talks to them, and they're invited to the wedding."

"This explains so much about you." I smiled and shook my head.

Taylor scrunched up his forehead, creating a small furrow between his eyebrows.

"You're a natural caretaker," I said, "and you're always trying to make the people around you happy. You dote on Margo. You showed up for me tonight the moment I asked. I'm pretty sure if you looked up the word responsible in the dictionary, your photo would be there."

Taylor grimaced. "I grew up fast. I don't love that for me, but it is what it is."

I squeezed his shoulders. "Baby, you're an incredible, kind, generous, and dependable person. Despite the difficulties you faced as a kid, you managed to get yourself and Margo through it. I think you're one of the best men I've ever met, and I'm not just saying that because you make me come my brains out."

Taylor blushed and tucked his chin to his chest, but I chased him with my lips, trailing kisses along his jaw.

"What did you want to be when you were a kid? Like when you used to daydream about being a grown-up, what did you imagine?" I could tell I needed to change the subject to something lighter, and I noticed Taylor's little sigh of relief.

"I was a theater kid, but behind-the-scenes stuff. I loved the costumes the most. If I could have done anything, it would have been working on designing costumes for movies or plays. It combines history and fashion in a way that's always fascinated me."

"I could see that." I grinned. "I always love what you're wearing when we go out."

"My clothes are so boring." Taylor cracked a small smile. "Pretty sure you'd think I looked hot in a paper bag."

"You would, but that doesn't disprove my point."

IN AN OUT-OF-CHARACTER MOVE, I'd arrived first—early!—to volleyball practice. As I was walking to our usual meeting spot, I felt that familiar jolt of anticipation when my phone buzzed in my pocket. When I pulled it out, I was immediately disappointed. Mamá let me know that the Lopez family would be attending the block party with their daughter.

> GABRIEL
>
> I'm coming to help Papá with the asada. I'm not interested in Daniela.

Silence followed, and I knew from experience that it didn't mean the conversation was over. It meant she was upset and wanted to punish me by giving me the silent treatment. I tossed my phone into my gym bag and plopped down in the sand to wait for the rest of the crew to show up for volleyball practice.

Our family was from the mountains, but I was an ocean baby. Michoacán would always be home in a deep, ancestral way, but I loved having my toes in the sand and listening to the waves crashing against the shore. The hustle and bustle of the beach on a Saturday was a lot, but we could always carve out enough space to set up the net. Even on the weekends when we didn't have a tournament, we made time for a practice game and some drills.

I hadn't been waiting long when Oscar arrived and threw his gym bag down beside mine. He had the carrying case with our net and the mesh bag of volleyballs over his shoulder. I grabbed his hand so he could pull me to my feet.

"Hola, primo," he said, pulling me into a hug.

"I'm glad you're here to help me stake out our spot. It's such a nice day that the beach feels especially crowded."

"Yeah, yeah, I was a little late, so what? It's not like anyone else was on time."

"Hey! I was on time." I wanted credit for this win. I genuinely was almost always late. If I started a project, especially for Plant Daddy, it felt like I became blind to the time, and before I knew it, I was behind schedule. Today, because I'd been chatting with Taylor over breakfast, I was out the door before I'd had the chance to get distracted.

"You gonna be at the block party next weekend?" I asked, tugging the net from the bag.

Oscar grabbed the other side of the net and walked it backwards. "Yeah, I don't think I'll be able to get out of it."

Oscar's parents were awesome. My parents hadn't wanted me to come out to anyone, but when I told my Tio and Tia that I was bi, they responded that they didn't care what the Catholic Church said. I was perfect, and they loved me. When Oscar came out as gay a few years later, they said the same, and I know it was his parents' reaction to me that helped him come to terms with his sexuality. It was the one thing I'd done before him. Once the golden child had come out, my parents started to change their tune and were at least outwardly more supportive.

"Thank goodness. I don't want to deal with that mess alone. Mamá won't get off my case about settling down with some church girl."

Oscar cringed. "Do they know about Taylor?"

"I'm bringing him as backup."

Oscar whistled, likely in acknowledgment of the impending drama. We fell back into our usual banter while we set up the net, and by the time we were finished, the rest of the team had arrived.

"Let's get the game going," Lucas called out.

Brian was shirtless, of course, because he always was. Alex pulled off her shirt, too, leaving her in a black sports bra.

The three of them claimed one side of the net, and Kat joined Oscar and me on the other. The league we played in was a recreational one, but we all loved the trash talk and the camaraderie. And, since it was a queer league, we got our fair share of eye candy at the tournaments and social events.

We spent about an hour and a half volleying back and forth, practicing our positions, and rotating out every fifteen minutes or so. By the time we were done, I was caked with sweat and happy as a clam.

"Anyone want to grab a smoothie?" I called out as we packed up the net.

"Kat and I are out," Alex said. "We have to work this afternoon, and I need to shower first."

"David and I have dinner with his folks in Venice tonight, so we're out too, unfortunately." We didn't see much of David, even though Lucas and his husband had been together for five years. He struggled with social anxiety and didn't make it to many of our games. "They're in town for the weekend, so we're playing tour guide. I was barely able to sneak away for this."

Fortunately, both Brian and Oscar were in for smoothies, so I helped Oscar carry our gear back to his car, and we walked down the boardwalk to the smoothie shop. I was hoping to have more distractions from Taylor, who seemed to dominate every spare thought in my brain. Of course, the guys wanted to hear all about how that was going.

"Is the sex good?" Brian asked.

Oscar frowned. "I don't want to hear about my cousin's sex life."

"I'm not talking about the sex," I said at the same time.

I wanted to gush about how incredible Taylor was, but I also wanted to keep him to myself. I'd never felt protective of a sexual partner before. Part of the reason Brian asked was that I usually shared details about my conquests without prompting.

Taylor was so much more than a conquest, though.

Brian narrowed his eyes in my direction as if he could tell exactly what I was hiding. "You always want to talk about sex. Either it's terrible, or you're falling for him, and I'm guessing you wouldn't be with him if it were terrible... which leaves one option."

People assumed that because of Brian's Playboy ways, big muscles, and tattoos, he was a bit of a himbo, but he was far too observant and intelligent for his own good.

I coughed and took a big gulp from my water bottle, considering how to respond. "I'm not sure what we're doing. I've never had an exclusive thing like this before, so it's uncharted territory, but I'm having a good time with him."

"Pretty sure no one is supposed to know what they're doing when they're falling in love," Brian replied. "Not that I'd know."

"I didn't say anything about love," I said quickly.

Whenever I'd gotten close to official boyfriend status in the past, I'd always run away, especially after Maria. Ever since she shut me down, reminding me I wasn't husband material, I'd avoided repeats altogether.

Taylor was the only one I'd wanted to repeat and repeat and repeat.

"Earth to Gabriel," Oscar said.

I'd zoned out, staring at the smoothie shop menu, and we'd reached the front of the line. We ordered and found a small table on the back patio.

"He deserves so much better than me." I sighed. "I'm about to turn thirty, and I don't have anything to show for it."

"Ok, first of all, you are a catch," Brian thrust his finger at my chest. "And I bet Taylor knows it too because he wanted to lock this awesomeness down immediately."

I lifted my eyebrows skeptically.

"Second of all," Oscar says, piling on. "You can't let what our family says get in your head. You're a college graduate, you have a career you enjoy, and you pay your rent. Just because you're not a millionaire with three kids by now doesn't mean shit. None of that matters if you're miserable."

I took a long sip from my smoothie. "Easy to say when you're a fancy lawyer and everyone in the family worships you."

Oscar reached out and slapped the back of my head. "Don't sabotage a good thing because you believe lies about yourself. Who cares what our family thinks? What matters is what you and Taylor think."

I let their words marinate in my mind as we finished our smoothies and moved to less sensitive subjects. Brian was interviewing for a new international route with his airline, which was a big deal. If he got it, he'd have to start traveling almost every week, but he assured us he'd still be around for weekend games as often as he could. Oscar was recovering from a rough breakup by adopting a new dog and needed to show us all six hundred photos he'd taken over the last three days.

And the whole time, I thought about what love was supposed to feel like.

15

TAYLOR

At this point, I'd helped Margo and Benji make all the major decisions they needed to for the wedding, which was only a few weeks away. Now, it was death by minutia. I felt like a dead man walking between wedding errands for Margo and making time for Gabriel, while inputting two years of receipts into the accounting software I'd set up for him.

I hadn't heard back from the doctors about all the tests they'd run, so I convinced myself nothing was wrong. I'd made it this far without the house of cards collapsing.

Of course, I wouldn't be able to outrun the burnout forever.

When I walked out into the kitchen Friday morning to grab coffee, Kai took one look at me and spun me right back around. He barricaded me in my bedroom and called Gabriel to let him know I was sick and that he needed to make sure I stayed in bed. I barely got my socks off before I fell back to sleep.

Mid-afternoon, I woke up to my phone ringing.

"Hey." Gabriel's voice washed over me when I answered. "Can you come to the door? I have soup."

Was I dreaming? I rolled out of bed in the now-wrinkled

jeans I hadn't managed to take off, and when I opened the door, Gabriel was there.

"What are you doing here?" I asked.

"Kai told me you were sick, remember? I took the afternoon off and made you chicken and rice soup. Added extra garlic, too."

"You took the afternoon off. To make me soup?"

"That's what I said." He pushed the back of his hand against my forehead. "Do you have a fever? Are you delirious?"

"I don't know." I stepped back as Gabriel shouldered his way inside.

"Let me put this on the stove to warm up, and then we'll get you into something more comfortable. I can't believe you passed out in jeans."

"It came on so fast. One second, I was fine. The next, I passed out."

It was a testament to how tired I was that Gabriel's hands were on me, undressing me, and it barely registered with my dick. He pulled a pair of sweatpants up my legs, lifting each foot to help me step in, and slipped a loose tee over my head. Finally, he pulled one of his college sweatshirts out of his overnight bag, and I eagerly put it on.

"Are you staying?" I asked hopefully.

"Just being prepared." Gabriel smiled softly. "I want to take care of you."

My heart fluttered all over the place. I hadn't had anyone take care of me since I was fifteen. Maybe younger than that. My parents weren't the caretaking type.

He slid under my arm and wrapped his arm around my waist, pressing his body against my side. "Come on, let's go eat."

I was exhausted, and my head ached, but the soup was incredible and soothing—worth dragging myself out of bed for.

The way Gabriel played with the hairs on the nape of my neck while I ate almost brought me to tears.

Once I'd eaten two full bowls of the best soup I'd ever tasted, Gabriel herded me back to bed. He settled with his back against my headboard and pulled my head into his lap. "Nap some more, baby."

"Are you an angel?" I knew I was feeling a little loopy from the cold medicine I'd taken, but with my arms around his muscular thighs and his fingers running lightly over my scalp, I felt like I was in a dream.

"No, baby. Just a regular guy."

"Nothing is regular about you. You're the best guy."

Gabriel chuckled. "Get some rest. I'll be here when you wake up."

I kissed his leg. "Thanks for being here, angel."

His fingers paused in my hair, then started the same soothing pattern up again.

I was half asleep when I heard him whisper, so I could have imagined when I thought I heard him say, "Anything for you."

I SLIPPED in and out of consciousness for the rest of the evening, and every time I opened my eyes, Gabriel was there. He made sure I took my meds and drank water, and he woke me up every so often to eat, even if it was just salty crackers. Once, I could hear him laughing with Kai out in the kitchen. I'd like to get used to this.

Gabriel in my space, Gabriel with my friends, Gabriel always.

I'd been so lonely for so long, holding myself back and keeping myself separate to protect myself from the pain of loss that inevitably follows love. But work wouldn't bring me soup when I was sick. Work wouldn't hold me when I was covered in snot. Until I'd met this chaotic bisexual who turned my world upside down, all my evenings had been spent alone unless Kai or Margo had dragged me out with them.

I was vaguely aware that I was supposed to be meeting Gabriel's parents this weekend, and I wasn't sure how good of an impression I'd be making in this state, but I couldn't stay awake long enough to worry.

IN THE MORNING, I awoke to find myself tangled around Gabriel, with my head on his chest and my arm thrown over him. I was sweaty and gross as I slipped out of his arms and crept into my en suite to take a shower.

The hot water massaged the tension from my shoulders, and once the clamminess was gone from my skin, I felt like a new man. I found Gabriel still in bed, scrolling on his phone. I was wrapped in a towel, using another small one to dry my hair, and I watched his eyes track my body with interest. I was ready to get naked and jump him, but he popped out of bed before I could. He gave me a quick kiss and passed by, scooting into the bathroom so quickly that I was left blinking at the closed door.

"Hey!" I cried, frustrated.

He laughed on the other side of the door, and I heard the shower run again. I ditched the towel and crawled back into bed. Gabriel emerged, wearing only low-slung grey sweats and holding a cup of water and a dose of cold meds.

"You look criminally good in those," I said, licking my lips.

"Hold your horses, cowboy. You're still on bed rest."

I smirked. "Good thing what I want to do to you involves being on this bed."

He burst into laughter and handed me the pills. Then he tossed me a pair of boxers and his sweatshirt.

"Come on, we're going to go sit on the couch and watch Drag Race. I'm still catching up on the last All-Star season."

I groaned. "Why do I have to put clothes on?"

"Have you forgotten you have a roommate? He may be at work right now, but I'm sure he'd rather not have your balls all over his couch."

Grumbling, I slipped on the boxers and hoodie, secretly glad they smelled like Gabriel. I suppose that if I had to wear clothes, this was a worthwhile compromise.

"How are you feeling this morning?" Gabriel asked as we walked to the living room.

I settled on the couch and pulled a blanket over myself. "So much better. I can't believe I slept that much."

"You were in full koala mode," Gabriel said. "I'm pretty sure you slept like thirty hours. I'm not surprised, though. You've been burning the candle at both ends."

I sighed, preparing for him to reprimand me.

"I swear I'm not trying to lecture you." Gabriel sat down, and I lifted the blanket so he could tuck in next to me. "I wouldn't want to talk you out of being there for Margo or putting in a hundred and ten percent at work, and I'm certainly not going to let you get out of seeing me. I care about you and want you to take care of yourself, too."

I sighed again, and he pulled me into his arms.

"I'll try," I muttered.

When he grabbed the remote and pulled up Drag Race, I finally processed what day it was.

"Wait, don't we have that thing with your parents tonight?"

"Yeah, that's tonight," Gabriel said. "I told them you were sick, and I would do my best to make it, but I was waiting to see how you were feeling."

"I'm not on my deathbed. You could go without me."

"Nope, package deal. I'm not walking into that mess alone. It's fine if you're not feeling up to it. It's not like I was looking forward to it."

Usually, I was the one with my arm around Gabriel, so I often found myself looking down at his eyes through those thick, dark lashes. Today, I was curled up at his side, so I tilted my head up to meet his eyes.

He gave me a soft kiss on the top of my head. "No pressure, let's see how you're feeling this afternoon, and we'll make a game-time decision."

"Ok." I kissed him, trying to deepen into something more, but Gabriel held back.

He huffed. "I'm not falling for your tricks."

As we shared banter about the drama on TV, I kept moving my hand up his thigh, and he kept sliding it back down to his knee. By the time we broke apart for lunch and another serving of that delicious chicken and rice soup, I felt like myself again.

"I think I'm feeling well enough to head to your parents' party tonight if you want," I said as I stood from the couch and stretched.

Gabriel leaned forward and kissed along the sliver of my stomach that was revealed.

"I don't want," Gabriel said. "But if you're sure..."

I grabbed his hands and pulled him up into a hug. "I'm sure. I feel fine."

We dressed, and I texted Kai to let him know I was alive before we left the house. Gabriel looked so good, especially with the way those jeans hugged his ass. The longer we were together, the harder it was for me to resist pushing for more. I wanted inside him so badly.

I wore a boxy plum-colored T-shirt—one I'd bought online on a whim during a recent online shopping spree—and fitted jeans. The tiniest sliver of my hips peeked out above the waistline of my pants when I moved just right, and based on the way Gabriel's eyes heated when he saw me, I knew he approved. I was a little nervous to show up at Gabriel's parents' house looking so obviously gay, but I decided to lean into it for a few reasons.

One, I was gay. There was no *dressing straight* to meet the parents of the guy I was seeing. It was what it was, and they needed to deal, or I'd have things to say.

Two, ever since Gabriel and I had that conversation about my childhood, I'd realized that just because I'd had to leave some of my dreams behind, it didn't mean I couldn't enjoy fashion or dress with a bit more personality.

I could feel Gabriel's anxiety spiking as we made our way down to Santa Ana. I was driving this time and reached over to calm his bouncing leg with a hand on his knee. He stilled and grabbed my hand tightly. I was glad I could be with him as we walked into the lion's den, and I sent a silent thank you up into the universe that whatever bug had attacked me was a short-lived one.

"Could you put some music on, angel?" I asked, and he blushed.

"I shouldn't let you call me that," he grumbled as he pulled up his music-streaming app.

"Why not?" I chuckled. "I can tell you like it."

The silence I received from him was answer enough.

Gabriel didn't sing along to the stereo like he usually did, but at least I was able to coax a few laughs and smiles from him as we chatted on the drive. My sense of impending doom started to grow, as much as I tried to hide it.

What exactly were we walking into that my expressive, effervescent beam of sunshine was folding in on himself?

16

GABRIEL

As we walked up to my parents' house, I kept my eyes peeled for Oscar, hoping he'd arrived before us and could mediate if things got out of control.

Of course, we didn't run into him before we reached my parents' front steps, and Mamá rushed out the door to greet us. My heart was racing, and I could tell I was squeezing life out of Taylor's hand, but I couldn't stop myself.

Instead of complaining, he leaned over to whisper in my ear, "You say the word, and we're out. Ok, angel?"

I nodded even as I had to release his hand to accept my mom's hug.

"Mijo, it's good to see you," she said. "Papá is ready to start the carne asada."

"Mamá, this is my boyfriend, Taylor," I said, gesturing toward him.

"Mucho gusto, Señora Rivera." Taylor smiled. "I took Spanish in high school, but I'm sorry to say it's not great. I'll need to practice."

She gave him a suspicious once-over. "A qué se dedica, mijo?"

"Mamá, inglés. He's an accountant."

She hummed and squinted.

I sighed. "We're going to find Papá."

Taylor took my hand, and I pulled him away. It grated on me that my mom wasn't even trying to see how awesome he was. Wasn't even giving him a chance. We found my dad in the backyard, hovering over a cooler where the beef and chicken were ready to be grilled. Knowing him, it had been marinating for a few days in the fridge. As stressed as my family made me, the food was always unmatched.

"Papá, how can we help?"

"Hola, Señor Rivera. I'm Taylor. Nice to meet you." Still with a smile on his face, Taylor reached out his hand.

My dad shook his hand, giving Taylor a small smile, but staying quiet—not unusual for him. At least he was being nice.

"Can you each grab a cooler, and we'll carry them out front?" Papá asked.

I squeezed Taylor's hand before releasing it to grab the first cooler. Taylor bent down to pick up the other without complaint, and I momentarily got distracted by his arms flexing with the cooler's weight.

I was happy we could get wrapped up in grilling and didn't have to wade into the crowd of neighbors lining the street. Families played corn hole, and the abuelito who lived on the corner was handing out paletas to any kid who passed by. My dad made polite conversation with Taylor as he manned the grill. He'd got my dad talking about the Mexican soccer team and listened intently despite not being much of a sports fan.

"I didn't know you were into soccer," I whispered, teasing.

"Everyone knows they're the hottest athletes, so my interest is more anthropological." Taylor lowered his voice as if to avoid my dad hearing, but the snort from the neighboring grill seemed to indicate that he hadn't been as quiet as he'd hoped.

"Hotter than volleyball players?" I asked, hand to my chest, feigning offense.

"I was speaking in generalities. There is a particular volleyball player who, in my opinion, could give any soccer player a run for his money."

"I guess I'll accept that," I said with a wink.

He raised his voice back to a normal level to include my dad in the conversation again. "The only sport I follow much is basketball. My sister's fiancé is a big fan."

"Lakers?" my dad asked.

"Yup, are you a fan too? Maybe we could get tickets to a game sometime."

Papá nodded and tipped his beer toward Taylor as he turned the chicken he'd been supervising on the grill. He was a man of few words, preferring to let my mom steamroll the conversation most of the time. As he and Taylor fell back into a comfortable silence, I realized I'd maybe assumed my dad's opinions were the same as my mom's since she was so loud, and he never contradicted her. At least it felt like he was trying.

That gave me the confidence to step away for a moment to grab us another round of beers. I kissed Taylor on the cheek and told him I'd be right back. I wanted to be quick; I wasn't trying to get cornered by my mom or thrust upon any bachelorettes while I was defenseless.

Jogging up to the drink fridge in the garage, I surveyed the options. Taylor wasn't a big beer drinker, but it was either that or tequila. My parents kept my favorite lager stocked at their house, and my dad had been converted too. Since Taylor was driving today, I avoided the tequila and grabbed three beers. I closed the fridge with my hip and turned, immediately spotting the Lopez family chatting with my mom in the yard.

After passing my dad his beer, I made a big show of wrapping my arms around Taylor from behind and rising onto my tiptoes to reach over his shoulder and kiss his cheek. He glanced around, like he was trying to figure out who I was performing for, as he turned to face me.

"The family my mom is playing matchmaker with just showed up," I whispered.

Taylor chuckled and took the beer, bringing the bottle up to his lips. I couldn't look away from his mouth. How did everything this man did hypnotize me? He blushed when he caught me staring.

I was both relieved and anxious when I heard Oscar greeting the next-door neighbors. While he'd never bought into the competition set up between us, my parents were insufferable about it.

Mamá followed behind him as he made his way over.

"Taylor, man, good to see you again," Oscar said, going in for a hug.

"Likewise. What a pleasant surprise. Do you live nearby?"

"Nah. My parents do, though." He threw an arm around me. "Got roped into helping, same as this one."

Taylor laughed, tilting his face up to the sun. I lived for the moments when his shoulders relaxed. The man carried the weight of the world.

"You didn't work today?" my dad asked Oscar by way of greeting.

Of course, we were going straight there.

"Nope, I have a paralegal now to help with paperwork," Oscar said. "Means I don't have to work as much on the weekends."

Papá was pleased by this, of course. It meant Oscar was rising in the ranks, another step higher on the unreachable pedestal my parents had placed him on.

"He got a promotion," Mamá added.

"Congrats," Taylor said, lifting his beer to toast him.

"When are you getting a promotion, mijo?" My mom so helpfully directed the spotlight onto me.

"I'm not trying to get a promotion, Mamá. I just started this job a few months ago."

She clicked her tongue in censure.

"The gardens are beautiful right now," Taylor said, looking at my dad. "Have you been to see the new exhibit he designed? I've seen photos, and it's incredible."

I could kiss that man. Neither of my parents had ever expressed much interest in what I did at work.

Of course, my mom continued talking as if Taylor hadn't spoken. "Why can't you show a little initiative like your cousin? We worked so hard so you could go to school, and now what are you doing? Not an important career like Oscar."

I wanted to disappear. It wasn't even the hundredth time I'd heard her say the same things, but to be dressed down in front of Taylor stung. I knew I wasn't good enough for him, and my mother laid out all of my shortcomings. I wanted to deny her claims, but it all felt so true.

I sipped my beer and slumped my shoulders.

Oscar was tense, as if not knowing what to say, and my dad remained silent as usual, poking at the meat on the grill. I could practically see steam coming out of Taylor's ears as his knuckles whitened on his beer bottle. The noises of the party amplified around us as someone started blasting classic merengue hits from a speaker, but I didn't absorb any of it.

I sighed and walked away from the conversation. It wasn't worth the confrontation.

Of course, that took me right into the path of Daniela, my mother's eligible bachelorette. This was turning out to be worse than a telenovela.

"Seems like you need an escape," she whispered, touching my arm. "Do you want to dance?"

"I'm here with my boyfriend," I said.

"Nonsense, mijo. It's just a dance," my mother said, appearing behind me and snatching our beers out of our hands.

"I'm not interested," I said again, stepping back.

"Excuse me," a deep voice cut in from behind me. It was the voice I most wanted to hear, and it instantly calmed my heart. Taylor wrapped his arm around me possessively.

"He promised me the first dance," Taylor said, forcing calm into his voice and looking into my eyes. "Although I don't know the steps."

I knew he was way out of his comfort zone, but I couldn't be more grateful.

"I got you, baby," I said.

I was desperately nearing the end of my rope, but I couldn't help but smile at Taylor. He was trying so hard to shield me from my parents' nonsense.

"Now I look like a fool in front of the Lopezes," my mother hissed. "Why didn't you tell me you had a boyfriend?"

"You didn't ask." I threw my hands up in frustration. "You don't care about my life aside from how you can brag about it to your church friends, and I'm never doing anything impressive enough for you!"

My mom began ranting in Spanish about how I'd set her up to embarrass her, and I couldn't help but shrink back as I felt the attention of all the neighbors turn our way, curious to hear the gossip.

I could feel the exact moment Taylor snapped. He dropped his arm suddenly from my shoulders and grabbed my hand.

"Señora Rivera?" he said, interrupting my mom's tirade.

The shock on her face was priceless.

"Gabriel is one of the most incredible people I know. Maybe it's taken him longer to find his stride, but it's because he refuses to settle. Not many people have the courage to keep trying things until they discover what they truly love, but Gabriel does. If you took five minutes to try to learn more about your son, you'd see that."

My mother sputtered.

But Taylor wasn't finished. "You act like he's not serious about his life, but he throws his whole heart into everything he does. I feel honored to be with Gabriel. He could have chosen anyone, and I'm the lucky person here with him. Are you kidding me? He's smart and determined and caring. I don't know how you could be anything but proud of him."

You could have heard a pin drop in the yard. I'd never seen Taylor this upset; it was like there was a storm cloud in those blue eyes.

I'm pretty sure there were hearts in mine.

It finally hit me how right he was, and how much I was letting my mom's disappointments color the life that I loved.

"Taylor's right, Mamá." All the frustrations I'd kept such a tight lid on finally spilled over. "I'm thankful for how hard you worked to create the life we have here. All I've ever wanted is to make you and Papá proud, and I hope someday you see that. But the whole reason I didn't tell you about Taylor was that I knew it wouldn't be enough for you. I knew you'd be disappointed, like you have about every other decision I've made, even though I'm happier than I've ever been."

I turned to Taylor and took his hand. "This isn't a set-up. It's real. And we're leaving."

Taylor followed behind as I practically dragged him across the lawn. Once we'd rounded the corner and made it down the street to his car, the tears finally spilled down my cheeks. Taylor's arms were around me in an instant.

I released an embarrassingly loud sob into his neck. The whole afternoon: all of my mother's nagging, my dad's silence, all my insecurities dragged out in the street. I couldn't hold it in anymore.

Mostly, I was overwhelmed with the way Taylor had supported me and defended me and held me through it all. He said he was the lucky one, but we'd have to fight for the position. Maybe we were both lucky.

"I need you," I said, finally.

"I'm here." He used his thumbs to wipe the tears from my cheeks.

I kissed him, desperate for his lips on mine.

When I finally pulled back for a breath, I whispered against his lips, "Take me home."

17

GABRIEL

I didn't specify or particularly care which home Taylor was taking me to. Both our places had beds, which were the essential ingredient. The last twenty-four hours had been too much, between Taylor's sickness and this drama with my family. I was emotionally raw.

All I wanted was to escape into familiar territory—a fun, playful, naked territory.

When we pulled up in front of my place, my whole body went limp with relief. Taylor took my hand and followed me up to my door. As soon as we were inside and we'd both taken off our shoes, I jumped into his arms. He grunted in surprise as he caught me around my waist, and my legs wrapped around his hips. He turned and pressed me into the wall. My arms went around his neck and pulled his face to mine.

Thankfully, once Taylor got on the same page, he seemed to be all in.

I moaned as his tongue parted my lips and thrust against mine. This was exactly what I needed. Every nerve ending in my body was alive. Taylor was like fire against me, and I went willingly into the flames.

When Taylor started kissing down my neck, I tilted my head and caught sight of us in the rattan mirror near my entryway. My hair was definitely not street-worthy in its current state, but I was quickly distracted by how hot we were together. Taylor's ass looked so good in those jeans as he rutted up against me, and I moaned at the way the muscles in his back and arms bunched as he supported my weight.

"We're wearing too many clothes," Taylor finally said between panting breaths.

No need to tell me twice. I slid down his body and pushed him into my bedroom, going straight to my nightstand and throwing the lube and a condom onto the mattress before ripping off my shirt. Taylor arched his brow, and I laughed. He may have been smirking, but that adorable blush was giving him away.

He reached behind his head to pull his shirt off, too. "Tell me what you want, angel."

"I want you to fuck me," I said, my hands dropping to undo my pants.

His eyes darkened as I slowly pulled down my jeans and briefs together. My cock was already rock hard against my abs as I fell backward onto the bed. Hands behind my thighs, I lifted my legs and held them open, and I knew Taylor was getting a hell of a view. He was naked and on top of me almost immediately.

Up until this point, it had felt like something was holding Taylor back in our physical relationship. We'd made each other come countless times in the last few weeks, but it was always with our hands or mouths. Not that I was complaining. Taylor's mouth was perfection as he licked down my neck, flicked my nipple ring with his tongue, and covered my stomach with open-mouthed kisses.

But there seemed to be a line drawn in the sand, and I wasn't sure what it would take to pull us over it.

"Taylor," I gasped. I arched my back up off the bed when his mouth grazed against the tip of my cock, his tongue swirling around the head. "What are you waiting for?"

He chuckled, his breath teasing the inside of my thigh, and held a hand up. I practically threw the bottle of lube at him. The click of the lid and the slick sounds of him warming the lube in his hands had my muscles clenching and relaxing like a Pavlovian response. He sat back on his heels between my legs, and the look on his face as his eyes slid over my body made me hold my breath in anticipation.

"I can't believe you're real," he said in a hushed voice.

I wriggled on the bed, trying to get closer to him. "Touch me, baby. I promise I'm real."

His hair was already wild, and his freckles looked like stars under the blue skies of his eyes.

"You took such good care of me." He bent over to kiss my chest. "Now I'm going to take care of you."

I squeezed my eyes shut against the flood of emotions he whipped up inside of me. Sex had never been like this before.

Finally, he grabbed the base of my erection with his slick hand and stroked, drawing a moan from me. Then I felt two fingers making gentle circles around my hole. I turned to liquid under his touch, and there was no way I was holding back the gasp of relief when he pressed inside me at last.

"You don't need to be precious with me, Tay." I chuckled, trying to lighten the mood. "I fuck with dildos bigger than you."

I attempted to push myself onto his fingers harder and faster, but he arched an eyebrow and held my hips down. This sweet, romantic shit was a lot, and I felt exposed. A part of me wanted to roll over so he could rail me hard from behind, and I didn't have to look into his eyes.

"I don't care." Taylor pressed his fingers against my prostate. The corners of his mouth tilted up. "I'm going to be precious if I want to. At least this first time."

I was a pile of moans, grunts, and pleas for more as he worked in a third finger. His eyes were glued to my face, reading my expressions and reactions until his hands left me. I was close to sobbing in frustration until I heard the tear of the condom packet.

I pushed myself up on my elbows so I could watch him roll the rubber down his cock. He braced himself on one arm by my head as he lined himself up. I felt the pressure and warmth of him against my hole, and I relaxed with a deep exhale. I wanted this more than I'd wanted anything before. His eyes searched mine, looking for who knows what.

He must have found it because the next moment, he pressed into me. I inhaled sharply as the head of his cock breached the ring of muscle.

Taylor's jaw tightened. "God, Gabriel, how do you feel so good?"

It was impossible to breathe until he was fully inside me, his hips flush with my ass. He leaned over me, panting, and I soaked up how good it felt to have a man's weight on top of me.

Not just any man, though—it was Taylor. Inside me and over me and everywhere that mattered. I wrapped my arms around his waist and lifted my head to kiss him. It was a sloppy, perfect kiss.

"I need you to move," I said as I writhed underneath him. "I'm going to lose my mind if you don't."

Taylor nodded and shifted up onto his elbows to pull his hips back. He adjusted his angle slightly, thrusting back in, and I lost my goddamn mind anyway.

I loved the side of Taylor I got to see during sex. When I first met him, it was like I was seeing this veneer—not a mask exactly, more like the full picture of him through a fog. He was quiet, blushing, and shy. Here, in the private moments no one else got to see, Taylor was a man unleashed.

He was always the one giving to others, but in bed together, he took what he needed. I'd let him take anything he wanted.

"Gabriel, fuck." Taylor grunted as I dragged my nails along his back.

His thrusts started slow and steady, but soon, he pushed my legs back toward my chest with his arms behind my knees, and he was taking me hard. I soaked in the way the cords of his neck strained, the way his eyes alternated between squeezing shut in pleasure and searching mine like they held the answers to the universe.

It was too much.

"Stop, stop," I breathed, and Taylor pulled back, his eyes filled with concern.

"Did I hurt you?" he asked.

"No, I just wanted to get more comfortable." I gave him a cheeky grin before flipping to my hands and knees.

"You're not going to hear me complain." Taylor swatted my ass, spreading my cheeks with his hands and sliding back inside me.

This was better. This was safe. Pressure built at the base of my spine, spreading like a wave from my prostate, and I reached down to jerk myself off. Taylor filled all my senses as my orgasm overwhelmed me: the feel of his weight, the smell of his vanilla body wash, the taste of his sweat, and the sound of his groans as he sped up his thrusts.

Before I could recover, he'd flipped me onto my back again, shoving back inside me as he came.

His face reminded me of a time-lapse video I'd watched recently of a flower blooming. There's all this anticipation, the plant twisting in the sun with its green leaves and little buds.

The petals burst open, and all at once, it's more stunning than you could have imagined. Even in slow motion, it happens quickly. Coming underneath Taylor was like a whole field of wildflowers blooming at once.

A superbloom.

It was hard to believe I'd found anything beautiful before seeing this.

I grunted when Taylor collapsed onto my chest, and I felt our hearts racing in sync. He nuzzled his face into my neck.

"Let me go get a washcloth," he said. "I'll be right back, I promise."

He pressed himself up and brushed a few of my curls back from where they'd stuck to my forehead. My eyelids were heavy. I could hear Taylor shuffling around my apartment and the sink running in the bathroom before I felt his weight back on the bed. I cracked one eye as he wiped me down softly.

"Hi," he said with a gentle smile.

"Hi," I said back.

The post-orgasm haze wrapped around us like a cloak as I opened my arms and pulled him to my chest. He tucked his head onto my shoulder and threw a leg over my thighs. His hand mindlessly toyed with my nipple ring as our heartbeats slowed. Nothing could be better than this. I kissed the top of his head, and as his breathing turned to soft snores.

My phone vibrated from the nightstand. Taylor must have plugged it in while he was up getting the towel. I ignored it at first, not wanting to ruin the bubble Taylor and I had made for ourselves. After a few more texts came through in quick succession, I changed my mind.

I was surprised to find the messages were from Oscar.

> **OSCAR**
>
> Dude, your mom was flipping out after you left. What an exit.
>
> I like Taylor. Keep him around.
>
> Seeing the way he stood up for you made me realize I should have had your back more when your parents laid into you, especially when it was about me.
>
> I'm sorry, man.

While I was mostly terrified to hear about what had gone down with my parents after we bailed, it meant a lot to hear from my cousin. I knew he didn't buy into all the competitive shit my parents were always saying. He was my best friend, but it still stung when he kept silent.

> **GABRIEL**
>
> You were a kid, too.
>
> **OSCAR**
>
> But we haven't been kids for a long time. I've had lots of chances. I'll do better.
>
> I'm sure Mamá will be giving me the silent treatment in protest, so I don't think I'll have to hear anything about it for a while anyway.
>
> Oh, she was pissed. But your dad was not having it. He actually dragged her into the house so she would stop making a scene in front of all the neighbors. I've never seen him lose his cool like that.

Huh. That was surprising, but it didn't undo a lifetime of his going along with her drama. I wasn't holding my breath for a big declaration or apology from either of my parents. The reality was that eventually, I'd be back over there helping them like I always did, because I loved them.

Taylor shifted slightly, and I remembered that what had changed was that I had this incredible man by my side. Maybe I'd refuse to go home without him.

Yup, that was the perfect solution. Keep Taylor forever and drag him to all my family obligations like a bodyguard. *Ha.* There was no way he'd sign on for that, right?

I silenced my phone and slid it back onto the charger. Waves of emotions, both bad and good, had been frothing inside of me, and they crashed into the back of my eyelids as I drifted into sleep, protected and safe under Taylor's reassuring weight.

I could deal with all the rest of it tomorrow.

18

TAYLOR

The sun warmed my face, but it felt far too early to be awake. I turned over to discover I was in bed alone, and my heart panged. It was a strange sensation, and I rolled the feeling around in my chest, analyzing it. Usually, I'd be relieved to wake up alone after sex. This was different. This had been so far from my usual transactional exchange in every way. It wasn't the first time I'd stayed over at his place, but the emotions swirling in my stomach were new.

The apartment was quiet, and while I knew Gabriel couldn't have gone far, anxiety built in my chest. It did not feel like the right time to have a panic attack, but between Gabriel coming to my rescue when I was sick, my shocking outburst at his parents, and the mind-blowing sex, this existential crisis was coming whether I wanted it to or not.

The convenient thing about the gay community was that there were plenty of opportunities to get your physical needs met while avoiding emotional entanglement. However, the more entangled I got with Gabriel, the more I had to accept that I hadn't been getting my needs met by those nameless hookups.

I was lonelier than I realized.

It took a lot for me to open up to people, but Gabriel had worked his way under my skin almost immediately. And that was scary. That meant I could love him, and if I could love him, he could break me and ruin everything.

I'd seen it happen, and I did not want to ride that ride.

I threw the covers off my sweat-soaked body and stood up to rummage through Gabriel's dresser for some clean underwear. After slipping on a pair of navy boxer briefs, I made my way into the bathroom to splash my face off and brush my teeth with the spare toothbrush Gabriel had tossed me the first night I stayed over. Seeing it still tucked away on his bathroom counter gave me heartburn.

Ok. Emotional entanglements were a solvable problem. All I had to do was avoid the prolonged eye contact and romantic daydreams, and I'd be fine. Hadn't Gabriel been the one to say I needed to stay in the moment and have more fun? Just fun, no feelings. That would be my new affirmation. That was all this was. Exclusive, casual fun. Super hot sex with a super hot man who I could take as a date to my sister's wedding.

A super hot man with a dimpled smile and a nose ring and curls peeking out from his Dodgers hat, who appeared in the doorway with a to-go coffee cup and a raspberry scone.

Damn it, this was going to be more challenging than I thought.

"Morning!" Gabriel leaned forward and pecked my cheek before handing me the coffee and blatantly checking me out. "You look hot as shit in my underwear."

I laughed, wiggling my hips as I gratefully accepted the coffee.

"Sorry for leaving you to wake up alone, but the coffee shop around the corner has the best scones, and they always disappear fast on Sunday mornings. I didn't want to risk it."

I smiled to cover the flurry of emotions still swirling in my stomach and pushed around him to grab my clothes.

Once I was dressed, Gabriel dragged me out into his living room and onto the sofa. He picked up his iced latte, arranged his legs over my lap, and leaned back against the arm of the couch. "If you were a sea creature, what kind of sea creature would you be?"

By this point, I was unsurprised by random thoughts spilling from Gabriel's brain. I was sure there were three raccoons in a trench coat up there—and I meant that as a compliment. My mind, in comparison, was like a collaboration between the sloth who worked at the DMV in Zootopia and the annoying HR lady from Monsters, Inc.

I clearly needed more coffee.

"An octopus, I guess."

"I could see that." Gabriel swirled the ice in his coffee and flashed a teasing smile. "You're smart, and your powers of suction are renowned among the animal kingdom."

I gaped at him.

"I think I'd be a dolphin," he said. "They seem like they are always down to party."

"You are unlike anyone I've ever met," I said honestly.

Those dimples popped beneath his scruff as he smiled at me and shrugged.

My insides were in turmoil as I repeated my new affirmation: *just fun, no feelings, just fun, no feelings*.

I couldn't help kissing him, though. He tasted like coffee and sugar.

Gabriel seemed lighter today than he had in weeks, and I realized how much this issue with his parents had been weighing on him. But we didn't talk about his family. We didn't talk about the sex. It was a morning of light banter and catching up on our weeks, accompanied by a side of snuggles.

That felt like a different kind of intimacy, and soon, the walls started to close in around me.

"I—" I cleared my throat and looked down at my phone. "Margo needs me."

"Right now?" Gabriel leaned up to look at the screen. "Is everything ok?"

I locked my phone and moved his legs off my lap to slip it into my pocket. "Just wedding things, but she says it can't wait."

I pop the last bite of scone into my mouth.

"Do you want me to come wi—"

"No!" I answered too quickly, and my cheeks flushed. "Sorry, it's just... she needs me."

The smile remained on Gabriel's face, but a bit of the sparkle left his eyes. "Ok. Text me?"

"I will. Promise." I hoped it was a promise I could keep.

Just fun, no feelings.

Yeah, right.

KAI POPPED his head into my bedroom after work to find me pacing back and forth, the doctor's email pulled up on my phone. I was too nervous to open it.

"Girl, what's with all the pacing? You are supposed to be relaxing. Margo is going to kill you if you're a walking corpse at her wedding."

I huffed, tossing my phone to him. "I might be a walking corpse either way."

"Oh shit," Kai said, spotting the email immediately. "Do you want me to open it?"

"Yeah, I'm not going to otherwise." I leaned my face into the wall, unable to make eye contact as he read the results.

"Good news first. No cancer."

Muscles I didn't even know I was clenching relaxed, and I slid down the wall to sit on the floor. Kai squatted down beside me.

"Bad news, there's something wrong with your heart. Myocarditis is what it says. They want you to come in for a follow-up EKG." He dropped the phone into my lap. "Want me to come to the appointment? I bet Margo would go with you, too, although I'm guessing you don't want to stress her out with more doctors. Or how about Gabriel?"

"I'm a grown man. I don't need a babysitter to take me to the doctor."

"It's not about need. We want to, Taylor. That's what it looks like when you care about someone." Kai reached out and tugged on my earlobe.

I deflated with a sigh. "No need to weigh down something that's supposed to be fun with my baggage. What Gabriel and I are doing isn't that serious."

I was lying through my teeth.

Kai narrowed his eyes. "Isn't it?"

"Since when did you become a romantic? I thought you were out in these streets being a ho."

I needed to deflect from my discomfort.

"Oh, I'm enjoying the ho life, but that's not because I don't believe in love. It's because I'm in love with someone I can't have."

My eyes widened. This was the first I'd heard of that.

"Anyway, we're not here to talk about me. I know your parents did a number on you, but they're assholes who blamed their kids for not being able to make a relationship work." Kai carried on like he hadn't blown my mind. "You're nothing like them."

I banged my head lightly against the wall until Kai slipped his hand back there. I wanted to strangle him, but I knew he meant well, even if he didn't know shit about how spectacularly I could implode a relationship.

"Please take care of yourself," Kai said with a cheeky grin. "If you die, I can't afford the rent on my own."

Never underestimate your best friend's ability to guilt you into things.

I pushed to my feet. "Fine, consider this intervention successful. I won't go to the doctor's unsupervised."

I WENT to the doctor's office unsupervised.

Once Kai had confirmed I didn't have cancer—which I'd been sure about from the beginning, mostly—I figured the doctor's visit would be routine. Doubts crept in when I sat on the exam table, the paper crinkling under my legs as I waited for them to tell me the results of the echocardiogram.

"You're in the clear," the doctor said as she peered at her clipboard.

"The clear?" I echoed. "What does that mean?"

"Everything came back normal on your EKG." She slid me a stack of papers. "This was likely a stress-related incident. These pamphlets have information for you about stress management and sleep hygiene."

I should have been thrilled. I'd be able to start work again, and my goals had only been delayed by a few weeks. Instead of relief, I felt dread.

My ears rang in the silence of the exam room once I was alone, the papers the doctor gave me hanging loosely in my hands.

I wished she'd been able to give me a diagnosis, a clear reason my heart had freaked out on me, and how to avoid it happening again. All I got was the ominous warning that once I had myocarditis, I was susceptible to it again. I'd have to keep an eye out for heart palpitations, shortness of breath, and chest pain for the rest of my life—an open-ended threat with no real answers.

How, exactly, was I supposed to avoid stress?

My three deep breaths weren't doing enough to calm the sensations in my chest.

As I exited the lobby, blinking into the bright sun, I could have sworn I was hallucinating. There was Gabriel, sitting on a bench right outside the front door, his eyes closed, and his face tilted up toward the sky.

"You keep showing up at places I don't give you the address of," I said. "Are you my boyfriend or a stalker?"

Gabriel opened one eye to squint at me. "Why not both?"

"Not that I'm complaining,"—I joined him on the bench and bumped his shoulder with mine—"but what are you doing here?"

"I thought you might need me." Gabriel shrugged and smiled softly.

"I won't admit to anything." I dragged him up onto my lap and wrapped my arms around his waist.

The truth was, I did need him here. That was almost as scary as this open-ended diagnosis.

"But I am happy to see you," I said, my heart pounding.

Gabriel placed his hand there, and I swore it started beating faster.

"So, what did the doctor say?" he asked.

I sighed. "Basically, everything looks normal now, but it could happen again, but she can't tell me why it happened in the first place, and I'm supposed to avoid stress."

Gabriel frowned, rubbing calming circles over my chest. "That's not very helpful."

As much as I loathed to admit it, the more I shared with

Gabriel, the better I felt. The way his comforting presence loosened the ball of anxiety in my stomach was like a drug, but did I really want to become addicted? I couldn't answer that, but I couldn't make myself stop.

"I know what will make you feel better," Gabriel said definitively. "Tacos."

"I was hoping you were going to say a blow job," I teased, pasting on a smile.

My stomach grumbled, and Gabriel burst out laughing.

He playfully slapped my chest. "I'm open to suggestions on dessert later."

19

GABRIEL

On Tuesday morning, as I was walking into work, Taylor texted to ask what my favorite part of the botanical gardens was. That was a hard question to answer; each exhibit had its own charm, and I felt like I was choosing between my children. But I always came back to this one grassy hill near the butterfly garden. I loved to lie there on my breaks, staring up at the clouds.

One day, I wanted to bring him here for a picnic. I knew it was strange to want to spend my time off at my job, but I'd loved coming to the gardens long before I started working here. Every time I scanned my employee ID to walk through the back office, I had to pinch myself.

Today, I was working in one of the small greenhouses where we cultivated annuals in preparation for summer installations I knew would become the backdrop for so many people's special moments.

Proposals, weddings, graduation photos, and families with their kids.

It was the best thing I could have dreamed of when I was getting my degree.

I was lost in my task when my phone buzzed. My heart leaped into my throat when I saw that Taylor texted a photo: a view of his feet in the brown oxfords he liked to wear, laid out on a blanket in the grass.

On a hill, with a view of the butterfly garden.

Taylor was here.

Glancing up at the clock, I saw that my break was supposed to start in ten minutes. I stuck my head into my boss's office to let her know I was taking an early lunch and practically ran out into the gardens.

I saw Taylor before he saw me. He wore light grey dress pants and a green checkered shirt. His jacket was folded on the blanket behind him, and there was a paper bag containing what I guessed was takeout.

The bigger surprise, though, was that there was a woman with him. She had bright purple hair, piercings up the shell of her ear, a silk dress, a knit sweater, and combat boots. They couldn't have had more different aesthetics. This had to be his sister, Margo.

My pulse quickened, and for a moment, I considered texting Taylor with an excuse. Then his eyes met mine, a smile split his face, and his hair glowed in the sun. Damn, he was stunning.

Taylor gave me a small wave, and the woman beside him turned to follow his gaze. At least I'd washed the dirt from under my fingernails—no time to panic now.

"You know, I was just thinking this morning how much I wanted to bring you here for a picnic. Now you've gone and done all the work for me," I teased Taylor as I plopped down on the blanket next to him, on the opposite side of his sister. "Hi, I'm Gabriel."

"Margo. It's so wonderful to meet you." Her smile was bright and genuine. She kept looking between Taylor and me with barely contained enthusiasm.

"We got Thai food," Taylor said, giving me a quick kiss. "I hope that's ok. I have a few different options, and you can pick whatever you like."

"Sounds great to me," I said. "My lunch is only thirty minutes, but I can stretch it to forty-five if I skip my afternoon break. Sorry you drove all this way for such a quick visit."

Taylor pulled out an assortment of containers: pork dumplings, chicken satay, spicy drunken noodles, and green curry with rice. "I'm just happy to see you. I probably should have checked with your schedule before surprising you at your job."

"It was my idea," Margo cut in. "It's been eons since my brother had a boyfriend, and I was not about to let him hide you away."

"I'm not hiding him anywhere." Taylor looked at his sister with such affection, even though I could tell he was frustrated with her antics.

We were going to get along splendidly.

"Whatever you say. Anyway, I had to meet you as soon as possible so I could personally invite you to be Taylor's plus one at my wedding."

I almost dropped the dumpling I had lifted halfway to my mouth, and Taylor choked on air.

"Margo!" Taylor groaned as I chuckled. "I just convinced him to date me like ten minutes ago. Please don't scare him off already."

"You told me you were going to invite him," Margo said. "I'm cutting out the middle man. I can't wait to have you at the wedding. It's going to be such fun!"

I tangled one of my legs with his and bumped his elbow to draw his attention. "I'd love to be your date."

Taylor got that blush I liked so much across his freckled cheeks. I'd made a big deal about the boyfriend thing at first, but even if he wanted to keep pretending this was casual, I was all in. He was not about to scare me away with a little wedding date.

Oh, who was I kidding? I was terrified of being his wedding date.

Weddings were significant events. Serious events. Even though Margo seemed like a blast, and I knew we'd enjoy getting to know each other, what if it didn't work out? All Taylor's memories of his sister's wedding would be tainted forever.

We'd only been doing this exclusive thing for a few weeks, and I was way out of my depth. I focused on scooping the spicy noodles onto a small paper plate to gather my thoughts and hoped my face didn't betray my nerves. I promised myself I'd be the best boyfriend he'd ever had, and I was not going to let either of us down.

"I feel underdressed for this date," I said, eyeing Taylor's tie.

Taylor shrugged sheepishly. "It's weird to be back in the office every day."

"You have life in your eyes again," Margo said, smiling. "And I bet it has nothing at all to do with this handsome guy and all the fun he's forcing on you."

"I do what I can," I replied.

Margo and I chatted as Taylor quietly ate his noodles, his eyes flitting back and forth. Turns out we were both extroverted bisexuals with an allergy to boredom, and I was relieved to discover we had so much in common.

Taylor didn't seem like the kind of person who let many into his inner circle. I'd always believed that if an introvert adopted you, it was one of life's great honors. Like being chosen by a cat. Everyone knew you canceled all your other plans if a cat sat on your lap. Taylor hadn't sat on my lap yet, exactly, but the heat in his eyes as he watched me lick satay sauce from my lips told me he wanted to. And you better believe I wanted it, too.

Lunch passed far too quickly, and soon, Margo was kissing my cheek goodbye like we'd been getting brunch together for years. She rushed off in a flurry. I'm not sure if that was her general pace in life or if she was trying to make sure Tay and I got a moment alone. I could feel Taylor's reluctance to leave, and I didn't want to release my arms from around his waist.

I tucked my mouth by his ear and whispered, "I wish I had a few more minutes so I could take you somewhere and suck you off real quick."

Taylor swatted at my arm. "You can't say stuff like that when you can't follow through." I could feel him starting to get hard against my leg, and I chuckled.

"This was a wonderful surprise, baby." I reached up to brush his hair behind his ear. "Thanks for introducing me to Margo. I know how important she is to you."

"She cannot be stopped once she has an idea in her head." Taylor rushed to clarify. "Not that I didn't want you to meet her."

I kissed him softly. "I didn't think that, Tay."

"You know, you're the only person who calls me Tay. I normally hate it, but for some reason, it works when it's you."

"Boyfriend privileges." I teased my fingers along the length of him through his pants, and he groaned. I gripped his cock and pressed my body in close; I couldn't resist teasing him a little more.

"I'll call you when I get home tonight and apologize for getting you all riled up in the middle of a work day." I released him and stepped back.

"You are a menace," Taylor said as he moved the jacket he had draped over his arm to cover his erection.

"A very cute one." I winked.

Taylor leaned in to kiss me briefly once more before he turned to make his way out of the gardens. "I'll be looking forward to tonight."

En route to my desk, I swung by the bathroom to continue the torment. I stepped into a stall and unbuckled my work pants, pulling them down my thighs, just under my ass. After stroking myself a few times through my underwear, I snapped a photo and sent it to Taylor's phone.

Miss you already, I said. A string of swearing emojis followed, then the fire emoji. I sent him back a little purple heart.

Every so often, when I could step away from my task, I'd send Taylor another teasing, flirty, or downright racy text. He was getting progressively more growly in response, and I knew it would all be worth it by the time we were able to chat.

Taylor might have been back at work, but this was in no way a ploy to ensure he kept a little work-life balance and clocked out at a reasonable hour. I was not at all doing this for my boyfriend's mental health; I was doing it for my own purely selfish, physical motivations.

Wink, wink.

As soon as I got home, all bets were off. I no longer had to worry about getting myself too horny to be presentable at work.

GABRIEL

> Want to know what I'm thinking about?

TAYLOR

> No. You've been torturing me all afternoon, and I still have an hour of work left. I feel like I've been hard for three years.

> Mmm. Well, I'm home now. I need you to send me a photo so I can look at it while I finger myself.

> Goddammit, Gabriel.

> *Angel emoji* Of course, you're always welcome to watch.

There was a longer pause in our texting, and I resumed cooking my dinner. I wasn't in any hurry. I still had to eat and shower before I was ready to get naked in my bed. My dinner was a simple frozen gnocchi to which I'd added homemade pesto and roast chicken. I didn't have much energy for cooking on work nights, so I relied heavily on frozen and prepared foods, but I tried to make them my own by adding herbs or veggies I'd grown in my little apartment garden.

With past hookups, I would get itchy if someone wanted to see me more than once a week. I had more than one former sexual partner, both men and women, call me unavailable. I hadn't seen it as such at the time, especially since I was always upfront with people about keeping things low-key. I liked my life to be busy with lots of friends, social events, and activities.

Now that I felt this connection with Taylor, I knew what they meant. I'd always been holding a part of myself back. Since we'd crossed this threshold together, I found myself wanting to make space for him. I was greedy for Taylor's time and attention, and it was a wild, new sensation.

I didn't bother getting dressed after my shower, sprawling out on the bed underneath the fairy lights. I had them hung all over the apartment; the harsh overhead lights stressed me out. When you had the option for fairy lights, why choose anything else?

When my phone finally rang, I scrambled to the nightstand to reach it. I answered the video call breathlessly when I saw Taylor's name on the screen. "Hi."

"Gabriel." Taylor's eyes roamed over the screen, taking in my damp hair and lack of clothing. "You've been driving me crazy."

I stroked myself just beyond the camera, but I could tell by the way his pupils dilated that he could guess what I was doing. "I told you I'd apologize, didn't I? I know we're not together, but I want to make you feel good. To thank you for bringing me such a sweet picnic. I'd never leave you hanging."

Taylor visibly shuddered while he tracked the slow, steady movement of my bicep. It was finally time to make good on the torture I'd been inflicting.

"Can you take your clothes off, baby?" I asked. "Set the phone somewhere I can see you. I've been thinking about you all day."

20

TAYLOR

I followed Gabriel's instructions as if I were in a trance. Setting my phone on my nightstand, I undressed slowly, wanting to enact retribution for the way the man had kept me on edge all afternoon. It was like he had a sixth sense for when I was about to lose my erection, and he'd text me at that exact moment, getting me all worked up again.

"I want to see you too." I gasped as I pulled off my pants and boxer briefs, finally freeing my cock.

Gabriel whined softly as my cock slapped up against my stomach. Then the camera was pointed at the ceiling as he rearranged. He must have moved a chair to the foot of his bed, because when he set his phone down, I had a full view of him against his bed frame. Legs spread, his hand holding his thick, hard cock.

"You're so hot," I said.

"Get comfortable, baby. I want you to touch yourself for me."

Holy shit, this man. I sat at the end of my bed, leaning back onto one arm, and stroking myself with the other. I licked my lips as he grabbed lube from his bedside table and poured it onto his fingers. Slicking his dick first, he bent one knee and reached his lubed hand underneath to play with his hole.

We moaned together as he slipped his first finger in. After a few minutes of panting breaths and small grunts on both ends of the phone, he added a second finger. He had the sexiest ass I'd ever seen, and just watching him finger himself had me on the edge. I squeezed tightly around the base of my cock, holding myself back, then tugged on my balls.

Gabriel gasped, and his abs tensed.

I cursed the fact that I was across town and not in his bed. "Fuck. I need to be inside you."

"Soon, baby." Gabriel panted. "I can't wait to feel your big dick in me again. It's going to feel so good stretching my hole."

"Oh, shit." My hand moved faster and faster along my length, squeezing the tip just the way I liked.

Gabriel was a vision as he writhed on the bed, fucking himself on one hand while the other shuttled over his cock. I threw my head back as an orgasm rushed through me, the cum filling my hand and shooting up my stomach. I collapsed back onto my elbows but pried my eyes open so I wouldn't miss Gabriel's orgasm.

"Fuck," he cried. "Taylor."

I'd never get tired of the sound of my name on his lips as he came. He looked hot as sin sprawled out on the bed, hole stretched, dick softening, covered in cum.

I loved that he wanted to connect with me even when we couldn't be together physically, and I'd be finding ways to bring him picnics all the time if this was how worked up he got about it. I wanted to feel him under me again. I wanted to be the one with my fingers inside him.

For the first time, I found something more important than work. It wasn't the sex; I'd never found sex that motivating. It was the connection we shared. I tried to catch my breath, and we stared into each other's eyes with the same look of awe.

"Wow," I said, finally finding my voice.

"Seriously." Gabriel nodded. "That was incredible."

"I wish I could hold you right now."

Gabriel sighed and collapsed back onto the bed. I grabbed my phone and headed for the bathroom, keeping it on video while I wiped myself with a washcloth and brushed my teeth. I could still see Gabriel sprawled out on his sheets, and despite enjoying the view, I knew he was probably getting crusty.

"You need to get up and clean off before bed."

He whined about it but eventually rolled to his side to grab tissues from his nightstand. "Always taking care of everyone."

Only people I loved, I thought, but did not vocalize. I hummed and watched as he yawned, stretching under the cozy quilt I wanted to pull back and crawl under, too. I wanted to tuck him under my arm and pull him against my chest.

It was strange, that desire.

"Stay on the phone until I fall asleep?" Gabriel asked with half-lidded eyes.

"Of course, angel." I crawled under my blankets in my tragically empty bed, plugged my phone in, and propped it by my pillow. It wasn't long before Gabriel's soft snores came through the phone. He was the last thought in my mind as I drifted off to sleep.

BY THE WEDNESDAY of my first week back in the office, I'd wound myself tighter than a tornado between trying to compensate for the unexpected time off, responding to fifty wedding-related texts a day from Margo, and avoiding my feelings for Gabriel.

I'd spilled coffee no less than three times, I'd accidentally sent my lunch delivery order to the apartment instead of the office, and I'd run out of pages in my yellow-lined notepad.

When I texted Gabriel about my day from hell, I got a notification that he'd sent a food delivery my way with enough chicken shawarma to share with Kai.

I peered at the little tuxedo cat plushie Gabriel bought me that now lived on the corner of my desk.

How would Gabriel feel once he knew how close everything felt to falling apart, how close I was to the edge? Would he still want me when I couldn't afford fun dates or vacations or gifts because all the spare change went to Margo's debt? Would he stay when he found out how truly crazy my parents are?

A knock shook me from my thoughts.

Rachel peeked through the door. "Is now a good time?"

"Of course," I said, popping up to grab the stacks of receipts I still had stacked on the spare chair.

"I just wanted to check in and see how you were transitioning back to work." Rachel pulled up the chair and sat down.

"I'm fine." I shrugged. "The doctor gave me the all clear."

Rachel stared at me, one eyebrow arched. "That's not what I asked, but I'm glad to hear it."

I squared my shoulders. "As much as I appreciate your concern, I've got things handled."

"You're one of our best accountants," Rachel said. "You should be proud of your work. That's why I want to make sure you're managing your stress. We want to keep you around."

"Thank you," I murmured, my eyes cutting over to the plushie again. "I've got people taking good care of me, and I'm handing a few clients off to junior accountants."

Rachel paused for a moment, as if she might say something else, but in the end, she simply nodded. "Good."

I was thankful she didn't push me about therapy I couldn't afford or cutting my hours again, which I *also* couldn't afford.

Hopefully, when things calmed down with work, the wedding, and all these damn medical bills, I would be able to do something about it.

"Can I join this man's waitlist?" Kai joked as I handed him his sandwich.

"No waitlist. Currently sold out and not expected to be back in stock," I said, collapsing into the seat across from him in our small break room.

"So, it's serious now?" Kai raised his brows.

I didn't know how to answer Kai's question, so I took a huge bite of shawarma to buy myself time. He cackled, probably knowing exactly what I was up to.

"I don't know, man," I said. "He's incredible, of course, but…"

"But your parents messed you up, and now you think you don't deserve someone incredible."

I stared at my sandwich with a furrow between my brows.

"Look, I know you. Probably better than anyone else. And I know you'd do anything for someone you love. You are a catch. But the only kind of love you've let yourself have is platonic because you're convinced romantic love is going to turn you into your asshole parents. But it's not."

"You can't possibly know that," I grumbled into my lunch.

"Oh, I *can* possibly know that. Your parents have the combined emotional intelligence of a fence post. Meanwhile, I've watched you break things off with totally undeserving men in a kind, respectful manner."

"I didn't love any of those men."

"And you love Gabriel?"

My eyes darted around the break room, ensuring we were

still alone. "No? I *could* love him, I think. But it's too soon for all that."

Kai shrugged. "Emotions run on their own timelines. All I'm saying is: this man takes care of you, he sees you, and he wants to be with you. He buys shawarma for your best friend."

"Ah, see"—I pointed at him—"he's just buying your good graces with food."

Kai rolled his eyes and ignored my accusation. "You don't have to have it all figured out, but don't push him away because you think you'll become Mr. Hyde as soon as you have your first big fight. Be warned, if you let him go, I'm stealing him."

"I hate you."

"Love you, too." Kai stood and gathered the sandwich wrappers to take to the trash.

I threw my crumpled napkin at the back of his head, and he laughed it off as he headed back to work.

The deeper my feelings got with Gabriel, the larger the specter of the proverbial other shoe loomed in my mind, waiting to drop.

21

GABRIEL

> GABRIEL
> What color tie do I need to buy to match your outfit for the wedding?

> TAYLOR
> Burgundy

Really? A one-word answer?

Something was bothering Taylor, and I couldn't figure out what it was. Ever since he'd topped me, it felt like he was putting distance between us. I was trying not to let that hurt because... that night had the opposite effect on me. I'd never felt a connection like that before.

All I wanted was to see him, talk to him, touch him. As much as possible.

We talked every night before bed, just like we had before, but he seemed more eager to get off the phone. He made excuses when my friends went dancing earlier that week, even though Kai came out. It took him hours, not minutes, to text back. All of this was subtle and not entirely out of character, but I felt like I was losing my mind. When he told me about the inconclusive test results from the doctor, it made more sense, but something still lingered in the back of my mind.

How ironic that I, the guy who was convinced he didn't want to be tied down, was now complaining about my boyfriend not spending enough time with me. Thankfully, though, the wedding was only a week away, which meant one more thing would be off his plate.

I could wait it out, no problem.

GABRIEL

> Can I come to your suit fitting so I can see the exact color? We can pick one out together.

TAYLOR

> Sure

Taylor could have easily sent me a photo, but when he accepted my thin logic to spend some time together without a fight, I wasn't going to mention it. I also brought us smoothies for breakfast. I felt a bit like one of those penguins who kept bringing rocks to their partner for their nest.

Except these rocks were tasty snacks.

For as much as Taylor cared for others, he didn't do a great job of taking care of himself. I was happy to fill that gap, and I was pretty sure he secretly liked it.

When I pulled up to the suit shop, Taylor was waiting out front. The way he smiled when he spotted me and pulled me into a full-body hug went a long way toward easing that nervous feeling in my gut. I kissed him and couldn't help but go back in for more a couple of times.

"C'mon, I'm going to be late for my fitting." Taylor wriggled in my arms, but he was smiling.

I handed over his raspberry citrus crush and sipped on my rainbow sherbet smash with an innocent look on my face. I knew he could see the mischief in my eyes. Taylor touched his hand to my lower back as he ushered me into the small storefront. Everything felt normal, wonderful even.

I'd been overthinking, right?

"Good morning, gentlemen." A slim, younger man with pretty eyes greeted us. As he walked around the counter, he looked Taylor up and down. "How can I help you?"

"I'm Taylor. I have a final fitting for my suit today."

I wasn't the territorial type, but I scooted closer to Taylor and wrapped my arm possessively around his waist.

He looked down at me with raised eyebrows. "And this is my date, Gabriel. He's looking for a tie that will match. It's for my sister's wedding."

"Awesome, I can help you with that." Now, it was my turn to be checked out by the flirty salesman. "I'm Elie. I'll be right back."

He turned and disappeared into the back of the store.

Taylor let out a small bark of laughter as I pulled him into my arms and squeezed.

"Trying to mark your territory, angel?"

"Always." I grinned. "Would you rather I pee on your leg?"

Now, he was laughing in earnest, and I took the opportunity to stick my tongue down his throat.

"Damn, you two are hot together." Elie reappeared with a dark burgundy suit draped over his arm. "I'll hang this in the fitting room right here."

Taylor blushed, and I preened a little bit. I couldn't help it. Smiling widely, I took his smoothie from him so he could get changed.

I was sitting on a small leather settee when Taylor walked out in a perfectly fitted suit. The jacket highlighted the slope of his shoulders and his broad chest, the pants hugged his ass, and his bulge looked positively sinful. The color brought out the reddish undertones of his hair. My mouth watered as he stretched his arms out and spun slowly for my perusal.

"How are you the sexiest person I've ever seen?" I asked rhetorically.

"I'm glad you like it." Taylor smiled shyly.

"I more than like it," I assured him, trying to subtly adjust myself by shuffling around on the settee. "Margo better bring her A-game if she doesn't want you stealing the show."

"I have to agree." Elie checked over various seams. "The fit is outstanding."

I narrowed my eyes at him.

He giggled and winked at me. "Babe, I have a man. I'm not trying to steal yours."

I grunted and crossed my arms over my chest, making Taylor chuckle.

Once Taylor had changed back out of the suit, we picked out my tie. It had a subtle shimmery floral pattern in the same burgundy color as Taylor's suit.

I hung off of Taylor as we checked out, and Elie bagged the tie. He flirted equally with both of us; it must have been his personality, since he said he had a partner.

"Let's get out of here, caveman," Taylor said as we walked out the door. I could hear Elie cackling from behind the counter.

"Ugh, I'm sorry," I whined as I turned to him on the sidewalk out front, returning his smoothie that I'd been babysitting. "Blame it on my complete lack of experience in a relationship. I don't know how to act."

I would also blame the weird mood I'd been simmering in all week, but I'd already decided not to bring that up. Taylor took a long sip of his smoothie, tilting his head thoughtfully.

"You've been perfect," Taylor whispered. I might not have even heard him if I hadn't been looking at his face to see his mouth move.

"Do you have to get going right away? Let's drive down to the beach." I wasn't ready to let him go. "As your official instigator of shenanigans, I think it would be good for you."

I threw in some puppy eyes and fluttered my lashes for good measure.

I could see the moment Taylor surrendered to my charms.

"I could hang for a bit."

WE SETTLED ON THE SAND, and I immediately pulled off my shoes to dig my toes in. Taylor leaned his head on my shoulder, and for a few moments, we listened to the waves and the people.

He finally broke the silence. "How are things going with your business paperwork?"

"Ugh, I hate paperwork. I just want to do the fun stuff. But everything is filed. It doesn't feel real yet, though."

It meant a lot that Taylor kept track of what was going on in my life. The more time I spent with him, the more I felt like the distance I was feeling was something I'd imagined.

"Now I have to decide if I'm going to apply for any farmer's market booths or make social media pages," I said. "It feels like the list never ends."

"One step at a time. I'm proud of you."

We had our legs stretched out in front of us, leaning back on our hands, and he knocked his shoulder into mine and threw one of his legs over my thigh. Had I ever heard anyone say they were proud of me before? It hit me hard.

"Thanks," I said to the sea. I couldn't bring myself to look at his face. "So, what's next on Margo's to-do list?"

"We're mostly done now. Out-of-town guests will start arriving this week." Taylor ran his fingers through his hair. "I can't wait for all this wedding shit to be behind me."

"Do you think you'd ever want a wedding someday?" My heart was pounding as I asked the question.

I hadn't put much thought into whether I'd want a ceremony or a party or all that, outside of the many opinions my mother had expressed on the subject. Now, when I thought of marriage, I thought of Taylor. When had that happened?

"Eh, I don't think so. I used to think I wouldn't get married, ever, at all, but..."

Maybe I was a masochist, but I *had* to know what came next.

"But..."

"I know you haven't seen Margo and Benji together, but they're couple goals. Until they started dating, I'd only seen the horrible side of love. It's made me think that maybe if I could have something like that, it wouldn't be so bad."

"Not so bad, huh? Such a romantic."

Taylor sighed. "My parents were truly, truly awful to each other and to me."

I wanted to hug him. To reach inside his heart and patch up all the cracks.

At some point over the last few weeks, I'd learned that if I wanted Taylor to keep talking, all I needed to do was wait out the silence—a task that was hard for my squirrel brain but tended to pay off when I could make it happen. This time was no different.

"Honestly, if I ever get married, I'm not inviting any family—aside from Margo, probably. She'd kill me if I eloped without her. I'd rather have something quiet, somewhere outside at sunset. Love shouldn't be a show you put on for other people, you know?"

I relaxed my head onto his shoulder. "Yeah, that sounds pretty nice."

"What about you? Do you want to get married?"

My breath hitched.

It's not a proposal, Gabriel. Get it together.

He literally said he wasn't sure marriage was in his future. This was a theoretical question, and my body needed to get on board.

"My mom has always wanted me to," I said. "She's had lots to say about my being almost thirty and still single."

Taylor interjected: "Not single."

"Not single *now*. Anyway, I'd never thought about marriage one way or the other, except that I didn't want to do it just because my mom insisted that I had to. Imagining having another person by my side every day, knowing them better than anyone else, supporting each other through hard things, being able to kiss them whenever I want—I don't think I need a piece of paper from the government to have that. But I want it."

Taylor hummed as he finished his smoothie. We both avoided eye contact, keeping our faces turned toward the waves. I was still acclimating to the tide of feelings that came with this new relationship status.

I was almost positive I was in love and felt completely unprepared.

22

GABRIEL

Oscar had been trying to meet up ever since the block party, and I'd been avoiding him. I still wasn't sure how I felt about everything that went down, but he was my cousin and one of my best friends. He'd apologized for his part, and I was ready to give him a chance to live up to his promise.

Today, he was hanging out on my couch while I prepared my orange bitters for sale. A few of the other volleyball crew were coming over later for a pizza-and-movie night.

"Have you talked to your mom?" he asked.

"Going for the big guns right out the gate, primo?"

He laughed as he lifted his beer. "I think she feels bad about what happened."

"Eh, she feels bad about being called out in front of the whole neighborhood. And by my gringo boyfriend, no less." I poured a large jug of the steeped bitters through a strainer. "I've been saying the same things to her for years, and she's never listened to me."

"Maybe it just took time to sink in."

"Maybe. She hasn't called or texted or anything."

Part of me felt like if she was sorry, she'd reach out. But she had some old-fashioned generational beliefs, like the idea that it was the kid's job to reach out to the parents. She never called unless it was to guilt-trip me for not calling. She was probably stewing in silence about how this generation had no respect, even if, by some miracle, she was willing to acknowledge that she was wrong.

Oscar sipped his beer and shrugged.

In some ways, even though he'd come out as gay, the family still held him in higher regard because of his high-paying job and because he leaned masculine in his gender presentation. He didn't paint his nails or wear makeup. He didn't have visible piercings or tattoos, either. It wasn't an act for him, something he did to fit in. It was what he preferred, and I was jealous sometimes that he'd had it so much easier. Even though I was bi and had dated women in the past, I still presented as obviously queer. My macho family members had a hard time with that.

"Tell me how the new promotion is going?"

I changed the subject, and Oscar gave me a side-eye from over the kitchen island.

"Yeah, I'm pretty sure everyone is more excited about this than me, but hey, a promotion's a promotion." He leaned his head on the back of the sofa, staring at the ceiling.

I added agave to the bitters and stirred. "Why isn't that good news? I thought you liked working at this firm."

Oscar hummed thoughtfully. "I mean, I do. The work environment is not as toxic as a lot of other law firms, and it's nice that I'm not the only out LGBTQ lawyer in our office. It could be worse, for sure, but I've always wanted to do something to make a difference for our community, you know? I'm tired of dealing with divorce court and shit."

"Huh."

"I know you've always been compared to me, but I've always

envied the way that you have done your own thing." He picked at the label of his bottle, appearing uncharacteristically nervous. "I know you went through a lot trying to choose your major, but you didn't give up until you found something that fit. I got the first job I could, and I've played it safe since. I should have told you sooner how much I admire you."

I was shocked at Oscar's confession and knew I had to be staring at him with wide-eyed confusion. His decisions and achievements had always been held up as the gold standard in our family. I'd never stopped to consider that he was facing the same pressures as I was.

Oscar smiled ruefully. "You know I would have stayed in the closet much longer if you hadn't come out first."

"My closet was made of glass. I don't think I had much choice." I laughed because the other option—crying—was too embarrassing.

Oscar finished his beer and got up from the couch to grab another. He bumped my shoulder as he passed. "I mean, at least you have the option to date girls. You didn't have to come out, but I'm glad you did."

I wasn't sure I agreed, but I let it slide. "I'm glad you did, too. It's nice not being the only one in the family."

Oscar smiled. We'd always been close, but it looked like there were still some surprises to uncover in our relationship, and I was thankful we'd cleared the air. Hopefully, it meant we'd grow even closer.

Oscar stayed in the kitchen, leaning up against the counter with his beer. "Want to tell me what you're working on here?"

I gestured to the row of small bottles, labeled with today's date. "Just wrapping up the next batch of bitters. Taylor finally convinced me to get things set up officially with a name and an LLC and everything."

My phone buzzed with a text, and I grabbed it from the counter.

TAYLOR
I'm going crazy with all our family in town. Can I come over?

GABRIEL
Sure, some of the Baes are here for movie night, but you're welcome to join us.

Butterflies swarmed around in my stomach just knowing I'd get a little time with my man.

Oscar's voice floated into my consciousness. "I like him."

"Yeah." I sighed a little too dreamily. "Me too."

"Oh shit." Oscar laughed. "You are down bad. This is so cute. My cousin is in *loooove*."

"Shut up." I body-checked him out of the way and moved in front of the sink to wash my supplies.

"Are you going to let me pick the movie tonight?" Oscar asked as I handed him a towel.

Might as well put him to work if he was going to be all up in my business.

"Absolutely not. You're gonna pick some creepy horror movie, and I need to sleep. I have to be in top form for wedding date duties this weekend."

It was back to the same arguments we always dragged out for movie night, and arguing with a lawyer was a pain in the ass. It didn't matter in the end. Everyone got a vote. We'd be waiting to decide until the others arrived with the pizza, whether he liked it or not.

By the time we'd finished bickering, Alex and Kat were calling to have me buzz them into the apartment building. The first pizza was devoured immediately, and we took the second over to the coffee table once we'd voted on streaming the latest spandex-wearing action-hero movie.

Grabbing a slice, Kat turned to me. "I need to know what you're wearing to the wedding this weekend. You have a bunch of events to attend, right?"

I laughed. "Yeah, I'll need outfits for the rehearsal, wedding, and brunch the next day. We picked up Taylor's suit last weekend, and it's unfair how good he looks in it. The only thing I've picked so far is the matching tie."

"I can help you choose." Kat pressed her hands together, pleading. "I haven't done anything fancy in a while, so I must live vicariously through you."

"I'll text you photos."

The doorbell announced Taylor's arrival, and soon we were smashed together on my big beanbag chair. I wish I had better seating for when I had friends over, but I'd prioritized my plant habitats over social space.

And it was a good excuse for extra cuddles.

Once the credits were rolling, Oscar jumped in with commentary. "The timeline of this movie made no sense."

"As far as I'm concerned, these superhero movies are more about the tight pants than the science," Kat said with a grin.

Taylor groaned. "I don't see how they could have made it from Tokyo to New York in that amount of time, even assuming they could fly faster than a jet."

"The magic of cinema," Kat said with a flourish of jazz hands.

"I regret not voting in your favor on the horror movie," Alex said. "Whatever we just watched was the true horror."

We laughed as we gathered the pizza boxes and paper plates.

"Ok, friends," I said, ushering them toward the door. "Closing time. You don't have to go home, but you can't stay here."

It was late already, and I was hoping I'd catch a few minutes alone with Taylor.

As soon as my friends called their ride shares and I'd scooted them out my door, I collapsed back onto the couch, pulling Taylor with me.

Was this what love would always feel like? A tightness in my chest when we were apart for too long? If I had my way, we'd be living together by next tax season, so I'd at least get cuddles at night. How strange to be thinking that far ahead, making plans.

I could only hope Taylor felt the same.

"Hi, angel," Taylor said as he curled into my side, and I breathed a sigh of relief.

As he told me about his day, I fell asleep to the sound of his voice, still stretched out on the couch. Zero regrets.

23

TAYLOR

I stood in front of the mirror, fussing with my hair.

Kai stuck his head into the bathroom. "You look great."

Tonight was Margo and Benji's wedding rehearsal. I wore wide-legged, high-waisted grey dress pants and a light pink dress shirt. It was more feminine than I usually dressed around my family, but I was out of fucks for what they thought of me.

"Thanks," I said, finally surrendering the comb.

I took a quick mirror selfie to send to Gabriel, and he immediately sent a string of fire emojis in response.

Margo looked stunning in a white pantsuit with a peplum jacket, and Benji complimented her with a dark red dress shirt. She'd dyed her hair lavender for the wedding. They'd leaned into the Valentine's Day color palette, but with a more modern edge than basic fire engine red and baby pink. The rehearsal was held at the art gallery where the wedding would take place, and we'd walked to a neighboring rooftop restaurant for dinner.

I was glad my parents weren't walking Margo down the aisle. They'd given her away when she was a child and didn't deserve to do it now. I'd managed to avoid talking to them before we started, and for that, I was feeling pretty lucky. I was still simmering and stressed, but I tried to focus on logistics during the rehearsal. The wedding day-of coordinator was a friend of Margo's from high school, and I was her main point of contact so Margo could relax and have as much fun as possible.

Only a few more steps and my weekend duties would be over—and my responsibilities to Margo would be over, too. I wasn't sure what I'd do without constantly fretting over her. She was ready, but I wasn't. I still had the medical loans to worry about, but those would be paid off next year if everything went as I planned. I was still waiting on all the bills from my own hospital stay, which sat at the back of my mind like a heavy stone.

I grabbed two cocktails at the bar—one for Margo and one for me—and wove through the party to find her.

Unfortunately, that's when my luck ran out.

"Taylor," my mother called out.

"Diane," I responded.

I didn't call her mom; she hadn't wanted to be a mom to me, so I'm sure she didn't mind. I turned toward her voice and took her in. I hadn't seen her since Margo's college graduation, I think. That was probably the last time my parents had been in the same room, too. She was decked out in a bedazzled floor-length gown and a designer handbag, definitely overdressed for the evening. I'm sure it was to prove a point to my father.

"Do you think you could let Margo know that I'm going to miss brunch on Saturday morning?" she asked in the syrupy voice she used when she wanted something. "I've been invited to go boating in the Riviera, so I'll have a plane to catch."

I clenched my jaw. Of course, she was leaving early, and of course, she'd made it my responsibility to break the news and make excuses for her.

She continued. "I don't want to bother her before the wedding, so I thought you could let her know that morning."

"I'm sure she'll figure it out when you're a no-show."

"Oh, but it's not because I don't want to be there. My boyfriend couldn't adjust his schedule, you understand. He's a busy man."

"Of course. Drinking wine on a yacht is more important than your daughter's wedding. I'm sure she'll understand." I was tired of this already. "Speaking of your daughter, I want to get this drink over to Margo before the ice melts, so I'm going to go do that now."

Before she could say anything else, I strode off. I spotted Margo by one of the fire pits in the restaurant's outdoor area. The view from the balcony of downtown LA was unmatched. I don't know how Margo got a deal on this place, but she could make friends with anyone, so I was unsurprised that she'd talked an event planner or customer service person into helping her out.

I was interrupted again by my father, John, and his new wife before I could escape. What was this, an Olympic hurdles event? I dragged a big sip from my drink.

"What did Diane want?" were the first words out of John's mouth.

"I'm not your message boy anymore. You can go talk to her yourself if you'd like."

He huffed. "I don't have anything to say to her."

"Great, she didn't have anything to say to you either."

"Doesn't Pam look lovely?" John asked, gesturing to his wife.

"Sure," I said, glancing at her.

It only took a quick look to see the diamonds she was decked out with.

If I didn't have these drinks in my hands, I'd be clenching my fists. I had been giving them tens of thousands of dollars a year toward Margo's medical debt, living in a crappy apartment, and eating ramen, while my parents both showed up flaunting their money. Assholes. At least I was paying the loan directly through the website, so I knew my money was going where I intended it.

"Look, I have a drink for Margo, and I don't want to keep the bride waiting. I'll catch up with you both later."

When I finally pushed out onto the balcony, my shoulders relaxed. Margo was still at the fire pit, so I walked with quick, purposeful strides in her direction to avoid being stopped yet again.

"About time you joined us, bro," Margo teased as I handed her a drink. "Your boyfriend was getting bored."

"My... what?" I finally processed who else was standing around the fire.

Gabriel was grinning ear to ear. "Oh, you've forgotten me already?" He slipped under my arm and kissed my cheek, and—what had I been so worried about again?

Curse Margo for setting me up like this, but it was a welcome surprise.

"I could never." I nipped at his lips. "I'm glad you're here."

"Hey, no one is allowed to be a cuter couple than Benji and me tonight," Margo shouted. "Babe, come over here and be cute with me!"

Benji laughed from across the balcony.

"My almost-wife is calling, and I must go," he told his groomsmen as he walked over to join us.

The group whistled and hollered.

"Benji, this is Gabriel," I said when the catcalls from the other group died down.

"Great to meet you, man," Benji said, tipping his glass. "I've heard a lot about you."

This was all I needed. My best friends, a cocktail, and a fire. Kai was missing, but otherwise, this moment was perfect. Forget the madness inside.

Gabriel's hand trailed up and down my back, and I relaxed under his touch.

"Are you two ready for the big day tomorrow?" Gabriel asked Margo and Benji.

They looked at each other with hearts in their eyes, and my chest squeezed.

"Oh yeah," Benji said. "I can't wait to marry Margo. She's incredible."

"It took you long enough to ask me," Margo teased before turning to me. "Have you said hi to Mom and Dad?"

"Yeah, I was ambushed by both of them on my way out here," I said.

"You're so hard on them."

"Not hard enough," I muttered.

"Are you going to introduce me?" Gabriel asked, squeezing my waist.

I groaned. "Do I have to?"

When a few more guests joined our fire pit circle, Gabriel dragged me by the hand to an unoccupied corner of the balcony.

"Be careful, or you're going to give a guy a complex," he whispered in my ear as he pulled me close.

"You know that your character isn't the one on trial here, right?" I whispered.

"I know, Tay." Gabriel traced my face with his eyes. "Are you doing ok?"

I leaned my head back against the stucco. "Not really, but it's fine. My parents have managed to do the bare minimum to keep Margo believing the best of them, but my mother has already told me she's leaving early to go on a cruise with some guy."

Gabriel leaned on his side, squeezing my hand and running his other hand down my forearm, his fingers brushing over my skin.

I inhaled deeply, grounded by his touch. "My father is trying to make my mother jealous for no reason, considering they haven't been together for almost twenty years and he's remarried. And that's only the start. I'm not a violent person, but it makes me want to punch something."

Another squeeze from Gabriel's hand, another deep breath.

"It's hard to be around them and not slide back into the mind of that abandoned fifteen-year-old who was trying to keep it together for his kid sister." I finally released the last of the tension and anger with a sigh. "Anyway, there's only one more loose end, and then I don't have to deal with my parents ever again."

"You're a good brother," Gabriel said.

It made me want to cry, but I blinked it back.

"Thanks for being here. I didn't know how much I needed you." I rolled my head against the wall so I could look at him.

He leaned forward and kissed my shoulder. "Of course. Any time you need reminding that your needs are worth taking care of, I'll be here."

"Are you sure you haven't had a boyfriend before? Because you're excellent at it." My free hand lifted to the back of his head, threading through his curly hair, and my thumb traced his dimple.

His hazel eyes dropped to my lips. "You're the first."

I didn't deserve an angel like Gabriel, and I wasn't treating him remotely like he should be, especially since I was the one who had initially pushed the issue and made that grand gesture in front of his whole neighborhood. Now, it felt like I was waiting for shit to hit the fan. All we needed was one crisis to turn us into my parents, and the best thing that had happened to me would be over.

Dread curled around my heart. My mind wanted to push Gabriel away in that moment, but my body turned it into desperation, and I pulled him into a kiss, forcing my tongue into his mouth.

"Holy shit," Gabriel said when he reluctantly pulled back to breathe. "We need to stop, or I'm going to embarrass myself."

The rest of the dinner passed in a blur. I put on a public smile for my sister's benefit and listened quietly as Gabriel endeared himself to the whole bridal party seated at our table. Thankfully, I didn't have to give a speech until tomorrow night, so I had some time to get my emotional shit together.

I was vaguely aware of my parents eyeing me from their separate tables throughout the evening, but I was done worrying about them. I would finish paying off Margo's debt, and then I would be free. Both Margo and I would be free.

24

TAYLOR

It turns out I didn't have to worry about introducing Gabriel to my parents after all. When I snuck out from the back room where the bridal party was getting ready the morning of the wedding, I discovered my parents had already dragged him into their drama.

John shot daggers at Diane, who was hanging onto Gabriel's arm. Pam was hanging back in a suspiciously cream-colored dress. While Gabriel had a polite smile plastered on his face, I could tell he was uncomfortable.

"Is this man bothering you?" Diane said to Gabriel with a syrupy voice, squeezing his arm. "I'd apologize for my ex-husband, but..."

"Ok, both of you. Seriously?" I stepped in between Gabriel and my mother, tucking him under my arm protectively. "Why don't you go find your seats? You can play concerned parents some other time."

"Oh, but honey, we're just trying to get to know your date," she continued with that cloying drawl.

Gabriel wrapped himself around my waist and squeezed.

"Nope," I said firmly. "Not today. Today is about Margo, and I won't have either of you causing problems. Go sit. The ceremony is about to start."

I didn't know if Gabriel had noticed that he'd tucked his pinky finger inside the waistband of my pants, right near my hip bone, but I sure did. The tiny touches against my skin calmed me.

When my parents finally left to find their seats, Gabriel leaned toward my face and spoke in a low voice. "I've never heard your dom voice before, but damn, how are you so hot when you're all stern like that? I'm never going to be able to fight with you."

I couldn't help but laugh, breaking the tension, which is what he'd probably been hoping for. The man was a miracle worker on my nerves.

"It's my secret evil plan," I whispered back.

It was the first time I'd seen him today, so I stepped back to take in his whole look. He was wearing a navy suit that fit him to perfection, with the burgundy floral tie we'd picked out together. He'd even painted his nails to match the tie. His hazel eyes looked absolutely captivating with a touch of smudged dark brown eyeliner. It didn't help that he was looking at me like he wanted to devour me.

"Are you done eye-fucking me?" I lifted a brow. "We need to get lined up for our grand entrance."

Gabriel twirled his finger, indicating I should spin for him. "Almost."

I obliged, one corner of my mouth lifting into a smile.

"Ok, now I'm done." He pecked my cheek. "I'm going to go find a seat."

Soon, it was time for the ceremony to begin in the main gallery. I squeezed Margo's hands before making my way down the aisle, and I couldn't help but find Gabriel's face in the small crowd. He winked at me when I spotted him sitting on the aisle in the second row, and I almost stumbled.

I never pictured myself walking down an aisle. I guess since I'd spent so much time avoiding getting into the kind of relationship that might lead to marriage, it hadn't crossed my mind.

You have to be in love to reach this point, and I didn't want love. Right?

Every time I did the accounting of my life, I'd placed love firmly in the liabilities column. But I was looking across at Benji's face the moment Margo appeared at the door, and I was tempted to reconsider. The gratitude, awe, and adoration in his expression were impossible to ignore. I turned to Margo, noticing her eyes sparkling with unshed tears as she walked toward her husband-to-be.

I considered it the greatest accomplishment of my life that I'd been able to preserve that romantic optimism for her. I was like a parent whose child still believed in Santa, knowing it was all a farce but getting so much enjoyment from their naive belief in magic. I never wanted Margo to stop believing.

I bent down to adjust the train of Margo's gown, then grabbed her orchid bouquet as she took Benji's hands.

"Margo, the day I walked into Graphic Design 101 and saw you in the front row, I knew my life had changed for the better..." Benji began.

It was impossible to keep tears from falling as I listened to the two of them exchange heartfelt vows. It felt like I was swimming in a pool of emotion more than I was hearing individual words. I could reach out and touch the love that Margo and Benji had for each other. I never remember my parents having that, even before everything crumbled.

"Benji, you are my rock and my steadfast joy," Margo said, beginning her lengthy vows. "I am so thankful you claimed you didn't have a pen that day, so you'd have an excuse to sit next to me..."

Would it be possible for me to believe again? Maybe the liability that came alongside love, the vulnerability that left you open to heartbreak and pain, didn't outweigh the asset love could be in your life.

Had I been doing the accounting all wrong?

I glanced out at the guests in attendance, and of course, my gaze immediately fell on Gabriel. He wore the softest expression as he watched my sister and Benji exchange rings. What was he thinking at that moment? As if I'd called out to him, he shifted his gaze to mine. If his eyes could become even fonder, I watched it happen as he smiled at me. He blew me a little kiss, and my heart cracked open.

I could see it. The two of us exchanging I love yous. Exchanging keys to our apartments. Exchanging rings. Gabriel, sitting on the window seat of our imaginary future home, maybe with a cat, surrounded by his plants. I could see it as if it were a memory, and I was terrified.

Applause jolted me from my imagination as Margo and Benji shared their first kiss as husband and wife. Joining the celebration, I handed Margo her bouquet and watched them make their way down the aisle, stopping for more kisses along the way.

The ceremony did a number on my emotions, and my insides were all jumbled up, but I was happy to have Gabriel's hand in mine again as we mingled during the brief cocktail hour.

"Are you nervous to give your Man of Honor speech?" he asked with a mischievous twinkle in his golden eyes.

"Finding nice things to say about Margo is not hard... public speaking is another story." I grabbed two glasses from a passing tray and handed one to Gabriel. "The champagne will help, though."

"I know I just met Margo and Benji, but you could feel how much they love each other," he said wistfully as he accepted a glass. "I felt lucky to witness it."

"It was beautiful, and everything's gone so smoothly—knock on wood. I know she worked hard on making this day special."

"You put in your fair share of blood, sweat, and tears for today." Gabriel tugged me close by the lapel of my jacket. "Give yourself some credit."

"The suit looks just as good out here in the wild as it did in the store," a familiar voice called from behind us, and we turned to see Elie from the suit shop.

Before Elie could swoop in for a hug, Gabriel leaned into my face and licked my cheek, shocking me into laughter.

"Oh, honey. I know he's yours, but if you're going to put on a show for me, I'd like to bring a guest. Come meet my husband, Theo."

I NOTICED that Margo had taken my suggestion and seated our parents at tables as far apart as possible. I'd been so frustrated that she wanted to invite them, but I'd done it to myself by shielding her from how terrible our parents were when we were young. At least she'd refused to have either of them walk her down the aisle, and they weren't invited to do speeches or dances. No special attention directed their way was ideal for me, although it was not ideal for them. They wanted to take the credit for Margo surviving and thriving as the kick-ass person she became.

After dinner was served, the DJ introduced me and thrust a mic into my hand. My palms were covered in sweat, and I rubbed my free hand against my pant leg. I'd ditched the suit jacket and rolled up my sleeves, but I still felt hot. I did not love the spotlight. But I could do this for Margo. I locked eyes with her as I spoke.

"Margo, you've been my favorite person since I was eight years old. Meanwhile, you've been lucky to know your favorite person your whole life."

Guests chuckled as I gestured to myself, and Margo raised her glass with a smile in her eyes.

"There was a time when I thought this day wouldn't come, that I'd be robbed of the magic of watching you grow up and cover the world in your bright light." My voice cracked. "Lucky for me, and for Benji, you're a fighter. You've always thrown yourself fully into every experience, you've faced every fear with courage, and you love harder than anyone I've met. As the Emperor said to bi-icon, Li Shang, in your favorite movie, Mulan: 'you don't meet a girl like that every dynasty.'"

I chuckled wetly through blurry eyes. "It's been such a gift to witness you fall in love, and I couldn't ask for a better brother-in-law than Benji. When you came home from college on break and couldn't stop gushing about this adorable web designer in your class, I had a hunch he was going to be special. Here we are, years later, celebrating the next chapter in your story, and I'm so honored to be a part of it. May you have many more happy years together. Cheers!"

I raised my glass in a toast, and all of Margo and Benji's friends and family joined in applauding them as they kissed.

Breathing a sigh of relief, I practically dove back into my seat. Gabriel's arm immediately went around my shoulder, and his fingers traced up my arm.

"You did great, cariño."

He'd never called me that before. I may not have remembered much from my Spanish class, but my gut clenched at the evident affection in his voice.

"I'm glad you're here with me." I couldn't help telling the truth, even though I felt myself being pulled into the undertow.

I had to kiss him, too, tasting the sparkling wine on his lips and threading my fingers through the hair at the back of his neck. He'd opened a few buttons on his dress shirt, making my throat dry. Everything was completely out of control as he grabbed my hand and tugged me out onto the dance floor. I was drowning, and Gabriel was fresh air incarnate.

I couldn't ignore him any more than I could ignore breathing.

25

GABRIEL

This turned out to be a surprisingly beautiful wedding. I'd been to family weddings with my parents when I was younger, but this was a totally different experience. Most of my friends, aside from Lucas, were unmarried, still playing the field and having fun. This was the first wedding I'd attended as an adult, and with a boyfriend I was almost positive I was in love with. It was a lot to process.

I had chosen a seat on Benji's side for the ceremony so I could see Margo's—and, more importantly, Taylor's—face. If I had let my mind wander a little bit as Taylor made his way down the aisle, imagining that I was the one standing at the end waiting for him, no one had to know.

When his eyes caught mine, I stopped breathing.

Maybe that was the reaction I was supposed to have for the bride, but I was more invested in her Man of Honor. Margo looked stunning in an ultra-modern mesh dress with a full skirt and sexy geometric panels. When I glanced over to look at Benji, he wore the biggest smile and was fighting back tears.

I'd met Benji for the first time last night at the rehearsal, but it was impossible not to feel the love between them when they shared their vows. Taylor had tears streaming down his face as he looked at his sister. It seemed like he was as overwhelmed as I was, but probably for a different reason.

After Taylor's speech was finished, I was ready to get the party started and help my man relax. He'd done so much to make this day perfect for Margo, and he needed to let loose. Of course, I was the man for that job—instigator of shenanigans reporting for duty.

As soon as I got the chance, I pulled him out onto the dance floor.

Dancing with Taylor was forever going to be one of my favorite things. It reminded me of our first date, except this time, I didn't have to wonder if he'd kiss me. I could go ahead and kiss him myself, which I did. Often.

When the family with young kids had left, and the older family members had said their goodbyes, the party truly got started. Kai was there, and hilariously, so were Elie and his partner, who must have been friends of Margo's. Since she and Taylor were both queer, most of their friends were too. We basically turned the after-party into a gay club, and I was here for it.

My hands were all over Taylor as I ground my hips against him. I'd been watching him be sexy, sweet, and so strong through the wedding weekend. He'd worked so hard to make this weekend amazing for Margo, and it had gone off without a hitch. As far as I was concerned, the man deserved a reward, and I had come prepared.

I licked up his neck, and I could feel the vibration of his groan against my tongue. We'd both lost our suit jackets and ties.

If we were going to make this a gay club dance floor, I was going to pull one of the classic gay club moves. Enough of all this lovey-dovey stuff. It was time for orgasms and a distinct lack of pesky feelings.

"Come with me," I leaned in to say to Taylor before grabbing him and pulling him into a small supply closet I'd scoped out earlier.

As soon as we were inside, I pushed him against the door.

"What are you doing?" Taylor whispered.

"You've done so much today." I slowly dropped to my knees in front of him and raised my hands to his belt. "I figured you deserved a treat. You'll have to be quiet, though."

I started on his buckle, and Taylor was breathing hard as he looked down at me. I felt like the most powerful man in the world. The music pounded in the room down the hall, but it was muffled in the closet as I slid his open pants down over his thighs, revealing his beautiful cock.

He hardened under my tongue as I licked up his length. The burst of salty precum on my tongue made me moan, and I couldn't help taking him to the back of my throat. I didn't want to make him come, but I wanted to bring him right to the edge. I wanted him to be as wrecked as I was.

I bobbed my head and twisted my tongue until he was thrusting into my mouth, and I couldn't help unbuckling my pants to relieve the pressure on my erection. But when his thighs vibrated under my hands, I pulled off.

"*Gabriel.*" Taylor groaned above me, and I loved the sound of my name all ragged and strung out.

I stood up and pressed him against the door, taking his mouth in a passionate kiss. We made out, tongues tangling, cocks pressed against each other with only my briefs between us until I couldn't take it anymore. I reached into my back pocket to pull out the condom and packet of lube and thrust them into Taylor's hand before dropping my pants and turning to brace against the storage shelves behind us. He gasped as I spread my legs.

"I need you to fuck me, Tay."

I felt his hands knead into my ass, spreading my cheeks, and he swore.

"Goddamn, you're so sexy. Have you been like this all day?" Taylor said in awe as he traced the top of the butt plug he'd discovered.

"I snuck away before the reception. Hurry up and get inside me."

His fingers pressed against the plug, and I arched my back.

I could hear the tearing of the condom packet and then the lube. Taylor gently pulled the plug out of my ass and grabbed a roll of paper towels from over the top of my head, presumably to wrap it up before it thudded to the floor. Finally, I felt the pressure of the head of his cock at my hole.

"Taylor," I whined as I tried to push back against him, and he held my hips in place.

"I'm right here, angel." And then, he was pushing inside me.

I pressed my mouth into my forearm to muffle my moan as his hips met my ass. He leaned over me and wrapped his arms around my middle, nuzzling his face into the back of my neck and kissing my shoulder blades.

There were moments when it felt like Taylor was holding me at a distance, afraid to get too close, but when we were together like this, it was like he couldn't get close enough. He was such a tender lover, which shouldn't have surprised me, knowing his personality—always wanting to give and give and never take—but I lived for the moments when his control slipped, and he couldn't help but meet those base needs.

I squeezed around him, urging him to move. "Come on, baby. We have to get back out there before someone comes looking for us. Fuck me like you mean it."

"So bossy," Taylor muttered as he slid back slowly.

"Occupational hazard of banging a vers dude." I chuckled. "Sometimes we can't help topping from the bottom."

He huffed a laugh as he entered me again with a quick thrust, and I moaned.

"Yes, more, baby."

One of his hands left my hips and ran up my spine, pushing my shirt up with it. He grabbed a large handful of my hair and pulled my head back.

"Hold on, and be quiet," he whispered before he started thrusting into me with abandon.

Once he started nailing my prostate, it was almost impossible to keep silent.

"Shhh," Taylor said, and then he slipped two of his fingers into my mouth. I sucked on his fingers eagerly, feeling so full of him everywhere.

"Fuck, I'm so close." He groaned against my back. "You're too sexy like this."

I was teetering on the edge of orgasm when I felt Taylor surge inside of me and let out a quiet gasp as he came. He was much better at being quiet than I was, but then again, I was the one being railed. I desperately needed friction on my dick, but I was afraid I would collapse if I removed one of my arms from the shelves. Taylor pulled his fingers from my mouth and released my head.

"Spit," he said, holding the hand I'd been sucking on in front of my mouth.

"Fuck," I breathed out, spitting on his hand.

He slicked my cock with spit and stroked me, his other hand gripping my chest, pulling me up against him. I could barely stand, but he supported my weight as he jerked me off. His body was so firm and strong, and his soft grunts in my ear finally tipped me over the edge.

"Taylor," I practically shouted, immediately covering my mouth. My cum covered his hand as I came and dripped onto the concrete floor of the storage closet.

"You are terrible at being quiet," Taylor said affectionately as he held me, and we both came down from the high.

"Have you met me?" I arched an eyebrow.

He laughed as he bent down to grab the roll of paper towels, using them to clean off his hand, wipe me down, and dispose of the condom.

"Sorry," he said. "I know paper towels are kind of scratchy."

"Eh, it's better than going back out to the dance floor all sticky." I smiled as I pulled up my pants and rearranged my shirt. "That was one of the hottest things I've ever done."

Shy, blushing Taylor was back in full force as he tucked his chin to his chest and smiled. Once he was dressed again, I pulled him into a hug, covering his face in soft kisses.

"Ready to get back out there?"

He huffed. "I think I've met my extrovert quotient for the next year. I don't want to talk to another person but you and Kai for at least a month."

I couldn't help grinning that I'd made the shortlist. "What about Margo?"

"Oh no, I don't want to hear about her wedding night or her honeymoon or her matrimonial bliss anytime soon," Taylor said, cringing. "That woman has no filter, and there are some things I don't want to know about my sister. I'll talk to her after tax season is over."

I laughed, unlocked the closet, and after glancing both ways to make sure we were clear, I dragged him back to the dance floor.

26

TAYLOR

My alarm sounded on the nightstand beside me, and I groaned in protest. My body was too heavy to move, my eyelids were itchy, and my head throbbed. I was exhausted, but there was no way I had a hangover. Or at least not an alcohol hangover. Maybe a social and emotional one.

Gabriel rolled on top of me as he stretched out across the bed to reach my alarm and hit snooze. I wasn't quite ready to open my eyes, so I let myself sink under the comfort of his weight as we came back to reality.

Once all my obligations had ended, the party turned out to be pretty fun. I couldn't believe that Gabriel and I had fucked in a closet at my sister's workplace, but it was one of the hottest encounters of my life, finding that plug inside him. And as far as I knew, we hadn't been caught, so all's well that ends well.

I wouldn't be able to take advantage of the fact that we'd tumbled into bed naked, much to my disappointment. There was one last wedding event to attend, although the morning-after brunch was much more casual than everything else had been. Thankfully, it was just downstairs, which is why we'd decided to book a room instead of heading to either of our apartments.

"Shower?" Gabriel mumbled into my chest.

"Yeah," I begrudgingly agreed. "But you need to get off me first."

"I could get *you* off first."

I slapped his ass playfully and shoved him toward the bathroom as he grumbled.

"Shower, then coffee," I said.

We still managed to squeeze in quick handjobs when the body wash situation got out of control. It was almost impossible to keep myself from touching Gabriel when he was naked in front of me. He pulled a casual set of joggers and a matching sweatshirt out of his overnight bag to wear to brunch, and I threw on my softest sweater before grabbing my hotel key and phone. I had a feeling we both needed the cozy vibes this morning.

I laughed out loud when I found Margo and Benji both wearing sunglasses inside at the breakfast table. The party likely lasted until three or four in the morning.

Margo whined, pointing at me. "Hey, no loud noises."

"Dear sister, what do you mean? Are you not feeling well this morning?" I teased, and she threw a blueberry muffin at my head, which Gabriel caught when I ducked out of the way.

"Thanks." He grinned and took a massive bite of the muffin. "Where's the coffee? I'm ready for an IV drip of caffeine and a mimosa."

We made a pass through the buffet line before joining the rest of the group at the table. It was most of the bridal party, along with Benji's parents, my father, and Pam. Deciding I was going to have to take the bullet for my mother yet again, I rounded the table and bent over Margo's shoulder.

"Hey, Mom told me yesterday that she's not going to make brunch. She had a flight to catch this morning."

"I guess she reached her limit on family time." Margo sighed. "At least she made it to the wedding."

I rolled my eyes. "Ah, yes, bare minimum. Great job, Mom."

"Did she say why?" Margo looked up at me expectantly.

This was where I usually made an excuse for our mother: create an emergency or a work thing that sounded important. But I was tired.

"European yacht trip with the latest boyfriend," I said.

"She has always been so selfish," John said, unhelpfully. He must have overheard.

Margo's shoulders slumped, and she turned back to her pancakes.

"Nope, no." I pointed at my father. "We are not doing this."

Gabriel jumped in from the other side of the table. "Hey, Margo. Can you tell me more about the exhibit that was hanging in the gallery last night? The work was so compelling."

I breathed a sigh of relief when Margo's eyes lit up, and she appeared to be successfully distracted from our parents' shortcomings.

"He's an up-and-coming artist, Ciarán Kelly. He explores the interconnection between the natural world and humanity, especially through the lens of England's colonization of Ireland. It's this really fascinating blend of postmodern and traditional styles, don't you think?"

"Totally," Gabriel said. "As a plant nerd, I noticed the nature themes right away. The oil painting of the tree rings was my favorite."

I could kiss that man.

Wait, I *could* kiss that man. I leaned over and pecked his cheek in gratitude before digging into my meal.

The conversation lingered on art theory for a while before shifting to the highlights of the epic wedding. Everything about the day had gone perfectly, and it was reflective of Margo and Benji's love. I was not one to wear rose-colored glasses, but I couldn't help but let my guard down a little bit in the face of their obvious, contagious joy. Leaning back, I put my arm around Gabriel's chair as he finished his meal, and I sipped my coffee, letting the conversation drift around me.

I should have known better than to get too comfortable while my father was still around. That was when it all went to shit.

"I'm gonna find the restroom," I whispered to Gabriel before excusing myself from the table.

I hadn't made it too far down the hallway when John called out my name. I paused and waited for him to catch up.

"I wanted to ask you a favor," he said.

I rolled my eyes. "Oh, here we go."

"This is important," he said in a sharp voice. "Pam and I are buying a vacation home together in Palm Beach. We're trying to get our credit score up so we can get a better interest rate, and it would go a long way if that medical loan were paid off."

I stared at him in disbelief, blinking at him for a moment while he shrugged meekly as if this whole situation was normal and he was put out to be asking me.

"Are you kidding me?" I hissed. "I've been paying off that loan for a decade, making way more than the minimum payment. I've been busting my ass, living with a roommate, putting my life on hold to pay off this loan as fast as possible. Meanwhile, you have the spare change for a vacation home, and you're here asking me for *more*?"

"I know how expensive weddings are, so I didn't want to have to ask Margo for a contribution, but—"

"You will absolutely not be going to Margo about this," I seethed.

"Going to Margo about what?" Her voice filtered down the hallway, and I covered my face with my hands.

"I needed Taylor's help with something, but he wasn't very willing." John infused his voice with feigned disappointment. "I merely suggested that perhaps you'd be more supportive."

Margo lifted her sunglasses to her head, and her eyes narrowed and flitted back and forth between our father and me. I clenched my jaw and crossed my arms, leaning against the wall.

"In my experience, Taylor has always been helpful and supportive," she said skeptically.

"Well"—John huffed—"this is such a small thing, Taylor. I don't know why you can't make it happen."

He wasn't backing down, Margo wasn't taking a hint, and it was apparent this train wreck was happening no matter how much I wanted to avoid it.

"Fine, make your request. Let's see how reasonable Margo thinks this *small thing* is." I braced myself.

"What the hell is going on?" Margo asked, sounding tentative and not a small bit freaked out.

"Pam and I want to buy a vacation home in Florida this year," John started. "It's just that the medical debt is affecting our credit, and we were hoping to have it paid off before we applied for the loan. I was asking Taylor for a little bit of help finishing it off."

A furrow appeared between Margo's eyebrows. "Medical debt?"

"From your chemotherapy, of course," John said as if he wasn't dropping a bomb on his child, who had almost died of cancer. "There's not much left now."

"Taylor..." Margo looked at me with those big, wide eyes.

All I could see was my kid sister clinging to her life in a hospital bed. I could tell the moment that she realized I wasn't as surprised by this revelation as she was.

"You knew about the debt?" she whispered.

"Yeah, I knew." I sighed, resigned. "There was about two hundred thousand dollars in loans left when I graduated from college, and I've been making payments since. I was planning on finishing it off next year, but daddy dearest wants me to work faster so he can get his little beach house."

I couldn't keep the resentment out of my voice.

Margo shrieked, "*You've* been paying it?"

"I know it's technically your responsibility," John cut in like an idiot. He didn't know his daughter at all. "But when Taylor and I talked about it, he offered, so…"

"My responsibility?" Margo's eyes widened, her lips opening and closing several times, but then her voice hardened, her jaw set. "How much is left, Dad?"

John hesitated at the sharpness of her words, but I egged him on. "If you don't tell her, I will. Seeing as you were so eager to make this her problem."

"Twenty-five thousand. We're almost there, kiddo."

I scoffed. "*We*."

"Don't think I'm not pissed at you," Margo growled at me. "You've been covering for this asshole for my whole life. Jesus Christ, Taylor. Two hundred thousand dollars? You better not pay another penny."

John looked between us, as if rethinking his strategy. "It seems irresponsible to back out of a commitment."

I leaned up against the wall, exhausted. All the battles I'd been fighting, all the secrets I'd been keeping, were out in the open. I hadn't held it together after all, but I realized I'd been doing it for the approval of a man who didn't care one iota about me.

"Margo is right." I rubbed a hand across my face. "I'm working myself to death, and I can't do it anymore. You're on your own. And Margo's not paying you either."

"It's just a shame," John hedged. "After everything we've done, turning your back on your family."

"After everything *you've* done?" Margo practically yelled. I couldn't tell if she was going to cry or commit murder. "Taylor has been a better parent to me than either you or Mom has been. I've given you both the benefit of the doubt for years, but I'm guessing that's mostly due to Taylor's little white lies. I'm over it. If you thought I'd take your side over his, you're delusional."

John mumbled under his breath, slinking down the hallway back toward the brunch.

"I wasn't going to let you pay for it," I whispered, my anger at my father deflating in the face of Margo's heartbreak. "I couldn't. And I've been managing just fine."

"You call a hospital stay and heart problems *managing*?" Margo pulled me into a hug. "You really are an idiot, you know that?"

"I didn't mean to ruin your wedding weekend. I was trying so hard to keep their bullshit contained."

I was still tense, but I wrapped my arms around her.

Nothing good could come from love. Maybe for other people, but not for me. Sure, I knew Margo loved me, and she was on my side for now. Eventually, Margo's new life would get too busy for me, despite the best of intentions. She'd have kids, PTA meetings, soccer practice, and family vacations.

And I'd be alone.

"You didn't ruin anything, Taylor." Margo squeezed my waist. "Our parents did that all on their own."

I wasn't about to cry and make Margo's morning worse, so I kissed the top of her head and stepped back. "Get back in there and enjoy your brunch. I still have to use the restroom since our wonderful father cornered me before I could make it there."

But instead of rejoining the party, I slipped upstairs to the hotel room, packed my things, and ran.

Once the tears started, they wouldn't stop.

27

GABRIEL

When Margo reappeared at the brunch table, she looked upset, and there was still no sign of Taylor. Their dad had left with his wife, acting cagey, and I was starting to get worried that something had happened.

I leaned across to Margo and asked as quietly as I could, "Everything ok?"

Margo sighed. "No, but it will be. Taylor just ran to the restroom. I'm sure he'll fill you in on the drama later."

I was skeptical, but I wasn't about to harass her about it. I struggled to focus on any of the conversation around me as the time stretched on. Taylor still hadn't appeared, and a pit started to form in my stomach. A quick text to him had gone unopened, so it was time to send out the search party.

"Hey, Margo. I'm going to go make sure Taylor is ok."

She looked around the table as if realizing he'd never returned, and her forehead creased. "Thanks for coming. My brother's had a really shitty morning, and I appreciate you looking out for him."

"We'll see each other soon, I'm sure. The wedding was a blast, thanks for having me. And congrats!"

I pulled an Irish Goodbye on the rest of the crew, too stressed to hang around.

First, I checked the bathrooms in the lobby, which were vacant. Next, I took the elevator up to our room. My heart was pounding as I swiped my key, not knowing what I'd find. Obviously, whatever had happened this morning with Margo and his dad had rattled him. I was not expecting an empty room. It only took a few minutes to process that only my belongings were left.

Taylor was gone. His key card was placed neatly on the desk.

Damn it, that man needed to stop running. When was he going to realize that I was going to keep chasing him?

GABRIEL

Where'd you go, baby? Everything ok?

TAYLOR

Sorry, needed to get out of there. I'm fine, just tired.

Yeah, sure. I was buying that. I threw everything haphazardly into my bag, rushed through checkout, and called a car. In the past, if someone I'd been seeing had pulled away like this, I would have deleted their number.

Taylor had repeatedly pushed me away, and I wasn't taking no for an answer. I kept showing up.

Was I making too much of an effort? What if Taylor didn't want to be chased, and I was pressuring him, making this into more than it was? I felt like my feelings were reciprocated when we were together, but could I have been the only one who'd fallen?

I didn't need to be a horticulturalist to know that plants could die both from neglect and from too much attention, and Taylor was more than a very complicated houseplant. Instead of being able to feel the moisture in the soil around him or assess the color of his leaves, I had to get the man to communicate.

Taylor could be more finicky than a fiddle leaf fig, and it wouldn't matter to me.

I loved him, and I was going to get him.

I TRIED CALLING him once before I grabbed my keys and headed his way, but it went to voicemail. When I knocked, I could hear loud emo music from inside, but no one came to the door. Then I tried calling Kai, but he wasn't home. Not sure what else to do, I slid down the wall and waited.

I finally heard Kai's voice from near the elevators as he approached their apartment.

"We need to get you a key. What's going on?"

"I'm not totally sure. There was some drama with Taylor's dad this morning at brunch, and then he hightailed it out of the hotel without saying goodbye, so it must have been bad. I haven't been able to get a hold of him, but I know he's in there unless you like to leave music playing when you're not home."

"No, that's definitely Taylor's playlist when he's in a mood." Kai unlocked the door and ushered me inside. "C'mon."

The music got even louder as we made our way into the apartment.

Kai grimaced. "No wonder he didn't hear you calling or knocking."

I wasn't sure what to expect as I made my way into Taylor's bedroom. I tested the doorknob gently, crossing my fingers that it wasn't locked. When the handle turned, I breathed a sigh of relief and cracked the door open.

Taylor was curled up in bed, buried under the covers, with the music blaring from the speakers on his dresser.

I turned down the volume and moved to sit beside him. "You want to talk about it?"

Taylor sighed. I wanted to know what was going on in that busy head of his, but I wasn't going to push him. I ran my hand down his back.

"There isn't anything to talk about," Taylor finally mumbled from under the covers. "I've failed."

"Baby, you are a lot of things, but a failure isn't one of them," I teased gently. "C'mon. Let's go do something fun, and then maybe you'll feel better. Once you get your mind off things."

Taylor threw the covers off and sat up in bed. "This is serious."

I flinched. "I... I know that. I'm just trying to help."

"I've let Margo down." Taylor buried his face in his hands. "I don't know how to make it right."

"Seriously?" Now I was mad. "Do you think I can't understand what it feels like to be a disappointment to the people I love?"

"Forced fun is not going to solve anything," Taylor said, exhaustion lacing his voice. "I need to be alone so I can figure out how to fix this. I don't want to let you down, too."

"Too late for that," I shot back, ignoring the hurt written all over his face. I was hurting, too. "I'll let you be miserable, since that's clearly what you want. Wouldn't want to *force* you."

Pushing myself up off the bed, I refused to look back as I left the room. I slammed his bedroom door behind me.

I'd spent the first thirty years of my life letting people treat me like less than because of how I chose to live my life, and I wasn't going to let anyone bring that energy into this next decade.

Even if it was the first man I ever loved.

Kai sat on the arm of the couch, looking concerned, but I wasn't in the mood to debrief. I slipped on my shoes without making eye contact and stormed out of the apartment.

28

TAYLOR

As soon as Gabriel slammed my bedroom door, I realized he was right.

I rushed out of bed, but by the time I'd put on my pants, he was gone. Kai eyed me from the couch.

I threw my hands up and retreated to my bedroom. "Yes, I know. I messed up."

"Glad I didn't need to say it," Kai shouted after me.

I grabbed my phone from my nightstand and dialed Gabriel's number, but it went straight to voicemail.

I tried Margo's number next, hoping she'd answer my calls.

"Hello?"

When her voice came through the phone, I broke down in a relieved sob.

"Taylor? Are you ok?"

I struggled to find the words. Finally, I landed on: "No."

"Where are you? I'm on my way."

"Don't leave Benji," I blurted. "You just got married."

"Yeah, and he'll still be here tomorrow when we leave for our honeymoon," Margo replied sternly. "You clearly need me, so tell me where you are."

I sighed and collapsed onto my bed. "I'm at home."

There was a wet spot beneath my face by the time Margo knocked on my bedroom door. I grabbed a shirt off the floor to wipe the tears and snot away before cracking the door open.

"Wow, you look even better than you did at the hospital," Margo deadpanned as she pushed her way in.

"Gee, thanks. I'm so glad I called you."

"Me too." She smiled as she rummaged through my dresser drawers to find a T-shirt. "Put this on, I'm not solving your crisis for you while you're shirtless."

Of course, she tossed me one of Gabriel's shirts.

"Whatever you want," I said as I pulled the shirt on, ignoring the way it burned my skin.

"Oh, it's whatever I want now?" Margo's voice was laced with sarcasm, but I deserved all of it. "You're clearly going through it, so I'm going to try to be nice, but don't think I'm not pissed at you about those loans you've been paying."

I flopped onto my back and threw one arm over my face. "Gabriel already let me have it, so you may as well take the opportunity."

"Don't be so dramatic, Mister Fall-On-Your-Sword." Margo poked me in the ribs, and I flinched. "Tell me what happened."

"I feel awful that I let you down with those loans. You were never supposed to know," I began. "Gabriel came over to try to cheer me up, but I blew up, and now he's pissed at me."

"First of all, you did let me down, but not in the way you think. All the people in your life who love you want to be here for you. *You're* the one who's pushing us away."

I peeked at her from under my arm. "Tell me how you really feel."

"I will," Margo said with a decisive nod. "I love you. That will never change. You're my big brother, and you've done more for me than any other human probably ever will."

"Not enough," I grumbled.

"Yes, enough! I'm tired of this one-sided relationship you've boxed us into. And I'm sure Gabriel feels the same way. I want you to need me like I need you!"

I let her words soak in. Nothing made me feel better than taking care of the people I loved, but had I been robbing them of the same joy by insisting I needed to fight all my own battles alone? Would Gabriel have been so upset if I'd told him what was wrong?

"Fuck," I muttered, rubbing my chest.

"Now, get up. Take a shower. Put some real clothes on and go fix things with Gabriel. You and I have a lifetime to work on our shit."

"Ok, ok. But please don't leave yet."

"Not a chance," she said. "I'm going to pick out your groveling outfit."

As I stood beneath the spray, I started to formulate a plan of how I could fix things with both Margo and Gabriel. I wrapped myself in a towel and reemerged with a new vigor.

Margo immediately let out a scream. "Gah! Put some clothes on."

"You said you were picking out my outfit. Was I supposed to teleport the clothes into the bathroom?"

I was so relieved that we were back to our usual banter.

"I'll admit I didn't think that through." She laughed, eyes closed as she held out a pile of clothes.

Another one of Gabriel's shirts.

"I'm starting to think you're doing this on purpose," I accused.

Margo smiled innocently. "It's physically impossible for a man to resist someone he loves when they're wearing his clothes. It's science."

I laughed, ignoring the L-word, as I carried the clothes she'd chosen into the bathroom to change.

"Actually," I shouted through the cracked door, "I have something you can help me with."

I'D THOUGHT I was nervous the first time I walked into The Whiskey Sour, when I was meeting Gabriel for our first date, but the stakes were much higher today.

On a Sunday afternoon, the place was deserted, but there was a head of curls I would recognize anywhere seated at the counter.

Alex was posted up behind the bar, her gaze icy as I approached.

"Let me know if I need to have this man removed," she said to Gabriel.

He looked up, his eyes tired and red as they met mine. "I will."

I slid into the seat next to him. All I wanted to do was fall to his feet and beg to kiss him, but that would come later. Hopefully.

"I'm sorry," I said, then I hesitated. My feelings were too big for words.

"A decent start," Gabriel said.

"Not enough," Alex piped up from where she was washing dishes.

I sighed, shooting her a glance. "I'm not done."

I turned in my seat to face Gabriel, trying not to get discouraged that he continued to stare straight ahead at the bottles lining the back counter.

Gathering my courage, I began again. "I'm sorry for pushing you away. I was hurting, but that's no excuse. I should never have implied that you weren't taking my feelings seriously or that you didn't care about what I was going through."

I ran my hand through my hair. "I've been on my own since I was fifteen, even younger than that if I'm honest. And letting someone in is something I'm going to need to practice. But I want to."

Gabriel dragged his fingers through the condensation on his glass, and I itched with the need to reach out to him.

"I can't say that I won't ever make this mistake again, but I can promise to stay in this with you."

I finally let myself touch his forearm with the tips of my fingers, and he let out a soft exhale.

"Our relationship means something to me, Gabriel." My voice cracked. "Let me show you how much."

Gabriel let his head fall forward, and my heart dropped.

Maybe he wouldn't hear me out after all.

The moments that followed felt like an eternity. The soft clicking of glasses from Alex at the dishwashing station was the only sound as I waited for Gabriel's verdict, and the silence stretched onward.

"Walk with me?" I asked, finally making eye contact with Gabriel in the mirror behind the bar. I gestured to Alex. "No offense, but I have some things to say I'd rather not have an audience for."

A lemon wedge hit me right in the temple, and Gabriel let out a small puff of laughter. Hope swelled inside me again. He threaded his fingers through mine and nodded his head toward the door.

I felt like I could fly.

29

GABRIEL

I wasn't sure what I was doing, letting Taylor keep talking, when everything inside of me was screaming to cut my losses and move on. My fucking traitor of a heart wouldn't let me.

Taylor, by his own admission, didn't let a lot of people in. But he came and found me.

So, I'd listen.

I led Taylor by the hand out of the bar and out into the afternoon sun.

"My parents never wanted kids," he said as soon as we were across the street. "I learned from early on that if I could stay quiet, be responsible, not cause trouble, the better things would go for me. Margo was an accident, and I was babysitting her almost right away."

My brows furrowed. "At eight?"

My extended family was so close that there was always an older cousin, aunt, or uncle—who may or may not have been blood-related—to step in. I couldn't imagine being left with a baby at such a young age.

"Yeah." Taylor tensed as I looked his way.

I threaded my arm around his waist and felt his muscles loosen.

"She was seven when she got sick—leukemia—and we couldn't stay under my parents' radar anymore. I think if I could have been her legal guardian at fifteen without a hassle, my parents would have done it, so they didn't have to go to the appointments. They'd drop us off, I'd do homework while Margo got her treatments, and they'd pick us up after it was done."

We stopped under a tree while we waited for the crosswalk light.

"I used my allowance to buy snacks Margo would tolerate," Taylor continued. "My parents believed kids should eat whatever the adults were eating, but she barely had an appetite from the chemo."

I couldn't help inhaling a sharp breath.

He gave a wry smile. "There was so much fighting in those days. It was like the cancer was the straw that broke the camel's back in their relationship. I thought it would get better when they finally divorced."

"I'm guessing it didn't?" I almost didn't want to hear more, but I wasn't about to stop him now that he was finally talking.

"Not by a long shot. I became their stand-in messenger boy, and they yelled their complaints at me. The cherry on top was when my father told me that Margo should be responsible for the remaining debt from her cancer treatments as soon as she turned eighteen. He was still mad that the debt had been assigned to him and not my mother in the divorce."

"What the *fuck*?"

If I had known this was what Taylor's parents were like before meeting them at Margo's wedding, I would not have been able to keep my cool. No wonder Taylor had been barely holding it together. I squeezed my arm tighter around him, pulling him close to protect him from the memories.

I hated that this made me love him more.

"Yeah. I'd just gotten my first job, and I was used to living on a ramen budget, so I talked Kai into living together to save on rent. I've been paying it down ever since, and Margo didn't know." He scrubbed his hand over his face. "Until today."

"There are so many things here I want to unpack." I tried to keep my voice calm, but I was livid with Taylor's piece of shit parents. "But for now, tell me about this morning."

He groaned and sank onto a sidewalk bench, awkwardly tucking himself against my side while he filled me in on the conversation with his dad and sister.

"I've been trying to protect her my whole life, and I failed. I'm her big brother. I'm supposed to take care of her, but I let her down."

I couldn't comprehend how he could think he was a failure when it was clear how many choices he'd made throughout his life to make sure she was safe.

"Hey, hey." I ran my finger over his cheek, wiping the tears that were building up again.

His freckles reminded me of the Milky Way when it was unobstructed by the lights of the big city. They were wild and perfect.

"You did so good, Tay," I said, and I meant it. "*So good.*"

Taylor sniffled. I might have been mad at him, but I could admit this.

"Your parents set you up for failure time and time again, and yet, you figured it out. Margo is an amazing human, thanks to you. I'm sure she doesn't think you failed her. I bet she thinks you're her hero."

Taylor rolled his eyes, but I carried on. "I'm serious, cariño.

None of this is your fault. None of it is proof that you're unworthy."

He looked up at me with those blue eyes that I couldn't help falling into. To me, he was the most worthy man to have ever existed. I was beginning to understand why he couldn't see it, but there was one final question I needed to know the answer to before I could forgive him: "Why did you push me away?"

I watched several expressions flit across Taylor's face while he formulated an answer.

"I've watched my parents turn into the worst version of themselves in the name of *love*. They claimed to love each other once upon a time, but it wasn't enough to keep them from ruining everything." He let out a frustrated sigh. "Now, my mother chases men's bank accounts all over the damn place. My father puts his new wife over his responsibilities to his kids. I can't let us become that. It would kill me."

I ignored my first thought: if he thought love would ruin our relationship, it meant he thought there was love in our relationship. That realization made my heart soar, but now was not the moment for those kinds of declarations.

Taylor deserved romance, a magical moment, not one where we were both tear-stained and exhausted. So, I'd wait.

The second thought left my mouth without permission.

"That's the stupidest thing I've ever heard."

From Taylor's shocked expression, I don't think he expected me to be so direct. "W-what?"

"You are not your parents. You have years and years of evidence to the contrary. Your love for Margo has made you a better person at every turn, with every opportunity for things to go differently. How you allow love to transform you is entirely your choice, and if you think it will magically ruin everything in our relationship, then respectfully, you're being stupid."

30

TAYLOR

I blinked at him. Gabriel just called me stupid, which I felt like I should be offended about, but his eyes were full of so much obvious adoration that I couldn't call up that emotion.

Instead, I broke out into a full-on belly laugh.

Gabriel stared at me for a minute, probably in as much shock as I was by this turn of events, but soon, he was laughing alongside me. My abs were sore, and we were falling into each other by the time I caught my breath. Each time one of us stopped, the other started back up.

It felt so good to do something other than cry.

"I can't believe you called me stupid." I swatted at his chest.

"I didn't call you stupid. I called those thoughts of yours stupid," Gabriel retorted, tapping on my forehead. "I'm not going anywhere. If you need to freak out, that's fine, but you don't need to do it alone."

I'd always done everything alone. It had always been me against the world, no one to depend on, no one to let me down. Could I really accept that after all this time, I didn't have to survive on my own anymore? I thought back to the ways Gabriel had shown up for me, brought me ice cream, delivered me snacks, and cradled me as I cried.

"Does that mean you forgive me?" I asked, daring.

"You really hurt me."

"I know."

"But yeah, I forgive you."

My eyes darted back and forth between his, trying to catalog the feeling that was burning and expanding beneath my ribs.

Nope, my emotional limit for the day had been met hours ago. It felt as if my body had suddenly been hollowed out and was ready to collapse in on itself.

My gaze tracked down to his lips, and my skin pebbled with goose bumps.

"Are you cold?" Gabriel asked as he trailed his fingers down my arm. I shook my head, but he still pulled off his hoodie and handed it to me. "What do you need?"

"I need you to show me," I whispered.

"Show you...?"

"That I'm not alone. I want to believe it."

"Anything you need, always."

He took my mouth in a kiss that would have knocked me over had I not been sitting down already. His lips were so soft against mine. When he pulled my lower lip in between his teeth, worrying it gently, I moaned and grabbed at him desperately.

I needed to feel him everywhere.

IT TOOK FAR TOO long to get Gabriel back into my bed.

As soon as we were there, I let him roll me onto my back. I spread my legs, inviting him between them, and he rolled his hips against mine in a way that made my back arch. The muscles in his arms bunched under my fingers as I squeezed his biceps and held on.

"Gabriel." I gasped. "You said you're vers, right?"

He smiled down at me, the bedroom light illuminating his hair with a heavenly glow. I grabbed his ass in my hands and pulled him closer.

He chuckled as he rolled his hips again, aligning our cocks together. "Yeah."

"I need you inside me so bad. Fuck me, *please*."

He leaned down to kiss me again, resting more of his weight on me. I felt so safe, completely surrounded by the heat of all those firm muscles.

"When was the last time you bottomed?"

I should have been more nervous, but I was sure that even if I were to fall off a cliff, Gabriel would catch me. I was teetering right on the edge.

"With a partner? It's been"—I was panting now—"a long time."

Gabriel nodded. Then, his hands and lips were everywhere at once. I closed my eyes as he sucked the soft skin of my neck into his mouth, and his fingers played along my sides. Gabriel licked down my pecs, pulling my nipples into his mouth one after the other. I rutted my hard cock into his chest, desperate for more friction, but he lifted himself enough to put space between us. I groaned in protest as he continued to kiss and lick down my stomach, paying attention to my belly button, the rainbow tattoo, and the line of my V.

"I've got you, baby," he murmured, looking up at me with a smile that looked way too innocent for his position.

Then, he kissed the tip of my erection, flicking out his tongue along the slit, and I threw my head back with a groan.

I was lost in the sensation of his lips and tongue on my cock, barely noticing his fingertips trailing down to caress my balls and apply gentle pressure to my taint. When a fingertip circled my hole, I lifted my feet up to the bed on either side of Gabriel's shoulders, giving him more access. It had been years since I'd been in this position. I needed to trust my partner to be willing to bottom, and it hadn't happened until now.

Today, getting Gabriel inside of me was the only thing I could think about.

When he moved away, I opened my eyes to protest, but he sat back on his heels and pointed at the nightstand drawer.

Ok, the man had a point.

I stretched out to grab the lube and tossed it lightly at him, along with a condom. He popped the lid, coated his fingers, and brought his mouth back down to my cock. I hissed at the cool lube against my hole, but it warmed under Gabriel's ministrations. He teased my rim, his touches winding me up so much that when his first finger finally breached me, I breathed a sigh of relief.

Gabriel was excruciatingly slow at first, pushing one finger all the way in, then pulling out with a slow drag.

Then, two.

Then, three.

I lost all track of time as he slowly stretched me open. Finally, he bent his fingers just so, stroking against my prostate, and I bit my lip and moaned. Now I knew what he must have felt like when I tormented him like this. And it was torture.

Before long, I was pushing back on his fingers, trying to fuck myself harder, but he held my body down with his free hand even as I writhed back and forth. My cock up into his mouth, then my ass down on his fingers.

"Damn it, Gabriel, I'm ready. I need to feel you."

He tore the condom packet and rolled it down his cock before flipping onto his back and pulling me to straddle him. "Ride me, baby. Show me what you like."

I shuddered as I lifted myself, and he used his hand to position himself under me. As I felt myself stretching with the head of his cock, I exhaled a long breath and pressed down. I couldn't look away from Gabriel's face as I lowered onto him, his jaw hanging open and his eyelids scrunched closed as if he was overwhelmed by the sensation.

He was so beautiful. I remember thinking on that first day that he was the most beautiful man I'd seen, and that was before I thought I'd see him like this, wanton and full of desire. Before I knew what made him smile. Before he called me stupid and made me laugh.

Now he was stretched out beneath me, muscles taught and curls fanning over my pillow. And I was entranced.

Finally, my ass was seated against his groin. He was fully inside me. I rocked my hips slowly, testing the movement, letting myself adjust to the stretch. His eyes slid open before his hand shot up to the back of my neck, pulling me down to kiss him. We made out lazily, in no hurry to move things forward. I wanted to stay in this moment, so connected to him that I might burst, forever.

"Taylor, I..." Gabriel tightened his fingers around my hips.

I kissed him once more because even though I thought I knew where this was going, it didn't mean I was ready to hear it. Leaning back to get better leverage, I lifted up and dropped back down. Slowly at first, testing the pressure, angle, and speed. Riding a man was not like riding a bicycle, it turned out, and in so many ways, this felt like the first time. Everything felt new and strange, but in the best way.

Once I got the variables dialed in just right, it was perfect. I moved faster and harder, tilting my hips so his cock rubbed against that perfect spot inside me every time. Finally, Gabriel started to match my thrusts, and I knew it wouldn't be long until I couldn't keep from coming. My orgasm was building like a warm heat at the base of my spine, the pressure pulling me right to the edge.

I gasped, barely coherent. "Oh my god. Gabriel, fuck."

"Touch yourself, baby. Cover me in your cum."

Gabriel's words dragged me over the cliff, and I grabbed my cock, stroking furiously, groaning as he thrust up into me until I shot my release across his chest. I barely had time to lift out of the orgasm fog. My eyes were still closed, my head hanging forward, and Gabriel locked my hips between his hands, thrusting frantically.

"You feel so good," he said through gritted teeth.

I brought my fingers up to his nipple rings and tugged.

My prostate felt sensitive and tender, almost more than I could take, but soon, he was spilling into the condom with a shout. I huffed out a breath as we both collapsed, but I wrapped my arms around him and squeezed like I'd never let him go. I never wanted to let him go.

"Angel, that was incredible," I whispered into his hair. "You're incredible."

He moaned, clearly unable to form words, and slipped out of me to dispose of the condom onto the floor. I'd feel gross about it later, but at the moment, I didn't want him out of reach. Gabriel slid off to one side, staying tucked under my arm. His fingers trailed up my thigh and down between my legs, softly massaging my hole.

The touch was so tender it made my eyes mist.

"I want us to get tested," he murmured as he slid one finger gently inside me again, continuing his massage.

"Yeah?"

"Yeah. I'm not going to lie. Imagining pushing my cum back inside you right now has got me almost ready to go again."

He was right; it did sound hot. My cock twitched against my stomach, and he chuckled.

"I'm on PrEP, but it would be better if we both got tested too." Gabriel pressed his hips against my thigh, and I could feel him half-hard against me.

"Ok," I said, but he continued as if he hadn't heard me.

"I know my topping probably isn't going to be a regular thing, which is fine. But I don't want that barrier anymore. I'd love feeling you cum inside me with nothing between us, too. I've never wanted that with anyone before."

Gabriel was cute when he was all nervous and rambling.

"Angel, it's ok. I'm saying yes. I want that, too."

"You do?" He tilted his head up from where it was resting on my chest, those damn hazel eyes so open and loving.

"Yeah, I do," I tilted his chin up and kissed him.

I was so fucking scared, but I was tired of running. Gabriel kept catching me, and this time, I would let him.

31

GABRIEL

Taylor insisted on being the next one to orchestrate our fun, so I met him on Thursday afternoon at an address I'd promised not to look up in advance. The significance of his leaving work right at five p.m. on a weekday to meet up, even though tax season was still in full swing, was not lost on me.

I stepped out of my ride share and spotted a sign touting vintage threads in the shop window.

"Hey, handsome," Taylor said to me as I walked up to the front door. He pulled me into a hug.

"I bet I can guess what we're doing here."

Now that the wedding was behind us, the countdown to my big birthday celebration had begun in earnest.

Taylor grinned. "You are refusing my help with your party—which is annoying, by the way—but I figured this was at least one way I could participate."

"You would go too hard." I shoved at him. "You need a break after all the wedding planning you just finished, and I'm not letting you burn out again."

Taylor tried but failed to hold in his smile.

"You only turn thirty once." He attempted to mimic my voice. "I'm going to make it a big fucking deal."

"Yeah, yeah, I know I said that, but it doesn't hold you personally liable."

Taylor rolled his eyes and interlaced his fingers with mine, leading me into the store.

"So, what are we looking for today?" he asked.

"Well, it's nineties themed, so let's start there. I'm hoping I stumble across something that inspires me because I haven't decided on a costume yet."

I scanned the racks. Sometimes you had to hit up the stores a few times before you found what you were looking for, but I'd been feeling lucky lately.

"What did you do for your thirtieth?"

"Just the matching tattoos with Margo," he replied.

I'd thought his little rainbow tattoo was adorable before, but now that I knew the story behind it, I loved it even more.

"No party?" I feigned shock, even though Taylor's deflection of attention from himself didn't surprise me in the slightest.

"Nope, it didn't feel like a milestone." Taylor tossed a sidelong smirk in my direction. "My life has been pretty routine until recently."

"I have no idea what you mean." I winked.

Taylor pulled out an oversized T-shirt with a geometric neon pattern and held it up to my chest. "I haven't been thrifting since I was a teen. My theater teacher encouraged us to find pieces for our school plays in stores like this one, then we'd modify them in class. I think the department had a nonexistent budget, but I loved the challenge."

"I've bought clothes secondhand my whole life," I said, taking the shirt from him and tossing it over my arm. An idea was starting to form in my mind. "Growing up, I hated it. Never felt as cool as the other kids in school with their new clothes.

Even though I went through a phase of buying the trendy stuff, now I shop almost exclusively at thrift stores again. Couldn't have the degree I have without doing my part for the environment."

I was distracted by the way Taylor's tongue stuck out ever so slightly while he was perusing the racks, deep in analysis mode. I thought he was stunning that first day in the fancy suit, but seeing him like this—wearing a casual white Henley and shorts, his eyes lighting up when he found something he liked—made him even more attractive.

When he pulled a plaid miniskirt off the rack and threw it over his arm, I raised an eyebrow at him.

"You're going to have to wait and see what that turns into." Taylor laughed and wrapped his free arm around my waist. "I know why you're doing this whole costume party thing, you know."

I hummed as I pushed hangers around on the next rack. "Why's that?"

"After I told you that story about my theater kid days, all of a sudden, we're planning a costume party? Nothing suspicious about that at all," Taylor teased.

"Not everything is about you, baby," I smiled widely.

Except this was a *tiny* bit about him, not that I would ever admit it.

"I know we haven't known each other for long, but you should know that I love a good costume party," I said. "Who says costumes are only for kids or Halloween? That's bullshit. What about those of us who are young at heart?"

"Ah, so definitely not a crisis of aging then, either." Taylor's eyes twinkled, and he poked my dimple with his finger. "Don't worry, angel. I'm having a great time over here in my thirties. You'll love it."

I huffed. "Why are you making this a big deal?"

"Because you told me you *wanted* it to be a big deal."

"Not like this." I shrieked in laughter as he tickled my ribs.

"Whatever, sure, you're doing none of this on purpose. Either way, I appreciate it. It's been fun to remember what I loved about those days. And maybe it is time for me to find a real hobby. I've been in a rut." He waved his hand over his clothes.

"I always think you look good. No more talking down about yourself on my watch."

"You are biased." He shot me a soft smile. "I feel like I'm always playing it safe. Basic, you know? At some point, it stopped being a priority. Plus, working as an accountant, you have to keep up professional appearances."

"Well, if you ever need an audience while you're testing out new fits, just ask. I'd be happy to ogle you for science."

I grabbed Taylor's necklaces and pulled his face closer so I could steal a quick kiss. His lips on mine always made my heart race. I couldn't resist dipping back for another and another until Taylor was laughing deeply.

"I'm sure you would," he said as he grabbed my hand and squeezed. "Thank you."

I didn't find everything I wanted for my costume, but I did buy a pair of jean overalls and talk Taylor into some criminally short navy shorts. He'd eyed them with skepticism, but when I whispered in his ear about how hot his ass would look in them, I could tell he was powerless to resist my charms. The shorts got added to his pile of purchases.

32

GABRIEL

The next day, Taylor drove us to my volleyball tournament. We were in his Honda Civic, with the windows rolled down and his hand on my thigh.

"Yesss," I shouted as the next song came on.

Taylor must have added it to the playlist we were working on for my birthday party. I could always count on Britney Spears to get me hyped up for game day. I started singing along, catching Taylor's fond glances in my direction whenever I opened my eyes.

"You know, that day I saw you singing in your car, I thought there was no way you were real." He shook his head, smiling ear-to-ear. "No one could be that happy to sit in traffic."

"It's not that I'm happy about it, exactly." I shrugged and rested my hand on top of his. "More that I can't do anything about it. Why sit and be frustrated over something I can't control when I could be having fun instead?"

He smiled and flipped his hand over so we could interlace our fingers. "You're choosing to keep smiling despite the problems." He squeezed my hand. "It's admirable."

I sucked in a deep breath. Everyone assumed that since I was generally cheerful, even when faced with situations that stressed others out, I was delusional, avoidant, or flippant. It was hard to explain how deeply I cared about things, despite what it looked like on the surface.

Somehow, Taylor understood.

We sat in comfortable silence until Whitney Houston came on, and then neither of us could resist singing along. Even with the rose-colored glasses I was wearing, I could admit that Taylor had a terrible voice. Hearing him belt along to the radio made my chest feel funny anyway.

When we finally reached the beach, we were nearly late.

"Sorry, parking was terrible," I said as I ran up to my teammates on the sidelines.

"I don't even want to know what kind of smutty excuse the two of you have this time," Alex said, rolling her eyes.

Brian cut in. "Oh, but I do. All the details, please."

"Nope, no time. We gotta get out there." Lucas shoved us all with maybe a little more force than was strictly necessary, but he had a point. The other team was already out on the sand.

We won our first set without much effort, but it was an unseasonably warm day, so I was dripping with sweat when we took the set break and switched sides. The crowds that gathered for our queer league's tournaments were always rowdy and loved a little show, which most of us were happy to play into. I lifted my crop top to wipe my forehead and laughed when Taylor catcalled me from the bleachers.

I grinned up at him before reaching into my bag to check my texts. He usually liked to send me a play-by-play of his escalating horniness to motivate me. I found his thread, which I expected, but there was also a text from my dad that made my stomach flip.

> **PAPÁ**
> I came to watch you play.

My brows furrowed as I looked up to scan the bleachers, and my eyes widened when they landed on a familiar face.

My dad was in the stands.

I didn't have time to respond before Brian tapped my shoulder to let me know our break was over. I tossed my phone in my bag and jogged to my starting position, shaking with nerves over the unexpected audience.

The second set was a disaster. I couldn't get to where I needed to be. I kept colliding with my teammates. And, of course, my energy affected all of them, shot after shot going wildly out of bounds. Finally, it was time to switch sides and regroup.

Lucas slung his arm around my shoulder and went into captain mode. "What's going on? You seem super in your head."

"My dad is here. I wasn't expecting him."

Lucas frowned. "All the more reason to rally, right?"

He was right. A few hours ago, Taylor and I were talking about my unrelenting optimism. Happiness was a choice I made. Yet I was letting this text affect my mood and my safe space here on the sand.

Time to choose something else.

"No, you're right. I've got this. Let's get back out there."

Lucas thumped my shoulder, and we got into position for the first serve. The third set was close, but we managed to win. By the fourth set, I was firmly back in the groove, and we defeated them soundly.

Our team was riding high after knocking the other team out of the tournament. Even David had made it today. Lucas picked him up with a twirl. I expected to find Taylor already by the sidelines, ready to join in the celebrations. When he wasn't in his usual spot, I scanned the bleachers again and found him talking to my dad a few rows back.

"Hey," I called out, heading in their direction.

Papá turned toward me, but I blew right past him and threw myself into Taylor's arms. My hands cupped his face as I kissed him, and he hugged me tightly against him.

"Great game, angel," Taylor said with a wide grin.

"Thanks." I smiled back before turning in Taylor's arms to face my dad.

I wanted to believe Oscar when he said my parents were repentant, but I still wasn't convinced. I had a feeling it was only to maintain appearances in the community. Papá was here, though, and that was something.

Oscar cut into our conversation and knocked into my shoulder. "Did you see that incredible save Gabriel pulled off at the end there? You were on your game today."

I laughed, knowing exactly what he was up to. "Thanks."

"Will you come to dinner, mijo?" Papá asked. "Mamá made enchiladas."

"Is Taylor invited?" I asked, and he nodded.

I looked at Taylor—for permission or reassurance, I wasn't sure.

He squeezed my hand and smiled. "I'm free if you're free."

Mamá still hadn't called or texted since the party, and I wasn't sure I'd ever get an apology. But when I looked at my dad, clearly out of his element but here to support me regardless, I thought this could be a new beginning.

"Ok," I said. "We can do dinner."

THE TABLE between us was piled high with food—rice, beans, salsa, and, of course, Mamá's enchiladas.

"Eat, eat." She gestured to our plates as she placed another casserole dish on the table, full of pollo placero.

Even with Taylor's hand on my thigh, I couldn't help bouncing it under the table, ready to crawl out of my skin. I scooped food onto Taylor's plate for him, since I urgently needed him to keep his hand where it was.

"Gabriel used to play soccer when he was in elementary school," Papá said. "I used to watch. Good memories. I was sad when he quit."

I cringed. It felt like my dad was calling me flaky, and all those insecurities scratched at my skin. But I was trying to give him the benefit of the doubt. He was right that those were good memories, after all.

"Yeah, I wasn't an athletic kid growing up at all," I said, deflecting.

"Really?" Taylor raised his eyebrow as he glanced over my body. I could tell he was trying to be subtle for the sake of my parents, but I got the implication. I definitely looked like I worked out.

"Really. I was a science kid." I chuckled awkwardly. "I didn't start exercising until I joined the volleyball team. It was initially for the social aspect, to make friends, but they indoctrinated me."

Mamá scooped more enchiladas onto both mine and Taylor's plates. She was quiet as she left the dining room.

"It's good your team is winning, mijo," my dad said finally, with a decisive nod.

I smiled, letting it be what it was. "Thanks, Papá. We have a lot of fun."

"Proud of you," Taylor spoke low for my ears only, and I squeezed his hand.

When my mom came back to the table, she had a small photo album in her hand. She flipped it open to a photo of me around age six in my soccer uniform, standing with my dad after one of our games. Mamá held the album out to Taylor, and he took it in his hands. When he looked up at me, his eyes were sparkling, crinkled at the corners in silent laughter.

My parents would never completely understand me, and I was coming to terms with that. They'd probably never be as outwardly affectionate and supportive as Oscar's parents. But that didn't mean they didn't love me in their way. There was a part of me that needed their affirmation and affection, but maybe I could try to accept them for who they were, too. I could love them, and they could love me, even if we didn't always know how to show each other.

For now, that was enough.

33

TAYLOR

Waking up with Gabriel in my arms was like a drug. My nose was buried in his hair, where the scent of the salty ocean and citrus shampoo lingered. It was my new favorite smell. When I rolled from where I was spooning him to lie flat, he followed immediately, sleepily tucking himself into my side. I ran my fingers along the solid muscles of his back and tipped his head up to kiss him gently awake.

"Is it morning already?" Gabriel murmured.

"Unfortunately. The good news is that there are mimosas in our near future."

Gabriel had stayed over so we could carpool with Kai to our monthly brunch. Margo and Benji were back from their honeymoon, and while I was hoping we didn't have to spend the whole time listening to the schmoopy romantic stories from their trip, at least I was also a little love-drunk. It was always easier to hear about other people's love when you weren't alone.

It made my heart hurt a little bit for Kai, who I knew was harboring an unrequited crush.

"Coffee, or I'm not going to make it that far," Gabriel mumbled into my armpit, and I couldn't help laughing.

"If we're lucky, Kai's already got it started."

"Kai," Gabriel shouted. "Is there coffee out there?"

He cackled, and I could hear it through the wall.

"You know it, honey," came the answer.

That was enough to coax Gabriel from my embrace. I was not going to be jealous of a beverage. I wasn't. I watched his ass with interest as he bent to grab his clothes from his gym bag and headed to the bathroom.

Thankfully, brunch at my sister's was a casual affair, so I threw on a pair of grey sweatpants and a black tee. The heat in Gabriel's eyes when I joined him at the bathroom sink made me want to drag him back to bed.

"Grey sweatpants should be illegal," he grumbled. He wore gym shorts slung low on his hips and a muscle tank with rainbow stripes across the chest.

"As if you have room to talk." I let my gaze travel indulgently across his body as I dragged my finger lightly from his belly button down to his waistband.

But going any further would have to wait. I had a birthday surprise to deliver, and for that, we had to make it to my sister's. Like a well-behaved boyfriend, I kept my hands to myself as I brushed my teeth.

"Yours is all fixed up, Taylor, but I didn't know how Gabriel took his," Kai said, handing us each a mug of coffee as we entered the kitchen. "I left some room for cream."

"Black is great, actually," Gabriel assured him.

I made a skeptical noise as I sipped my highly sugared, beige coffee. Thank goodness he had better taste in men than he did in coffee.

THE COFFEE DID nothing to help my anxious stomach as we made our way to Margo's place. I probably should have skipped the caffeine altogether, but then I'd be dealing with headaches, and that was worse. Gabriel looked quizzically at my tense shoulders and nervous expression when we stood on the porch.

"I know you're nervous about talking to your sister about the money," Gabriel said. "But she loves you. Everything will be fine."

He squeezed my hand as he lifted the other to knock. I shook the tension off with a smile as Benji opened the door to let us in.

"Welcome, guys!"

"Thanks for having me," Gabriel said as he shook Benji's hand.

"Of course, man. You're part of the crew now." Benji smiled, leading us into the kitchen.

My heart fluttered at thinking of Gabriel as part of our little family, and Gabriel's cheeks reddened. Maybe he was thinking the same thing? A guy could hope.

Margo was at the fridge when we walked in, pulling out the prosecco and orange juice. "We're gonna have to upgrade family brunch to three bottles if you start bringing someone around, too, Kai."

He let out a forced laugh. "Unlikely. I think you're safe. You all better not make me feel like a fifth wheel, though, or I will mutiny."

I didn't know what was going on with Kai, but I was still willing to come to his rescue. "Have you all figured out your costumes for Gabriel's party?"

Thankfully, my sister jumped on this change in topic, and Kai breathed a subtle sigh of relief.

"I found the best outfit the other day," Margo exclaimed. "And I even convinced Benji to match me. It's going to be amazing."

"Marital bliss, everyone." Benji rolled his eyes, but his tone was indulgent.

"Don't tell me there's trouble in paradise already?" Kai chuckled.

Margo and Benji grinned at each other.

"Just because we disagree on whether Clueless is one of the greatest movies of all time does not mean our relationship is about to collapse, thankfully," Margo replied.

With our plates and glasses filled, we sat around the table, and I was happy with how easily Gabriel fit right in. We'd spent a decent amount of time around Kai, Margo, and Benji by this point, so I didn't have a reason to think something would go wrong, but I'd never wanted someone to fit into my family that badly. Granted, Gabriel was so friendly and kind that I couldn't imagine anyone disliking him. I still had a protective anger toward anyone who'd made him feel like he was unworthy. Gabriel was everything.

When Margo stood to grab mimosa refills from the kitchen, she raised her eyebrow in question, and I nodded subtly in acknowledgment.

"Can I take anyone's dishes?" I asked, grabbing anything I could clear from the table and following Margo out of the room. It was a challenge with my hands shaking as they were, but I made it to the kitchen without incident.

Margo jumped right in headfirst, as she did with everything. "I've blocked Dad's number. I told him where he could shove that debt first, though."

"I hate that you had to do that."

"You've covered for them for long enough." She glared at me. "Let me be mad for you."

I knew I would let her have her way, as always.

"Fine," I said with a put-upon sigh.

"I have Gabriel's gift, but I have something for you, too."

Margo reached into her pocket and pulled out an envelope. Inside was a check for $5,000.

My mouth dropped open. "Margo, I can't accept this."

"You can and you will," she said. "I know I insisted you get a bunch of those extra tests at the hospital. This probably won't scratch the surface of the medical bills, but it's the least I can do."

"I love you, Margo." My voice cracked as I held my emotions. It seemed I had feelings in abundance these days.

With Margo's gift and my parents blocked at last, maybe I could see that therapist sooner rather than later.

"I know, big brother." Margo pulled me into a hug that I pretended to fight, even though we both knew I wanted it.

She squeezed me tight, and I squealed in a manly, grown-up way. Her bright laughter lightened the moment. Margo released me and reached into the back of her pantry to remove the black folder she'd stashed there.

"Here's everything you asked for. He's going to love it."

I let out a slow breath and nodded. Now was the moment of truth. I wasn't sure if Gabriel was going to be pissed that I'd gone behind his back or—as I was hoping—see this as a gesture of my unconditional support of his fledgling business.

Margo carried the Prosecco and orange juice, and I carried the folder, rejoining Gabriel and Benji at the table.

"What's that, baby?" Gabriel asked, gesturing at the folder.

"I got you something for your birthday. I know your party is coming up soon, but I wanted to give it to you now since Margo helped me with it. Sorry, it's not wrapped."

As I handed over the folder, Gabriel glanced around the table. Could he hear how fast my heart was racing?

I held my breath as he flipped it open, and he let out a gasp.

"Taylor," he whispered as he thumbed through the papers inside.

"Margo studied graphic design in college, so I paid her to help me make a logo and branding for Plant Daddy Botanicals. It's all in there. Of course, she can edit anything if you don't think it's perfect yet."

"Taylor may have sent me photos of the vision board you were working on," Margo said. "Hopefully, we're close to what you were imagining."

My heart sat in my throat as Gabriel took in all of Margo's design work. His face was unusually blank as he turned each page. Would he feel like I was forcing him down a path like his parents? Maybe this had been a terrible idea, and I moved my fingers under my thighs to keep myself from snatching the folder back and pretending none of this had happened.

Gabriel had tears in his eyes when he looked up at me, and I couldn't read his face to know whether they were good tears or bad tears.

"It's perfect," he said, finally.

Oh, thank god.

"I want you to know how much your passion and perseverance inspire me as you launch this new brand," I said. "You're working hard, and you deserve to be celebrated and supported. I got you all set up on your accounting software, but that's not nearly as exciting. I can show it to you later."

There was nothing I wouldn't do to see Gabriel's dreams come true, and I hoped this communicated that.

Setting the folder down, he practically leapt into my arms, squeezing onto my lap.

I laughed, deep and joyful. "If you let me scoot my chair back, you'll have more room."

"Nope, I live here now." He squeezed his arms tighter around me. "That was the best gift I've ever been given. Thank you for helping him, Margo. You're so talented."

I lifted my fingers to his cheek to wipe away the tear that had spilled over.

"Happy to do it," Margo replied. "Honestly, I don't get to do a lot of true graphic design in my work for the gallery, so this was a fun change of pace. Don't worry, I gave him the friends-and-family discount, so you can consider that my birthday present to you. We're so excited to see how your business takes off."

Gabriel glowed.

I made eye contact with Kai, and he lifted his mimosa in a toast. All my most important people were around the same table, and I basked in it.

For so long, I'd felt the burden of ensuring the people I loved were healthy and safe. I'd carried everything alone. But seeing Margo and Benji across from us, happily married and in this beautiful home, something deep inside me settled.

We made it.

Yes, the matter of my lingering medical bills needed to be resolved, but I was no longer on my own. It wasn't a failure if I needed help from my true family. Margo was safe and successful. I had a best friend who'd always stood by me, even when things were the darkest they'd ever been, and now I had a doting boyfriend and an awesome brother-in-law.

I'd been so focused on Margo not needing me anymore as we were gearing up for the wedding, so afraid I'd be left alone, that I didn't realize my family was growing instead.

"I'm proud of you," I whispered into Gabriel's ear, and he shivered, blushing. When I got him alone, I planned to show him how much.

Margo topped off our drinks, and we toasted to Gabriel's birthday and his new business. Gabriel stayed on my lap for the rest of our meal, and even though Kai made gagging noises every time I nuzzled into Gabriel's neck, I wasn't going to stop on his account.

In this moment, with Gabriel in my arms, life was good.

34

TAYLOR

Since Gabriel crashed into my life—thankfully not literally—I'd found myself in situations I'd never expected. My life pre-Gabriel was routine. Work, home, work, home, brunch at Margo's on Sundays, rinse, repeat. Now, I was attending volleyball games, playing mini golf, and planning to make my nineties drag debut at my boyfriend's birthday party.

Spare time was still lacking, but I could see the light at the end of the tunnel. The end of tax season was so close. For once, I had something to look forward to. Somehow, Gabriel was still here by my side through the late nights and weekend hours, and I wanted to believe that if someone could survive me during tax season, they were in it for the long haul.

I'd been worried when I asked Margo to design the logo for his business that I'd overstepped, but at every turn, Gabriel surprised me. He'd had the logo printed on labels and business cards and popped it into the header of the simple one-page website he'd made, where people could sign up to be notified when he had a new batch of bitters for sale.

Today, to celebrate another big order from his friends' bar,

Gabriel picked me up from my office in his yellow bug and dragged me to the park for an impromptu picnic. No one could get me to close my laptop quicker than he could.

He pulled a collection of meats and cheeses from a canvas tote bag for us to snack on, along with some boxed wine and grapes—although the grapes mostly ended up on the ground. Gabriel kept asking me to toss one into his mouth, and I had terrible aim. But we laughed and laughed until our bellies were full of cheese and our heads were buzzing.

"That one looks like a dragon breathing fire. Do you see its wings?" Gabriel pointed up at the sky from where we were stretched out on the picnic blanket.

Holding hands and leaning our heads together, we searched out a sunflower, the Eiffel Tower, and two cats sword-fighting. It reminded me of the fanciful daydreams of my childhood before I'd taken the weight of our family and my sister's life on my shoulders. How long had it been since I'd taken the time to stare at the sky? Gabriel made it easy to remember. Gabriel was magic in that way.

We'd been lying on the grass for a few hours watching the cotton candy sunset, and the sky was as dark as it would get in the city. No stars, just a faint orange glow of the city lights on the horizon. As the evening chilled, we'd wrapped ourselves tighter around each other. Now, we were on our sides facing each other on the quilted picnic blanket, faces close, with our legs tangled, and my head on Gabriel's bicep.

"What are you thinking about?" he asked.

While it was too dark to distinguish colors by now, I knew the hazel of Gabriel's eyes was one of my favorites. And those eyes watched me with an open, curious expression. I stroked through his hair, and he played with my hipbone, fingers pressing in.

"You," I answered, pulling him in for a kiss.

I lost myself in his kisses for a while. Gabriel had never held back, while I felt like I'd been pressing my finger in the crack of a slowly crumbling dam. I'd always said I didn't want love. Love was a weakness, a vulnerability.

But Gabriel showed me that it was also a strength. Sure, love could turn you into the worst version of yourself—I'd seen it happen with my parents—but it could also turn you into the very best version of yourself. Ultimately, I could decide which path I wanted to take. And with Gabriel's arms around me, his chest against me, his lips and tongue dancing with mine, I wanted to be better for him.

With that revelation, the dam broke, and the emotion I'd been running from hit me like a flash flood.

Holy shit. I loved him. I was in love with him.

"Gabriel..." I breathed as I pulled back in surprise.

Suddenly, we were doused in a spray of water as the park's sprinkler system turned on all around us. We shrieked and jumped into action, gathering our picnic and our blankets while the water soaked us. Gabriel dragged my hand as he laughed, running toward the sidewalk.

I let the picnic bag fall as I stopped, pulling him back. Our clothes were soaked through, and the sprinklers were still going, but I grabbed his waist and spun him around. Like I knew he would, Gabriel jumped in with me, giggling and running through the spray.

I became an adult at fifteen, whether I wanted to or not, thrust by a horrible crisis into a world I didn't choose. I forgot how to see the magic, or maybe I was forced to stop looking for it. I'd spent the last seventeen years as the responsible one, the dependable one, the problem-solver. I didn't regret the decisions I made to give Margo the life she'd fought so hard for, but somewhere along the way, I lost sight of who I was as a person outside of that role.

Being with Gabriel reminded me how to live again. I was finally breathing after drowning for eons. I couldn't hold back the tears of laughter as the two of us jumped around like wet dogs with a hose. Gabriel danced under the sprinkler water, and I floated higher.

Maybe I should have been more afraid of this feeling I'd been running from my whole life. But how could I when, in this moment, it felt like transcendence?

We were both gasping and panting by the time the sprinklers shut off. Gabriel's shirt clung to his muscular chest, and his curls were pasted to the side of his face. I'd never seen anyone so wonderful, and I was never letting him go.

"I love you." The words spilled out of my mouth with a sigh.

There. It was out in the open. I tensed, waiting to be hit by lightning. Another part of me drifted in a timeless, euphoric haze. Gabriel stood frozen, eyes wide, and the panicked part of me might have won out were it not for the broad smile on his face.

"Finally," Gabriel said as he pulled me to him, his eyes twinkling. "Feels like I've been waiting for ages."

"Excuse me, what?" I squeezed his sides as I laughed, finally releasing all the built-up tension.

"I've loved you since the day you yelled at my mom. It's about time you got with the program."

I kissed his lips, his cheek, his jaw. I held him close and whispered 'I love you' into his ear until he was shivering. At that point, I wasn't sure if it was from being cold and wet or my breath on his neck.

When we were finally popsicles, at least by Southern California standards, we took off our soggy shoes and padded barefoot back to the car, hand in hand.

∼

BACK AT GABRIEL'S APARTMENT, I peeled off our damp clothes and pulled him under the shower spray with me. The hot water and the proximity of all his smooth skin went a long way toward warming me up.

"I can't believe you kept that secret for weeks," I murmured as I ran my hands up and down his arms. "I had to blurt it out the moment I realized."

Gabriel smiled at me, water droplets catching in his dimples. "Well, I didn't think you were ready to hear it. And I wasn't ready to say it."

I ran my fingers through his hair, scratching his scalp and watching the shampoo foam up. He closed his eyes and leaned into my touch.

"Maria and I fucked around in college. It was a hookup thing, and we were having fun, but I caught feelings. When I asked her to be my girlfriend officially, she laughed. Told me I was a fun time, and I was way too messy for a serious relationship."

I was in danger of getting mad all over again. Apparently, people could walk all over me as much as they wanted, but they had better watch out if they came for the ones I loved.

"Your spontaneity is one of your best qualities," I said with a huff. "She didn't know what she was talking about."

Gabriel hummed as I continued to massage his scalp. "It reinforced so much about what my parents told me my whole life. I'd just come out. I was struggling in my engineering classes, and I felt like I was letting everyone down. Especially when Maria got engaged to her now-husband six months later. She wanted something serious... she just didn't want it with *me*."

I moved him under the shower spray so he could rinse out the shampoo.

"You deserve a partner who loves every part of you, who would never try to change you into someone you're not," I said.

"I'd been in stasis for so long, and I feel like I'm living again because of you. You're a fucking treasure."

I pulled him close and wrapped him in my arms. His ex may have been willing to walk away, but I was keeping him forever. He trailed his fingers down my back and squeezed my ass in his hands. I couldn't help laughing and squirming a bit.

Gabriel brushed a thumb across my cheek. "I love seeing you smile. You seemed so weighed down when we met."

"You make me smile all the time," I whispered against his lips as I leaned in to kiss him. "So perfect for me."

And it was true. I'd been so focused on how my parents' love had let me down that I couldn't see how the love from my true family—Margo, Kai, and now Gabriel—had helped me become a better person.

We kissed under the shower until all our fingers were pruned, and then we relocated to the bed, limbs and hearts intertwined.

"Remember when we watched that documentary about the monarchs together the other night?" I'd wanted to learn more about them since they overwintered in a part of Mexico not far from where Gabriel's family was from.

He nodded.

"You know how the first two generations spend their whole lives flying north for the summer? They've only seen warming weather, long days, and blooming flowers. They've never experienced winter themselves. But then the third generation is born, and something inside them tells them they need to fly south. The opposite direction of their parents and grandparents. Toward something they've never seen, for some reason they don't understand. Then they end up in these beautiful mountains with all these other butterflies and find a safe place to rest."

I pulled Gabriel close to me as I continued. "I know you feel like you've been swimming upstream your whole life, but maybe you're the winter butterfly. Maybe you're the one who has to fly south, and that's exactly what you were made for."

Gabriel's eyes were so wide that I wasn't sure I was making any sense, but he rolled me onto my back and settled his head onto my chest and his body between my legs. "I've never had anyone see me like you do, Tay. I love you."

"I love you too, angel." I ran my fingers through his damp hair as we traded sloppy, sleepy kisses.

When he reached between our bodies to stroke me to hardness, I groaned into his mouth. And when he straddled me and took me inside with nothing between us, I'd never experienced anything so perfect. So right.

What had I been so afraid of? This was the best feeling in the world.

35

GABRIEL

The party room at The Whiskey Sour had been completely transformed for my birthday celebration. Even though Alex and Kat had both taken the night off, they'd come in early with me to help decorate.

Alex fussed over Kat on a ladder while she hung streamers in teal, lavender, and hot pink. We put up posters from my favorite nineties movies, and I was so proud of the magic eight balls I'd tracked down to use as centerpieces. I'd even convinced Alex and Kat's boss to advertise a 90s theme night at the bar so we could play all the classic 90s dance music. I'd created a birthday cocktail using my Plant Daddy bitters—cosmos, of course, with a dash of my hibiscus lavender bitters.

The night was still young, and I was pretty sure the nostalgic theme night would draw a crowd.

Typical Aries behavior: hijacking a whole club for my birthday. Thank you very much.

When I woke up this morning, I was almost surprised that I felt no different. I'd half expected my joints to crack and my eyes to wrinkle from the moment I'd entered a new decade. In retrospect, that was a silly thing to fear. Taylor was two years older than me and, in my very unbiased opinion, he looked fantastic.

It felt impossible that this competent, smart, responsible, loyal man chose me, a chaos gremlin, to fall in love with. Even though my thirty-year-old body didn't feel any different, I felt like I was about to be graded on my life performance thus far and somehow fall short.

It turned out there was no report card delivery waiting to judge me for how well I adulted during my twenties. There was just the man I love waking me up with my dick in his mouth, in my cozy apartment surrounded by all my plant babies. He brought me pastries from my favorite coffee shop and a cozy playlist while we snuggled and ate breakfast in bed.

My parents called around lunchtime. I put the call on speaker, knowing Taylor would make me hang up the phone before they could make more of their passive-aggressive remarks.

"Feliz cumpleaños, mijo," Mamá said.

I clenched, waiting for the lecture that never came.

"Te deseamos lo mejor," Papá continued. "Te amo."

We chatted for about ten minutes, catching them up on my upcoming party, before hanging up. While things still felt strange between us, at least they managed to wish me a happy birthday without complaining about my life choices.

Maybe I didn't own a home, or dominate a high-powered career, or have two point five children. Maybe I hadn't made my parents proud by whatever made-up metric they'd created for me. But damn it, I was happy, and I was having a blast living this one wild life.

And if Taylor could love my little chaotic self, maybe I could let myself believe I was lovable.

It was the best birthday I could remember before we'd even made it to the party, which I realized with some shock. I'd always been happiest when surrounded by people—the more, the merrier. Somehow, staying in with Taylor had become more satisfying than being swallowed by a crowd of friends and acquaintances.

Not that I was ready to give that up entirely. I'd spent months waiting for this party.

Speaking of Taylor, I barely recognized him as he made his way from the front of the bar to our little roped-off party area. He'd wanted to keep his costume a surprise, and wow, I was surprised. Taylor was in full drag as Britney Spears from her iconic Hit Me Baby One More Time music video. Long blonde pigtail braids, that short, pleated skirt he'd thrifted, knee-high socks, and a dress shirt tied over a padded bra.

"Hot damn, you make a sexy Britney, baby." I pulled him into an enthusiastic kiss.

Taylor laughed as he pulled back, "Careful, don't mess up the makeup. I had to watch way too many YouTube tutorials to get this contouring right."

"Let no one say you aren't committed to the cause," Kai teased as he came up behind us.

He looked hilarious in his wide-legged Junco jeans, thick eyeliner, and Hot Topic accessories. The shoulder-length hair he usually kept up in a bun was hanging loose around his face.

Margo and Benji showed up dressed in complementary plaid outfits like Cher and Dionne from Clueless. The volleyball crew wore 90s-themed workout attire. Personally, I'd chosen a Fresh Prince of Bel-Air look: overalls, a colorful, oversized tee, and sneakers. It was so much fun watching everyone walk the 'runway' across the dance floor as they entered, and we filled the bar with whoops and screams each time someone arrived in costume.

Contrary to how it seemed, considering I'd planned this massive party at a bar for my birthday, I didn't want to be the center of attention. I just wanted an excuse to get all of our friends together in one place. So, I'd requested no singing or cake. Which, of course, my friends ignored.

Alex appeared from behind the bar with a cake shaped like the number thirty, covered in rainbow sprinkles. By the time I blew out my candles, Taylor had acquired a microphone from who knows where. I glared at Kat, and she shrugged innocently. I wasn't buying it.

"Thanks so much for coming out to celebrate Gabriel's forthcoming AARP membership," Taylor said, and our friends cheered. "This morning, Gabriel asked me if his adulting report card had been lost in the mail, and wouldn't it be nice if someone could tell us whether or not we were succeeding at the game of life? As far as I know, there isn't an official report card or rubric unless mine was also lost in the mail."

Taylor threw his arm around me with a laugh, and I grinned wryly at him.

"Gabriel, you're the one who taught me that the most important metric we should aim for in life is happiness and self-fulfillment—not some imaginary benchmark created by society or our family or by comparing ourselves to others. And in that case, I'd say you've not only passed with flying colors, but you've also been tutoring all of us in the subject. I can't wait to see what magic you make happen next. Happy birthday, angel."

I pulled him into a hug to hide my flushed face as our friends applauded and whispered in his ear, "Are you done embarrassing me?"

Taylor just laughed and nuzzled into my hair. "For now."

"Estas son las mañanitas..." Oscar sang dramatically off-key as he wormed his way into our hug. "Happy birthday, primo."

Taylor's eyes widened in amusement.

"You better not be groping my boyfriend." I narrowed my eyes at Oscar.

"I would never," he said as he lifted his hand onto Taylor's shoulder before leaning in and kissing each of us on the cheek.

"How many of those cosmos have you had?" Taylor said with a chuckle.

"I don't have to drive tonight," Oscar replied. "Which means I don't have to count."

I rolled my eyes affectionately before unwinding myself from his grasp and pushing us toward the dance floor.

Our costumed group made quite a scene on the dance floor, rocking out to the Spice Girls, Madonna, and Janet. I held Taylor close and let my hand wander up his skirt while we danced together, almost giving myself a heart attack when I felt the straps of a jock. His smug smile as he pulled my body flush against his told me he was getting exactly the reaction he'd planned on.

"You're just full of birthday surprises, aren't you?" I said, my mouth close to his ear.

"You only turn thirty once. I wanted to make it special."

I had only sappy things to say in response to that, and I was tapped out on sappiness for the evening, so I pulled his face to mine and kissed him hard. I devoured him, pouring all of my gratitude and love into that kiss. Taylor's body pushed against mine, his arms around my waist, holding me as close as I could get with clothes between us. The party drifted away around us, and I was lost.

It felt both impossible and inevitable that when I'd sent that paper airplane sailing through my highway hottie's car window a few months ago, I'd be here on this dance floor with him tonight. I hadn't thought hard about the spontaneous decision. Even in my wildest dreams, I might have imagined having a fun little fling, maybe a date for my birthday party. Falling in love wasn't even on my radar.

I'd been told by lover after lover that I was just a good-time guy. Someone you had fun with until a serious relationship came along. Too silly for a meaningful romance. Too spontaneous to settle down with. Yet those were Taylor's favorite things about me, what made me worth loving. And seeing myself through his eyes was a miracle. Everything changed because I didn't have to change for Taylor to love me.

I'd never be the spreadsheet guy in our relationship. I'd never remember to contribute to my 401(k). I'd probably always get sucked into new hobbies, buy a bunch of supplies, and have them collect dust in a random closet a month later. And I'd be the one dragging us skydiving, or go-kart racing, or salsa dancing.

Somehow, Taylor saw all of that and loved it. Loved me. For all those things I'd always seen as imperfections. He created this snug little safe space where I could truly let my freak flag fly.

As if reading my mind, Taylor wrapped me in his arms and said, "You make everything so much fun. I'm lucky to be here with you."

"Right back at you, baby."

The colorful lights of the dance floor shimmered in his blue eyes, and I knew I was exactly where I was supposed to be.

The End

EPILOGUE

GABRIEL
Three Years Later

There was a window seat in our new home that I absolutely loved, looking over the small backyard where I planned to put a garden. We were acclimating to life in Denver after a cross-country move last month. Kai relocated here not long ago, so it seemed as good a place as any. He and his partner were coming over for dinner later that evening, and the scent of enchiladas baking in the oven wafted in from the kitchen.

Neither Taylor nor I had wanted to leave LA, especially Margo and the Ace of Baes, but I needed some space from my parents, and Taylor wanted to give me a backyard. Even after Tay didn't have the medical loans weighing him down, we still couldn't afford a backyard in Los Angeles. So, I went full-time with Plant Daddy Botanicals, and Taylor joined Kai in his new accounting practice in Denver.

I was curled up with a blanket in that window seat, watching the leaves change. I wasn't sure I was prepared for my first winter, but I could talk Taylor into extra cuddles, so it wasn't all bad.

Speaking of the man making all my dreams come true, I had plans to propose soon. I figured it was time to show Taylor how serious I was about him, just in case moving across the country with him hadn't been convincing enough. I had a ring picked out and everything, hidden in a porcelain frog that my monstera, Magdalena, was guarding.

But every idea I came up with for the actual proposal didn't feel quite right.

I was startled out of my daydreams by a sudden movement and a tap on the window in front of me. A paper airplane had landed on the bench. My eyes darted around the living room, but I couldn't see Taylor. I couldn't help smiling, though, remembering the paper airplane that had started it all.

Sometimes, we still liked to send each other messages this way. I flipped through my mental calendar to see if I'd forgotten an anniversary. Nothing came to mind, but that didn't mean anything. I wasn't all that great at remembering dates.

My heart raced when I recognized the paper as the one I'd pulled from a recent journal and tucked into my nightstand drawer. I'd written out all the various combinations I could take for my married name just to test them out. You know, for science.

Gabriel Thomas
Gabriel Rivera-Thomas
Gabriel Thomas-Rivera

With that buzzy, lovey feeling in my chest, I flipped the airplane over to find four words written on the backside in Taylor's handwriting that froze me in place.

Will you marry me?

My mouth dropped open in shock.

"Are you serious?" I said aloud.

"So serious."

When I surveyed the living room again, I could see Taylor inside the doorway, down on one knee with a small black ring box in his hand. I attempted to jump up and run to him, but my legs tangled in the blanket I was wrapped in, and I collapsed on the floor. We ended up crawling toward each other, laughing.

When Taylor finally reached me, he pulled me into his arms.

"Gabriel, you gave me my life back, and now that I have it, there is no one I'd rather share it with forever. Be my husband?"

"Yes, *yes*, cariño," I rushed to say. "I will absolutely marry you."

Tears filled my eyes as he slid the gold band on my finger. I pushed his chest as they spilled over onto my cheeks.

"You ass, I was planning an epic proposal, and you beat me."

Now we were both laughing *and* crying.

"I'm sure you were, angel." Taylor rubbed his thumbs over my dimples and pulled me into a kiss.

I melted against him immediately. Feeling the security of his chest against mine and his strong arms around me, I almost couldn't believe I'd be able to kiss this man whenever I wanted for the rest of our lives.

"You can propose, too, if you want to," he said. "I am not opposed to wearing your ring sooner rather than later."

"I'd hope so, considering you just signed up to be my husband." My heart swelled. *Husband*. "I love you so much."

"Te amo."

He was pulling out all the stops tonight, even whipping out the Spanish. He'd been trying to learn more so he could communicate better with my family, and it made me swoon just thinking about it. I kissed him again, grabbing his ass and tugging him closer.

"How long do we have before Kai is supposed to show up?" I asked, as I broke the kiss to pull off his shirt.

Taylor grunted as I sucked a hickey above his collarbone. "About an hour, I think."

"Plenty of time." I sighed as my fingers worked on opening his jeans, pulling his pants down his thighs, and letting his cock free. "He's never on time anyway."

Taylor tore my shirt over my head next, then bent down to suck my nipple into his mouth, playing with the ring between his teeth. It sent shockwaves straight down to my dick, and I groaned. His hands slid under my sweatpants and pushed them down. We toppled over onto the rug with our legs still in our pants but unable to keep our hands off each other.

"I wasn't sure about proposing at home," Taylor said through heavy pants as he ground his hips against me. "But at the moment, I'm glad I did."

I laughed, but it was abruptly cut off with a moan when Taylor traced around my foreskin with his finger, collecting my precum. Then, his slick hand was around us both, jacking us off together. I awkwardly freed one leg from my sweatpants so I could hitch my leg up over his hips to bring us closer together and get some leverage to rut up into his fist.

Even after all this time, I still got feral when he touched me.

Maybe we should have had some drawn-out, romantic lovemaking after a marriage proposal instead of a quick and dirty orgasm on our living room floor, but it felt exactly right. Everything with Taylor felt right. In no time at all, the waves of pleasure spread through my body from my groin.

"Fuck, Taylor, I love you."

I practically shouted as cum poured out of me, pooling on his smooth stomach and dripping into his belly button. I pulled him into a fierce, claiming kiss and swallowed his moans as he followed me over the edge, his cum mixing with mine.

"I love you too, angel." He leaned back just enough to look into my eyes before diving into another deep kiss.

Once our lips were puffy and our heart rates slowed, we finally kicked off our pants completely. Taylor pulled me up from the floor, paper airplane in hand. Walking to the bookcase, he grabbed the shadowbox he'd given me for our first anniversary: a small wooden box with photos, ticket stubs from things we'd done together, and the Chinese takeout flyer I'd pulled from my glovebox and written my number on. He opened the top and added his proposal paper airplane to the pile.

I came up behind him, wrapping my arms around his waist and standing on my toes so I could peek over his shoulder.

"I like Thomas-Rivera," he said as we looked at the shadowbox together.

"Mr. and Mr. Thomas-Rivera." Warmth expanded in my chest.

Taylor turned his head to smile at me. "Yeah, that one."

"Sounds perfect."

And it was. We had our moments like any couple, but I'd never take anything as seriously as I took loving Taylor.

BUT WAIT, THERE'S MORE

Want to see what Gabriel and Taylor get up to after Gabriel's birthday party? Visit the link below to download this steamy bonus scene for free—yes, the skirt stays on.

www.bellamywestwrites.com/bonus/

Curious how the rest of the Baes get their happily-ever-afters? Oscar's story is coming Spring 2027. When you sign up for Bellamy's newsletter at the link above, you'll be the first to hear publishing updates.

ACKNOWLEDGMENTS

Dear reader, I can hardly believe you're holding my debut novel in your hands. I am tremendously proud of this story and these characters, and I am so grateful you took a chance on Taylor and Gabriel's love story.

To my beloved partner, thank you for your unending belief in me. You invite me to dream bigger every day, and you love me like I'm the main character. I am a lucky penguin.

To my incredible editor, Elle Lavandelle, thank you for pushing me to level up my craft in every way.

Thank you to my early readers: my sister, cousin, and dear friends who gave me the encouragement I needed to get to the finish line in this publication process. Thanks especially to Maria at Hear for the Reads, who corrected my mediocre Spanish and gave Gabriel's character a much-appreciated authenticity read.

This book is a dream come true for my childhood self, who said that writing a book was exactly what they wanted to do when they grew up. It's a dream come true for my teenage self, who desperately needed bisexual representation in media. I hope I'm making both of you proud.

ABOUT THE AUTHOR

Bellamy West (she/they) writes fun, flirty bi+ romance for readers who love found family banter, abundant queer joy, and happy endings for all. In her spare time, you can find her gardening, singing in an LGBTQ+ choir, or adventuring with the love of her life and their fluffy orange cat. 50/50 odds as to whether her travel mug has an oat milk chai latte or a margarita.

Accounting for Love is Bellamy's debut novel. They are currently working on a novella within the shared world of Sleighbell Springs, a multi-author series providing a peek into what the locals of a touristy Christmas town get up to during the other eleven months of the year.

If you enjoyed this book, please consider leaving a review on Amazon, Goodreads, or StoryGraph. Every review makes an impact for indie authors, and Bellamy is grateful for your support.

www.ingramcontent.com/pod-product-compliance
Lightning Source LLC
LaVergne TN
LVHW041908070526
838199LV00051BA/2543